DEATH IN ECST.

DAME NGAIO MARSH, one of the world's most popular detective novelists, has written twenty-four of her classical whodunnits since she published *A Man Lay Dead* in 1934.

Now in her seventies, she is New Zealand born and bred. Her first name (pronounced "Nye-oh") is a Maori word which can mean a tree, a bug that lives on it, a light on the water—or simply "clever".

Many of her stories have theatrical settings, for Ngaio Marsh's real passion is Shakespeare. Almost single-handedly she revived the New Zealand public's interest in live theatre, and it was for this work that she received what she calls her "damery" in 1966.

Her most recent detective story is *Grave Mistake*.

Available in Fontana by the same author

Last Ditch
Hand in Glove
Colour Scheme
Enter a Murderer
Off with His Head
Overture to Death
When in Rome
Artists in Crime
Black as He's Painted
False Scent
A Man Lay Dead

NGAIO MARSH

Death in Ecstasy

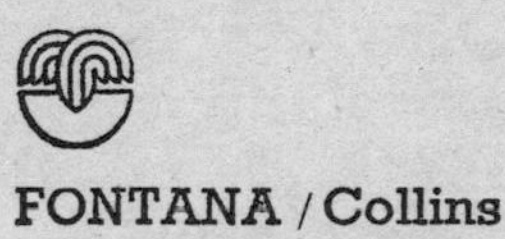

FONTANA / Collins

First published in 1936 by William Collins Sons & Co Ltd
First issued in Fontana Books 1962
Second Impression April 1968
Third Impression April 1975
Fourth Impression January 1976
Fifth Impression June 1979

Printed in Canada

For
THE FAMILY
in Kent

CONTENTS

PART I

PART II

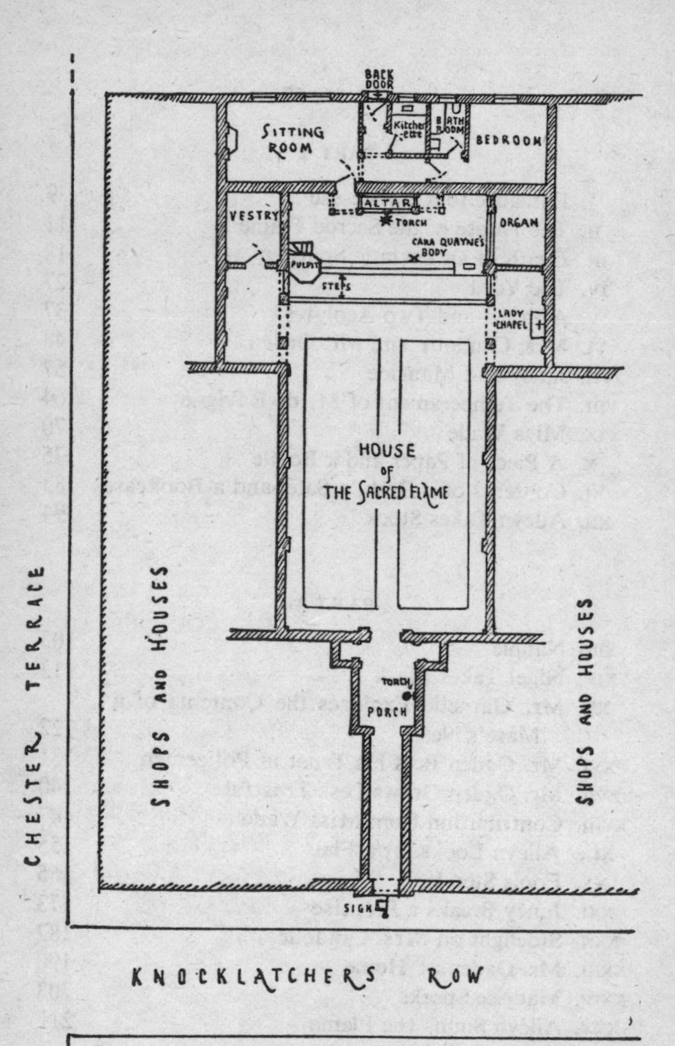
BACK DOOR
SITTING ROOM
Kitchen-ette
BATH ROOM
BEDROOM
ALTAR
VESTRY
TORCH
ORGAN
CARA QUAYNE'S BODY
PULPIT
STEPS
LADY CHAPEL
HOUSE of THE SACRED FLAME
CHESTER TERRACE
SHOPS AND HOUSES
SHOPS AND HOUSES
TORCH
PORCH
SIGN
KNOCKLATCHERS ROW

THE CHARACTERS IN THE CASE

Jasper Garnette		*Officiating priest of the House of the Sacred Flame*
The Seven Initiates	Samuel J. Ogden	*Warden of the House. A commerical gentleman*
	Raoul de Ravigne	*Warden of the House. A dilettante*
	Cara Quayne	*The Chosen Vessel*
	Maurice Pringle	*Engaged to Janey Jenkins*
	Janey Jenkins	*The youngest initiate*
	Ernestine Wade	*Probably the oldest initiate*
	Dagmar Candour	*Widow*
Claude Wheatley		*An acolyte*
Lionel Smith		*An acolyte*
Dr. Nicholas Kasbek		*An onlooker*
The Doorkeeper of the House		
Edith Laura Hebborn		*Cara Quayne's old nurse*
Wilson		*Her parlourmaid*
Mr. Rattisbon		*Her solicitor*
Elsie		*Mr. Ogden's housemaid*
Chief Detective-Inspector Alleyn		*Criminal Investigation Department, Scotland Yard*
Detective-Inspector Fox		*His assistant*
Detecive-Sergeant Bailey		*His fingerprint expert*
Dr. Curtis		*His Divisional Surgeon*
Nigel Bathgate		*His Watson*

FOREWORD

In case the House of the Sacred Flame might be thought to bear a superficial resemblance to any existing church or institution, I hasten to say that if any similarity exists it is purely fortuitous. The House of the Sacred Flame, its officials, and its congregation are all imaginative and exist only in Knocklatchers Row. None, as far as I am aware, has any prototype in any part of the world.

My grateful thanks are due to Robin Page for his advice in the matter of sodium cyanide; to Guy Cotterill for the plan of the House of the Sacred Flame, and to Robin Adamson for his fiendish ingenuity in the matter of home-brewed poisons.

N. M.

Christchurch, New Zealand

PART I

CHAPTER I

ENTRANCE TO A CUL-DE-SAC

On a pouring wet Sunday night in December of last year a special meeting was held at the House of the Sacred Flame in Knocklatchers Row.

There are many strange places of worship in London, and many remarkable sects. The blank face of a Cockney Sunday masks a kind of activity, intermittent but intense. All sorts of queer little religions squeak, like mice in the wainscoting, behind its tedious façade.

Perhaps these devotional side-shows satisfy in some measure the need for colour, self-expression and excitement in the otherwise drab lives of their devotees. They may supply a mild substitute for the orgies of a more robust age. No other explanation quite accounts for the extraordinary assortment of persons that may be found in their congregations.

Why, for instance, should old Miss Wade beat her way down the King's Road against a vicious lash of rain and in the teeth of a gale that set the shop signs creaking and threatened to drive her umbrella back into her face? She would have been better off in her bed-sitting-room with a gas-fire and her library book.

Why had Mr. Samuel J. Ogden dressed himself in uncomfortable clothes and left his apartment in York Square for the smelly discomfort of a taxi and the prospect of two hours without a cigar?

What induced Cara Quayne to exchange the amenities of her little house in Shepherd Market for a dismal perspective of wet pavements and a deserted Piccadilly?

What more insistent pleasure drew M. de Ravigne away from his Van Goghs, and the satisfying austerity of his flat in Dover Street?

If this question had been put to these persons, each of them, in his or her fashion, would have answered untruthfully. All of them would have suggested that they went to the House of the Sacred Flame because it was the right thing to do. M. de Ravigne would not have replied that he went because he was madly in love with Cara Quayne; Cara Quayne would not have admitted that she found in the services an outlet for an intolerable urge towards exhibitionism. Miss Wade would have died rather than confess that she worshipped, not God, but the Reverend Jasper Garnette. As for Mr. Ogden, he would have broken out immediately into a long discourse in which the words " uplift," " renooal," and " spiritual re-generation " would have sounded again and again, for Mr. Ogden was so like an American as to be quite fabulous.

Cara Quayne's car, Mr. Ogden's taxi, and Miss Wade's goloshes all turned into Knocklatchers Row at about the same time.

Knocklatchers Row is a cul-de-sac leading off Chester Terrace and not far from Graham Street. Like Graham Street it is distinguished by its church. In December of last year the House of the Sacred Flame was obscure. Only members of the congregation and a few of their friends knew of its existence. Chief Detective-Inspector Alleyn had never heard of it. Nigel Bathgate, looking disconsolately out of his window in Chester Terrace, noticed its sign for the first time. It was a small hanging sign made of red glass and shaped to represent a flame rising from a cup. Its facets caught the light as a gust of wind blew the sign back. Nigel saw the red gleam and at the same time noticed Miss Wade hurry into the doorway. Then Miss Quayne's car and Mr. Ogden's taxi drew up and the occupants got out. Three more figures with bent heads and shining mackintoshes turned into Knocklatchers Row. Nigel was bored. He had the exasperated curiosity of a journalist. On a sudden impulse he seized his hat and umbrella, ran downstairs and out into the rain. At that moment Detective-Inspector Alleyn in his flat in St. James's looked up from his book and remarked to his servant: " It's blowing a gale out there. I shall be staying in to-night."

CHAPTER II

THE HOUSE OF THE SACRED FLAME

In Chester Terrace the wind caught Nigel broadside-on, causing him to prance and curvet like a charger. The rain pelted down on his umbrella and the street lamps shone on the wet pavement. He felt adventurous and pleased that he had followed his impulse to go abroad on such a night Knocklatchers Row seemed an exciting street. Its name sounded like a password to romance. Who knows, he thought hopefully, into what strange meeting-place I may venture? It should be exotic and warm and there should be incense and curious rites. With these pleasant anticipations he crossed Chester Street and, lowering his umbrella to meet the veering wind, made for the House of the Sacred Flame.

Two or three other figures preceded him, but by the time he reached the swinging sign they had all disappeared into a side entry. As he drew nearer Nigel was aware of a bell ringing, not clearly, insistently, like the bell of St. Mary's, Graham Street, but with a smothered and inward sound as though it was deep inside a building. He turned left under the sign into shelter, and at that moment the bell stopped ringing. He found himself in a long covered passage, lit at the far end by a single lamp, or rather by a single light, for as he approached he saw that a naked flame rose from a bronze torch held in an iron sconce. Doubtless in deference to some by-law this unusual contrivance was encased in a sort of cage. Beyond the torch he saw double doors. A man came through, closed the doors, locked them, and seated himself on a stool under the torch. Nigel furled his umbrella and approached this doorkeeper. He was a thinnish young man, pale and spectacled, with an air of gentility.

"I'm afraid you are too late," he said.

"Too late?" Nigel felt ridiculously exasperated and disappointed.

"Yes. The bell has stopped. I have just locked the doors."

"But only this second. I saw you do it as I lowered my umbrella. Couldn't you open them again?"

"The bell has stopped."

"I can hear that very well. That, too, has only just occurred. Could not you let me in?"

"I see you do not know our rules," said the young man, and pointed to a framed notice which hung beside the doors. Nigel turned peevishly and read the sentence indicated by the young man: "The bell ceases ringing as the Priest enters the temple. The doors are then locked and will not be reopened until the ceremony is ended."

"There, you see," said the young man complacently.

"Yes, I see. But if you will allow me to say so, I consider that you make a mistake in so stringently enforcing this rule. As you have noticed I am a new-comer. Something prompted me to come—an impulse. Who knows but what I might have proved an enthusiastic convert to whatever doctrine is taught behind your locked doors?"

"There is a Neophytes' Class at six-fifteen on Wednesdays."

"I shall not attend it," cried Nigel in a rage.

"That is as you please."

Nigel perceived very clearly that he had made a fool of himself. He could not understand why he felt so disproportionately put out at being refused entrance to a ceremony of which he knew nothing and, he told himself, cared less. However he was already a little ashamed of his churlish behaviour and with the idea of appeasing the doorkeeper he turned once again to the notice.

At the top was a neat red torch set in a circle of other symbols, with most of which he was unfamiliar. Outside these again were the signs of the Zodiac. With a returning sense of chagrin he reflected that this was precisely the sort of thing his mood had demanded. Undoubtedly the service would be strange and full of an exotic mumbo-jumbo. He might even have got a story from it. A muffled sound of chanting beyond the doors increased his vexation. However he read on:

> In the Light of the Sacred Flame all mysteries are but different facets of the One Mystery, all Gods but different aspects of one Godhead. Time is but an aspect of Eternity, and the doorway to Eternity is Spiritual Ecstasy.
>
> JASPER GARNETTE

"Tell me," said Nigel, turning to the doorkeeper, "who is Jasper Garnette?"

"Our Founder," answered the young man stiffly, "and our Priest."

"You mean that not only does he write about eternity but he actually provides the doorway which he mentions in this notice?"

"You may say," said the young man with a glint of genuine fervour in his eye, "that this *is* The Doorway."

"And are you fated to stay for ever on the threshold, shutting out yourself and all late arrivals?" inquired Nigel, who was beginning to enjoy himself.

"We take it in turns."

"I see. I can hear a voice raised in something that sounds like a lament. Is that the voice of Mr. Jasper Garnette?"

"Yes. It is not a lament. It is an Invocation."

"What is he invoking?"

"You really should attend the Neophytes' Class at six-fifteen on Wednesdays. It is against our Rule for me to gossip while I am On Guard," pronounced the doorkeeper, who seemed to speak in capitals.

"I should hardly call this gossip," Nigel objected. Suddenly he jumped violently. A loud knock had sounded on the inside of the door. It was twice repeated.

"Please get out of the way," cried the young man. He removed the wire guard in front of the torch. Then he took a key from his pocket and with this he opened the double doors.

Nigel drew to one side hurriedly. There was a small recess by the doors. He backed into it.

Over the threshold came two youths dressed in long vermilion robes and short overgarments of embroidered purple. They had long fuzzy hair brushed straight back. One of them was red-headed with a pointed nose and prominent teeth. The other was dark with languorous eyes and full lips. They carried censers and advanced one to each side of the torch making obeisances. They were followed by an extremely tall man clad in embroidered white robes of a Druidical cut and flavour. He was of a remarkable appearance, having a great mane of silver hair, large sunken eyes and black brows. The bone of his face was much emphasised, the flesh heavily grooved. His mouth was abnormally wide with a heavy underlip. It might have been the head of an actor, a saint, or a

Middle-West American purveyor of patent medicines. Nigel had ample opportunity to observe him, for he stood in front of the torch with his short hands folded over an unlighted taper. He whispered and muttered for some time, genuflected thrice, and then advanced his taper to the flame. When it was lit he held it aloft. The doorkeeper and the two acolytes went down on their knees, the priest closed his eyes, and Nigel walked into the hall.

He found himself in a darkness that at first seemed to be absolute. In a few seconds, however, he could make out certain large shapes and masses. In the distance, perhaps on an altar, a tiny red light shone. His feet sank into a thick carpet and made no sound. He smelt incense. He felt the presence of a large number of people all close to him, all quite silent. A little reflected light came in through the doors. Nigel moved cautiously away from it towards his right and, since he met with no obstruction, thought that he must be in a cross-aisle. His eyes became accustomed to the darkness, he saw veils of moving smoke, lighter shapes that suggested vast nudities, then rows of bent heads with blurred outlines. He discovered that he was moving across the back of the church behind the last row of pews. There seemed to be an empty seat in the far corner. He made for this and had slid into it when a flicker of light, the merest paling of gloom, announced the return of the priest—surely Jasper Garnette himself—with his taper. He appeared in the centre aisle, his face and the rich embroidery of his robe lit from beneath by the taper. The face seemed to float slowly up the church until it changed into the back of a head with a yellow nimbus. The taper was held aloft. Then, with a formidable plop, an enormous flame sprang up out of the dark. The congregation burst into an alarming uproar. An organ uttered two or three of those nerve-racking groans that are characteristic of this instrument and red lamps came to life at intervals along the walls.

For several minutes the noise was intolerable, but gradually it revealed itself as a sort of a chant. Next to Nigel was a large lady with a shrill voice. He listened attentively but could make nothing of her utterances, which seemed to be in no known language.

" Ee-ai-ee-yah-ee," chanted this lady.

Presently the organ and the congregation together unexpectedly roared out a recognisable Amen. Everyone slid back from their knees into their seats and there was silence.

Nigel looked about him.

The House of the Sacred Flame resembled, in plan, any Anglican or Roman church. Nave, transept, sanctuary and altar—all were there. On the left was a rostrum, on the right a reading-desk. With these few specious gestures, however, any appearance of orthodoxy ended. Indeed the hall looked like nothing so much as an ultra-modern art exhibition gone completely demented. From above the altar projected a long sconce holding the bronze torch from which the sanctuary flame rose in all its naptha-like theatricality. On the altar itself was a feathered serpent, a figure carved in wood with protruding tongue and eyes made of pawa shell, a Wagnerian sort of god, a miniature totem-pole and various other bits of heathen bric-a-brac, as ill-assorted as a bunch of plenipotentaries at Geneva. The signs of the Zodiac decorated the walls, and along the aisles were stationed at intervals some remarkable examples of modern sculpture. The treatment was abstract, but from the slithering curves and tortured angles emerged the forms of animals and birds—a lion, a bull, a serpent, a cat and a phœnix. Cheek by jowl with these, in gloomy astonishment, were ranged a number of figures whom Nigel supposed must represent the more robust gods and goddesses of Nordic legend. The gods wore helmets and beards, the goddesses helmets and boots. They all looked as though they had been begun by Epstein and finished by a frantic bricklayer. In the nearest of these figures Nigel fancied he recognised Odin. The god was draped in an angular cloak from the folds of which glared two disconsolate quadrupeds who might conceivably represent Geri and Freki, while from behind a pair of legs suggestive of an advanced condition of elephantiasis peered a brace of disconsolate fowls, possibly Huginn and Muninn. Incense burned all over the place. Everything was very expensive and lavish.

Having seen this much, Nigel's attention was arrested by a solitary voice of great beauty. The Rev. Jasper Garnette had mounted the pulpit.

Afterwards, when he tried to describe this part of the service to Chief Detective-Inspector Alleyn, Nigel found himself quite unable to give even the most general resumé of the sermon.

Yet at the time he was much impressed. It seemed to him that these were the utterances of an intellectual. He had an extraordinary sense of rightness as though, in a series of intoxicating flashes, all mental and spiritual problems were reduced to a lovely simplicity. Everything seemed to fit with exquisite precision. He had a vivid impression of being personally put right. At first it appeared that the eyes of the preacher were on him alone. They looked into each other's eyes, he thought, and he was conscious of making a complete surrender. Later the preacher told him to look at the torch and he did so. It wavered and swelled with the voice. He no longer felt the weight of his body on the seat. Nigel, in short, had his first experience of partial hypnotism and was well under way when the large lady gave utterance to a stentorian sneeze and an apologetic gasp: "Oh, dear me!"

That, he told Alleyn, tore it. Back to earth he came just as Father Garnette spoke his final period, and that was the one utterance Nigel did retain:

"Now the door is open, now burns the flame of ecstasy. Come with me into the Oneness of the Spirit. You are floating away from your bodies. You are entering into a new life. There is no evil. Let go your hold on the earth. Ecstasy—it is yours. Come, drink of the flaming cup!"

From all round the hall came a murmur. It swelled and was broken by isolated cries. The large lady was whimpering, further along a man's voice cried out incoherently. The priest had gone to the altar and from a monstrance he drew out a silver flagon and a jewelled cup. He handed the flagon to the dark acolyte and passed his hand across the cup. A flame shot up from within, burned blue and went out. In the front rank a woman leapt to her feet. The rest of the congregation knelt. The woman ran up the chancel steps and with a shrill "Heil!" fell prostrate under the torch. The priest stood over her, the cup held above his head. She was followed by some half-a-dozen others who ranged themselves in a circle about her, knelt and raised their hands towards the cup. They, too, cried out incoherently. There was something indecent about these performances and Nigel, suddenly sane, felt ashamed and most uncomfortable. Now the priest gave the cup to one of the kneeling circle, a large florid woman. She, with the exclamation of "Y'mir," pronounced with shrill emphasis, took the silver flagon from the attendant acolyte, poured something into the cup and passed it to her neighbour. He was a dark and well-groomed man who repeated the ritual uttering a different word. So the cup went round the circle. Each Initiate took it from his neighbour, was handed the flagon by the acolyte, poured wine from the flagon into the cup, passed the cup to the next Initiate, and returned the flagon to the acolyte. Each uttered a single word. Nigel thought he detected the names of "Thor," of "Ar'riman" and "Vidur" among others so outlandish as to be incomprehensible. The circle completed, the priest again received the cup. The prostrate woman sprang to her feet. Her arms twitched and she mouthed and gibbered like an idiot, turning her head from side to side. It was a nauseating, a detestable performance, doubly so since she was a beautiful creature; tall, not old, but white-haired. She was well and fashionably dressed, but her clothes were disarranged by her antics, her hat had slipped grotesquely sideways and one of her sleeves was twisted and dragged upwards. She began to speak, a long stream of incoherences in which were jumbled the names of antique gods with those of present-day beliefs. "I am one and I am all." The kneeling circle kept up an obbligato of "Heils" in which, at the last, she joined, clapping her hands together and rocking to and fro.

Suddenly, perhaps at some signal from the priest, they were all silent. The woman stretched both her hands out and the priest gave her the cup.

"The wine of ecstasy give you joy in your body and soul!"

"Tur-aie!"

"The holy madness of the flame possess you!"

"Heil! Tur-aie! Tur-aie!"

She raised the cup to her lips. Her head tipped back and back until the last drop must have been drained. Suddenly she gasped violently. She slewed half round as if to question the priest. Her hands shot outwards as though she offered him the cup. Then they parted inconsequently. The cup flashed as it dropped to the floor. Her face twisted into an appalling grimace. Her body twitched violently. She pitched forward like an enormous doll, jerked twice and then was still.

CHAPTER III

DEATH OF AN ECSTATIC SPINSTER

At first Nigel, though greatly startled, imagined that this performance was merely the climax of the ceremony. He found the whole business extremely unpleasant but was nevertheless interested. Perhaps a minute passed before he realised that the woman's collapse was not anticipated by the congregation or by Father Garnette himself. A young man in the group of Initiates gave the first indication. He rose from his knees and stood looking from the woman to the priest. He spoke, but so quietly that Nigel could not hear what he said. The rest of the circle remained kneeling, but rather as though they had forgotten to rise or were stricken into immobility. The ecstatic fervour of the ceremony had quite vanished and something infinitely more disquieting had taken its place. The priest spoke. Perhaps because he had heard the words so often that evening, Nigel heard them then.

" Spiritual ecstacy. . . ." He pronounced this word " ecstasah." " Manifestation. . . ."

The Initiate hesitated and looked fixedly at the prostrate figure.

" My friends," said the priest loudly, with an air of decision. " My friends, our beloved sister has been vouchsafed the greatest boon of all. She is in ecstasy. Let us leave her to her tremendous experience. Let us sing our hymn to Pan, the God-in-all."

He stopped. The organ uttered a tentative growl. The congregation, murmuring and uneasy, got to its feet.

" Let us sing," repeated Jasper Garnette with determination, " the hymn——"

A scream rang out. The dowdy woman had broken away from the circle and stood with her head thrust forward and her mouth wide open.

" It's not. It's not. She's dead. I touched her. She's dead!"

" Miss Wade, quiet!"

" I won't be quiet! She's dead."

"Wait a moment," said a placid voice near Nigel. An elderly solid-looking man was working his way out of the row of pews. He pushed himself carefully past the large lady. Nigel moved out to make way for him and then, on a journalistic impulse, followed him up the aisle.

"I think I had better have a look at this lady," said the man placidly.

"But, Dr. Kasbek——"

"I think I had better have a look at her, Father Garnette."

Nigel unobserved, came up with the group under the torch. He had the sensation of walking on to a stage and joining in the action of a play. They appeared a strange enough crew, white-faced and cadaverous looking in the uneven glare of the single flame. This made a kind of labial bubbling. It was the only sound. The doctor knelt by the prostrate figure.

She had fallen half on her face, and head downwards across the chancel steps. The doctor touched her wrist and then, with a brusque movement, pulled away the cap that hid her face. The eyes, wide open and protuberant, stared straight up at him. At the corners of the mouth were traces of a rimy spume. The mouth itself was set, with the teeth clenched and the lips drawn back, in a rigid circle. The cheeks were cherry-red, but the rest of the face was livid. She may have been in a state of ecstacy but she was undoubtedly dead.

On seeing this dreadful face, the Initiates who had gathered round drew back quickly, some with exclamations, some silently. The elderly drab lady, Miss Wade, uttered a stifled yelp in which there was both terror and, oddly enough, a kind of triumph.

"Dead! I told you she was dead! Oh! Father Garnette!"

"Cover it up for God's sake," said the tall young man.

The doctor knelt down. He sniffed twice at the rigid lips and then opened the front of the dress. Nigel could see his hand pressed firmly against the white skin. He held it there for some time, seconds that seemed like minutes. Still bent down, he seemed to be scrutinising the woman's face. He pulled the hat forward again.

"This is turrible, turrible. This certainly is turrible," murmured the commerical-looking gentleman, and revealed himself an American.

"You'd better get rid of your congregation," said the doctor abruptly. He spoke directly to the priest.

Father Garnette had said nothing. He had not moved. He still looked a striking enough figure, but the virtue had gone out of him. He did not answer.

"Will you tell them to go?" asked Dr. Kasbek.

"Wait a moment."

Nigel heard his own voice with a sensation of panic. They all turned to him, not in surprise, but with an air of bewilderment. He was conscious of a background of suppressed murmurs in the hall. He felt as though his vocal apparatus had decided to function independently.

"Has this lady died naturally?" he asked the doctor.

"As you see, I have only glanced at her."

"Is there any doubt?"

"What do you mean?" demanded the priest suddenly, and then: "Who are you?"

"I was in the congregation. I am sorry to interfere, but if there is any suspicion of unnatural death I believe no one should——"

"Unnatural death? Say, where d'you get that idea?" said the American.

"It's the mouth and eyes, and—and the smell. I may be wrong." Nigel still looked at the doctor. "But if there's a doubt I don't think anybody should leave."

The doctor returned his look calmly.

"I think you are right," he said at last.

They had none of them raised their voices, but something of what they said must have communicated itself to the congregation. A number of people had moved out into the centre aisle. The murmur had swelled. Several voices rang out loudly and suddenly a woman screamed. There was a movement, confused and indeterminate, towards the chancel.

"Tell them to sit down," said the Doctor.

The priest seemed to pull himself together. He turned and walked quickly up the steps into the pulpit. Nigel felt that he was making a deliberate effort to collect and control the congregation and to bend the full weight of his personality upon it.

"My friends"—the magnificent voice rang out firmly—"Will you all return to your seats and remain quiet? I believe, I firmly believe that the great rushing powers of endless space have chosen this moment to manifest themselves. Their choice has fallen upon our beloved sister in ecstasy, Cara Quayne." The voice wavered a little, then dropped a tone. "We must strengthen our souls with the power of the Word. I call upon you to meditate upon the word 'Unity.' Let there be silence among you."

He was at once obeyed. A stillness fell upon the hall. The rustle of his vestments sounded loudly as he came down the steps from the pulpit. To Nigel he seemed a fabulous, a monstrous creature.

He turned to the two acolytes, who stood, the one mechanically swinging his censer, the other holding the jug of wine.

"Draw the chancel curtains," whispered Father Garnette.

"Yes, Father," lisped the red-headed acolyte.

"Yes, Father," minced the dark acolyte.

A rattle of brass, the sweep of heavy fabric, and they were swiftly shut away from the congregation by a wall of thick brocade. The chancel became a room, torch-lit and rather horribly cosy.

"If we speak low," said Father Garnette, "they cannot hear. The curtains are interlined and very thick."

"For Gard's sake!" said the American. "This is surely a turrible affair. Doctor, are you quite certain she's gone?"

"Quite," answered the doctor, who had again knelt down by the body.

"Yes, but there's more in it than that," began the young man. "What's this about no one leaving? What does it mean?" He swung round to Nigel. "Why do you talk about unnatural death, and who the hell are you?"

"Maurice," said Father Garnette. "Maurice, my dear fellow!"

"This woman," the boy went on doggedly, "has no business here. She had no right to the Cup. She was evil. I know you —Father Garnette, I *know*."

"Maurice, be quiet."

"Can it, Pringle," said the American.

"I tell you I *know*——" The boy broke off and stared at the priest with a sort of frantic devotion. Father Garnette looked fixedly at him. If there was some sort of conflict between them the priest won, for the boy suddenly turned aside and walked away from them.

"What is it?" Nigel asked the doctor. "Is it poison?"

"It looks like it, certainly. Death was instantaneous. We must inform the police."

"Is there a telephone anywhere near?"

"I believe there's one in Father Garnette's rooms."

"His rooms?"

"Behind the altar," said the doctor.

"Then—may I use it?"

"Is that absolutely necessary?" asked the priest.

"Absolutely," said Dr. Kasbek. He looked at Nigel. "Will you do it?"

"I will if you like. I know a man at the Yard."

"Do. What about the nearest relative? Anybody know who it is?"

"She lives alone," said a girl who had not spoken before. "She told me once that she had no relations in England."

"I see," said Dr. Kasbek. "Well, then, perhaps you"—he looked at Nigel—"will get straight through to the police. Father Garnette, will you show this young man the way?"

"I had better return to my people, I think," replied Father Garnette. "They will need me. Claude, show the way to the telephone."

"Yes, Father."

In a kind of trance Nigel followed the dark acolyte up the sanctuary steps to the altar. The willowy Claude drew aside a brocaded curtain to the left of the altar and revealed a door which he opened and went through, casting a melting glance upon Nigel as he did so.

"Nasty little bit of work," thought Nigel, and followed him.

Evidently Father Garnette lived behind the altar. They had entered a small flat. The room directly behind was furnished as a sort of mythological study. This much he took in as Claude glided across the room and snatched up something that looked like a sacramental tea-cosy. A telephone stood revealed.

"Thank you," said Nigel, and hoped Claude would go away. He remained, gazing trustfully at Nigel.

Sunday evening. Unless he had an important case on hand, Alleyn ought to be at home. Nigel dialled the number and waited, conscious of his own heart-beat and of his dry mouth.

"Hullo!"

"Hullo—— May I speak to Chief Detective-Inspector Alleyn? Oh, it's you. You are in, then. It's Nigel Bathgate here."

"Good evening, Bathgate. What's the matter?"

"I'm ringing from a hall, the—the House of the Sacred Flame in Knocklatchers Row off Chester Terrace, just opposite my flat."

"I know Knocklatchers Row. It's in my division."

"A woman died here ten minutes ago. I think you'd better come."

"Are you alone?"

"No."

"You wretched young man, what's the matter with you? Is the lady murdered?"

"How should I know?"

"Why the devil didn't you ring the Yard? I suppose I'd better do it."

"I think you ought to come. I'm holding the congregation. At least," added Nigel confusedly, "they are."

"You are quite unintelligible. I'll be there in ten minutes."

"Thank you."

Nigel hung up the receiver.

"Fancy you knowing Alleyn of Scotland Yard," fluted Claude. "How perfectly marvellous! You are lucky."

"I think we had better go back," said Nigel.

"I'd much rather stay here. I'm afraid. Did you ever see anything so perfectly dreadful as Miss Quayne's face? Please do tell me—do you think it's suicide?"

"I don't know. Are you coming?"

"Very well. You seem to be a terrifically resolute sort of person. I'll turn the light out. Isn't Father Garnette marvellous? You're new, aren't you?"

Nigel dived out of the door.

He found the Initiates grouped round the American gentleman, who seemed to be addressing them in a whisper. He was a type that is featured heavily in transatlantic publicity, tall, rather fat and inclined to be flabby, but almost incredibly clean, as though he used all the deodorants, mouth washes, soaps and lotions recommended by his prototype who beams pep from the colour pages of American periodicals. The only irregularities in Mr. Ogden were his eyes, which were skewbald—one light blue and one brown. This gave him a comic look and made one suspect him of clowning when he was most serious.

To Nigel's astonishment the organ was playing and from beyond the curtains came a muffled sound of singing. Father Garnette's voice was clearly distinguishable. Someone, the doctor perhaps, had covered the body with a piece of gorgeously embroidered satin.

When he saw Nigel the American gentleman stepped forward.

"It appears to me we ought to get acquainted," he said pleasantly. "You kind of sprang up out of no place and took over the works. That's O.K. by me, and I'll hand it to you. I certainly appreciate prompt action. My name's Samuel J. Ogden. I guess I've got a card somewhere." The amazing Mr. Ogden actually thrust his hand into his breast pocket.

"Please don't bother," said Nigel. "My name is Bathgate."

"Pleased to meet you, Mr. Bathgate," said Mr. Ogden, instantly shaking hands. "Allow me to introduce these ladies and gentlemen. Mrs. Candour, meet Mr. Bathgate. Miss Wade, meet Mr. Bathgate. Mr. Bathgate, Miss Janey Jenkins. Monsieur de Ravigne, Mr. Bathgate. Dr. Kasbek, Mr. Bathgate. Mr. Maurice Pringle, Mr. Bathgate. And these two young gentlemen are our acolytes. Mr. Claude Wheatley and Mr. Lionel Smith, meet Mr. Bathgate."

The seven inarticulate Britishers exchanged helpless glances with Nigel. M. de Ravigne, a sleek Frenchman, gave him a scornful bow.

"Well now——" began Mr. Ogden with a comfortable smile.

"I think, if you don't mind," said Nigel hurriedly, "that someone should go down to the front door. Inspector Alleyn is on his way here, and as things are at the moment he won't be able to get in."

"That's so," agreed Mr. Ogden. "Maybe one of these boys——"

"Oh, do let me go," begged Claude.

"Fine," said Mr. Ogden.

"I'll come with you, Claude," said the red-headed acolyte.

"There's no need for two, honestly, is there Mr. Ogden?"

"Oh, get to it, Fauntleroy, and take little Eric along!" said Mr. Ogden brutally. Nigel suddenly felt that he liked Mr. Ogden.

The acolytes, flouncing, disappeared through the curtain. The sound of organ and voices was momentarily louder.

"Do acolytes have to be that way?" inquired Mr. Ogden of nobody in particular.

Somebody laughed attractively. It was Miss Janey Jenkins. She was young and short and looked intelligent.

"I'm sorry," she said immediately. "I didn't mean to laugh, only Claude and Lionel are rather awful, aren't they?"

"I agree," said Nigel quickly.

She turned, not to him, but to Maurice Pringle, the young man who had spoken so strangely to the priest. He now stood apart from the others and looked acutely miserable. Miss Jenkins went and spoke to him, but in so low a voice that Nigel could not hear what she said.

"Dr. Kasbek," said the little spinster whom Mr. Ogden had called Miss Wade, "Dr. Kasbek, I am afraid I am very foolish, but I do not understand. Has Cara Quayne been murdered?"

This suggestion, voiced for the first time, was received as though it was a gross indecency. Mrs. Candour a peony of a woman, with ugly hands, uttered a scandalised yelp; M. de Ravigne hissed like a steam-boiler; Mr. Ogden said: "Wait a minute, *wait* a minute"; Pringle seemed to shrink into himself, and Janey Jenkins took his hand.

"Surely not, Miss Wade," said Dr. Kasbek. "Let us not anticipate such a thing."

"I only inquired," said Miss Wade. "She wasn't very happy, poor thing, and she wasn't very popular."

"Miss Wade—please!" M. de Ravigne looked angrily at the little figure. "I must protest—this is a—a preposterous suggestion. It is ridiculous." He gesticulated eloquently. "Is it not enough that this tragedy should have arrived? My poor Cara, is it not enough!"

The voice of Father Garnette could be heard, muffled but sonorous, beyond the curtains.

"Listen to him!" said Pringle. "Listen! He's keeping them quiet. He's kept us all quiet. What are we to believe of him?"

"What are you talking about?" whispered Mrs. Candour savagely.

"You know well enough. You'd have taken her place if you could. It's not his fault—it's yours. It's all so—so beastly——"

"Maurice," said Miss Jenkins softly.

" Be quiet, Janey. I will say it. Whatever it is, it's retribution. The whole thing's a farce. I can't stand it any longer. I'm going to tell them——"

He broke away from her and ran towards the curtains. Before he reached them they parted and a tall man came through.

" Oh, there you are, Bathgate," said Chief Detective-Inspector Alleyn. " What's the trouble?"

CHAPTER IV

THE YARD

The entrance of Chief Detective-Inspector Alleyn had a curious effect upon the scene and upon the actors. It was an effect which might be likened to that achieved by the cinema when the camera is shifted and the whole scene presented from a different view-point. Nigel had felt himself to be involved in a nightmare, but it now seemed to be someone else's nightmare of which he was merely the narrator. He wondered wildly whether he should follow Mr. Ogden's example and embark on an elaborate series of introductions. However, he avoided this complication and in as few words as possible told Alleyn what had happened. The others remained silent, eyeing the inspector. Janey Jenkins held Pringle's hand between her two hands; Miss Wade kept a handkerchief pressed against her lips; M. de Ravigne stood scornfully apart; Mrs. Candour had collapsed into a grand-opera throne on the left of the altar; Mr. Ogden looked capable and perturbed and the two acolytes gazed rapturously at the inspector. Alleyn listened with his curious air of detachment that always reminded Nigel of a polite faun. When Nigel came to the ecstatic frenzy, Alleyn made a slantwise grimace. Speaking so quietly that the others could not overhear him, Nigel repeated as closely as he could remember them the exclamations made by Pringle, Miss Wade and de Ravigne. Alleyn asked for the names of persons who should be informed. Beyond Miss Quayne's servants there seemed to be nobody. Miss Jenkins, appealed to, said she had overheard Miss Quayne saying that her staff were all out on Sunday evening. She volunteered to ring up and find out and retired to Father Garnette's room to do so. She returned to say there was no answer. Alleyn took the number and said he would see the house was informed later. As soon as he had learnt the facts of the case, Alleyn lifted the satin drapery and looked at the distorted face beneath it, spoke a few words aside to Dr. Kasbek, and then addressed them all quietly. At this moment Father Garnette, having set his congregation going on another hymn, returned to the group. Nigel alone noticed him. He stood just inside the curtains and never took his eyes off the inspector.

Alleyn said: "There is, I think, no reason why you should not know what has happened here. This woman has probably died of poisoning. Until we know more of the circumstances and the nature of her death I shall have to take over the case on behalf of the police. From what I have heard I believe that there is nothing to be gained in keeping the rest of the congregation here." He turned slightly and saw the priest.

"You are Mr. Garnette? Will you be good enough to ask your congregation to go home—when they have quite finished singing, of course. I have stationed a constable inside the door. He will take their names. Just tell them that, will you?"

"Certainly," said Father Garnette and disappeared through the curtains.

They heard him pronounce a benediction of sorts. Beyond the curtains there was a sort of stirring and movement. One or two people coughed. It all died away at last. A door slammed with a desolate air of finality and there was complete silence in the building, save for the slobbering of the torch. Father Garnette returned.

"Phew!" said Alleyn. "Let's have the curtains drawn back, may we?"

Father Garnette inclined his head. Claude and Lionel flew to the sides of the chancel and in a moment the curtains rattled apart, revealing the solitary figure of the doorkeeper, agape on the lowest step.

"Is there anything I can do, Father?" asked the doorkeeper.

"Lock the front door and go home," said Father Garnette.

"Yes Father," whispered the doorkeeper. He departed hurriedly pulling the double doors to with an apologetic slam

For a moment there was silence. Then Alleyn turned to Nigel.

"Is there a telephone handy?"

"Yes."

"Get through to the Yard, will you, Bathgate, and tell them what has happened. Fox is on duty. Ask them to send him along with the usual support. We'll want the divisional surgeon and a wardress."

Nigel went into the room behind the altar and delivered this message. When he returned he found Alleyn, with his note-book in his hand, taking down the names and addresses of the Initiates.

"It's got to be done, you see," he explained. "There will, of course. be an inquest and I'm afraid you will all be called as witnesses."

"Oh, God," said Pringle with a sort of disgust.

"I'd better start with the deceased," Alleyn suggested. "What is her name, please?"

"She was a Miss Cara Quayne, Inspector," said Mr. Ogden. "She owned a very, very distinctive residence in Shepherd Market, No 101. I have had the honour of dining at the Quayne home, and believe me it surely was an æsthetic experience. She was a very lovely-natured woman with a great appreciation of the beautiful——"

"No. 101 Shepherd Market," said Alleyn. "Thank you." He wrote it down and then glanced round his audience.

"I will take yours first if I may, Doctor Kasbek."

"Certainly. Nicholas Kasbek, 189a, Wigmore Street."

"Right." He turned to Miss Wade.

"My name is Ernestine Wade," she said very clearly and in a high voice, as though Alleyn was deaf. "I live at Primrose Court, King's Road, Chelsea. Spinster."

"Thank you."

Miss Jenkins came forward.

"I'm Janey Jenkins. I live in a studio flat in Yeomans Row, No. 99d. I'm a spinster too, if you want to know."

"Well," said Alleyn, "just for 'Miss' or 'Mrs.,' you know."

"Now you, Maurice," said Miss Jenkins.

"Pringle," said that gentleman as though the name was an offence. "Maurice. I'm staying at 11, Harrow Mansions, Sloane Square."

"Is that your permanent address?"

"No. Haven't got one unless you count my people's place. I never go there if I can help it."

"The Phœnix Club will always find you, won't it?" murmured Miss Jenkins.

"Oh, God yes," replied Mr. Pringle distastefully.

"Next please," said Alleyn cheerfully. Mrs. Candour spoke suddenly from the ecclesiastical throne. She had the air of uttering an appalling indecency.

"My name is Dagmar Candour. Mrs. Queen Charlotte Flats, Kensington Square. No. 12."

"C. a. n——?" queried Alleyn.

"d. o. u. r."

"Thank you."

Mr. Ogden, who had several times taken a step forward and as often politely retreated, now spoke up firmly.

"Samuel J. Ogden, Chief. I guess you're not interested in my home address. I come from the States—New York. In London I have a permanent apartment in York Square. No. 93, Achurch Court. I just can't locate my card-case, but—well, those are the works."

"Thank you so much, Mr. Ogden. And now you, if you please, sir."

Father Garnette hesitated a moment, oddly. Then he cleared his throat and answered in his usual richly inflected voice:

"Father Jasper Garnette." He spelt it. "I am officiating priest of this temple. I live here.

"Here?"

"I have a little dwelling beyond the altar."

"Extremely convenient," murmured Alleyn. "And now, these two"—he looked a little doubtfully at Claude and Lionel—"these two young men."

Claude and Lionel answered together in a rapturous gush.

"What?" asked Alleyn.

"Do be quiet, Lionel," said Claude. "We share a flat in Ebury Street; 'Ebury Mews.' Well, it isn't actually a flat, is it, Lionel? Oh dear, I always forget the number—it's too stupid of me."

"You *are* hopeless, Claude," said Lionel. "It's 17, Ebury Mews, Ebury Street, Inspector Alleyn, only we aren't very often there because I'm in the show at the Palladium and Claude is at Madame Karen's in Sloane Street and——"

" I do not yet know your names."

" Lionel, you are perfectly maddening," said Claude. " I'm Claude Wheatley, Inspector Alleyn, and this is Lionel Smith."

Alleyn wrote these names down with the address, and added in brackets: " Gemini, possibly heavenly."

M. de Ravigne came forward and bowed.

" Raoul Honoré Christophe Jérôme de Ravigne, monsieur. I live at Branscombe Chambers, Lowndes Square. My card."

" Thank you, M. de Ravigne. And now will you all please show me exactly how you were placed while the cup was passed round the circle. I understand the ceremony took place in the centre of this area."

After a moment's silence the priest came forward.

" I stood here," he said, " with the chalice in my hands. Mr. Ogden knelt on my right, and Mrs. Candour on my left."

" That is correct, sir," agreed Ogden and moved into place. " Miss Jenkins was on my right, I guess."

" Yes," said that lady, " and Maurice on mine."

Mrs. Candour came forward reluctantly and stood on Garnette's left.

" M. de Ravigne was beside me," she whispered.

" Certainly." M. de Ravigne took up his position and Miss Wade slipped in beside him.

" I was here," she said, " between Mr. de Ravigne and Mr. Pringle."

" That completes the circle," said Alleyn. " What were the movements of the acolytes."

" Well you see," began Claude eagerly, " I came here—just here on Father Garnette's right hand. I was the Ganymede you see, so I had the jug of wine. As soon as Father Garnette gave Mrs. Candour the cup, I gave her the wine. She holds the cup in her left hand and the wine in her right hand. She pours in a little wine and speaks the first god-name. You are Hagring, aren't you Mrs. Candour?"

" I *was*," sobbed Mrs. Candour.

" Yes. And then I take the jug and hand it to the next person and——"

" And so on," said Alleyn. " Thank you."

" And I was censing over here," struck in Lionel with passionate determination. " I was censing all the time."

" Yes," said Alleyn; " and now, I'm afraid I'll have to keep you all a little longer. Perhaps, Mr. Garnette, you will allow them to wait in your rooms. I am sure you would all like to get away from the scene of this tragedy. I think I hear my colleagues outside."

There was a resounding knock on the front door.

"Oh, may I let them in?" asked Claude.

"Please do," said Alleyn.

Claude hurried away down the aisle and opened the double doors. Seven men, three of them constables, came in, in single file, headed by a tall thick-set individual in plain clothes who removed his hat, glanced in mild surprise at the nude statues, and walked stolidly up the aisle.

"Hullo, Fox," said Alleyn.

"Evening, sir," said Inspector Fox.

"There's been some trouble here. One of you men go with these ladies and gentlemen into the room at the back there. Mr. Garnette will show you the way. Will you, Mr. Garnette? I'll keep you no longer than I can possibly help. Dr. Kasbek, if you wouldn't mind waiting here——"

"Look here," said Maurice Pringle suddenly, "I'm damned if I can see why we should be herded about like a mob of sheep. What has happened? Is she murdered?"

"Very probably," said Alleyn coolly. "Nobody is going to herd you, Pringle. You are going to wait quietly and reasonably while we make the necessary investigations. Off you go."

"But——"

"I knew," cried Mrs. Candour suddenly. "I knew something dreadful would happen. M. de Ravigne, didn't I tell you?"

"If you please, madame!" said de Ravigne with great firmness.

"All that sort of thing should have been kept out," said little Miss Wade. "It should never——"

"I think we had better follow instructions," interrupted Father Garnette loudly. "Will you all follow me?"

They trooped away, escorted by the largest of the constables.

"Lumme!" ejaculated Alleyn when the altar door had shut. "As you yourself would say, Fox, '*quelle galère.*'"

"A rum crowd," agreed Fox, "and a very rum place too, seemingly. What's happened, sir?"

"A lady has just died of a dose of cyanide. There's the body. Your old friend Mr. Bathgate will tell you about it."

"Good evening, Mr. Bathgate," said Fox mildly. "You've found something else in our line, have you?"

"It was at the climax of the ceremony," began Nigel. "A cup was passed round a circle of people, these people whom you have just seen. This woman stood in the middle. The others knelt. A silver jug holding the wine was handed in turn to each of them and each poured a little into the cup. Then the priest, Father Garnette, gave her the cup. She drank it and—and fell down. I think she died at once, didn't she?"

He turned to Dr. Kasbek.

"Within twenty seconds I should say." The doctor looked at the divisional surgeon.

"I would have tried artificial respiration, sent for ferrous sulphate and a stomach tube and all the rest of it but"—he grimaced—"there wasn't a dog's chance. She was dead before I got to her."

"I know," said the divisional surgeon. He lifted the drapery and bent over the body.

"I noticed the characteristic odour at once," added Kasbek, "and so I think did Mr. Bathgate."

"Yes," agreed Nigel. "that's why I butted in."

Alleyn knelt by the fallen cup and sniffed.

"Stinks of it," he said. "Bailey, you'll have to look at this for prints. Not much help if they all handled it. We'll have photographs first."

The man with the camera had already begun to set up his paraphernalia. He took three flashlight shots, from different view-points, of the body and surrounding area. Alleyn opened the black bag, put on a pair of rubber gloves and took out a small bottle and a tiny funnel. He drained off one or two drops of wine from the cup. While he did this Nigel took the opportunity to relate as much of the conversation of the Initiates as he could remember. Alleyn listened, grunted, and muttered to himself as he restored the little bottle to his bag. Detective-Sergeant Bailey got to work with an insufflator and white chalk.

"Where's the original vessel that was handed round by one of these two hothouse flowers?" asked Alleyn. "Is this it?" He pointed to a silver jug standing in a sort of velvet-lined niche on the right side of the chancel.

"That's it," said Nigel. "Claude must have kept his head and put it there when—after it happened."

" Is Claude the black orchid or the red lily?"

" The black orchid."

Alleyn sniffed at the silver jug and filled another bottle from it.

" Nothing there though, I fancy," he murmured. " Let me get a picture of the routine. Miss Quayne stood in the centre here and the others knelt round her. Mr. Garnette—I really cannot bring myself to allude to the gentleman as ' Father '—Mr. Garnette produced the cup and the—what does one call it? Decanter is scarcely the word. The flagon, perhaps. He gave the flagon to Master Ganymede Claude, passed his hand over the cup and up jumped a flame. A drop of methylated spirits perhaps."

" I suppose so," said Kasbek, looking amused.

" Well. And then the cup was passed from hand to hand by the kneeling circle and each took the flagon from Claude and poured in a libation."

" Each of them uttered a single word," interrupted Nigel. " I really have no idea what some of them were."

" The name of a diety, I understand," volunteered Kasbek. " I am not a member of the cult, but I've been here before. They pronounce the names of six dieties. ' Hagring,' ' Haco,' ' Frigga,' and so on. Garnette is Odin and the Chosen Vessel is always Frigga. The idea is that all the godheads are embodied in one godhead and that the essence of each is mingled in the cup. It's a kind of popular pantheism."

" Oh, Lord!" said Alleyn. " Now then. The cup went round the circle. When it got to the last man, what happened?"

" He handed it to the acolyte, who passed it on to the priest, who gave it to Miss Quayne."

" Who drank it."

" Yes," said Dr. Kasbek, " who drank it, poor thing."

They were silent for a moment.

" I said ' when it got to the last man '—it *was* a man you said? Yes, I know we've been over this before, but I want to be positive."

" I'm sure it was," said Nigel. " I remember that Mr. Ogden knelt at the top of the circle, as it were, and I seem to remember him giving the cup to the acolyte."

" I believe you're right," agreed the doctor.

" That agrees with the positions they took up just now."

"Was there any chance of Miss Quayne herself dropping anything into the cup?"

"I don't think so," Nigel said slowly. "It so happens that I remember distinctly she took it in both hands, holding it by the stem. I've got a very clear mental picture of her, standing there, lit by the torch. She had rings on both hands and I remember I noticed that they reflected the light in the same way as the jewels on the cup. I feel quite certain she held it like that until she drank."

"I have no such recollection," declared the doctor.

"Quite sure, Bathgate?"

"Yes, quite sure. I—I'd swear to it."

"You may have to," said Alleyn. "Dr. Kasbek, you say you are not one of the elect. Perhaps, in that case, you would not object to telling me a little more about this place. It is an extremely unusual sort of church." He glanced round apologetically. "All this intellectual sculpture. Who is the lowering gentleman with the battle-axe? He makes one feel quite shy."

"I fancy he is Wotan, which is the same as Odin. Perhaps Thor. I really don't know. I imagine the general idea owes something to some cult in Germany, and is based partly on Scandinavian mythology, though as you see it does not limit itself to one, or even a dozen, doctrines. It's a veritable *olla podrida* with Garnette to stir the pot. The statues were commissioned by a very rich old lady in the congregation."

"An old lady!" murmured Alleyn. "Fancy!"

"It is rather overwhelming," agreed Kasbek. "Shall we move into the hall? I should like to sit down."

"Certainly," said Alleyn. "Fox, will you make a sketch-plan of the chancel? I won't be more than two minutes and then we'll start on the others. Run a line of chalk round the body and get the bluebottle in there to ring for the mortuary-van. Come along with us, won't you, Bathgate?"

Nigel and Dr. Kasbek followed the inspector down to the front row of chairs. These were sumptuously upholstered in red embossed velvet.

"Front stalls" said Alleyn, sitting down.

"There are seven of them, as you see. They are for the six Initiates and the Chosen Vessel. These are selected from a sort of inner circle among the congregation, or so I understand."

Dr. Kasbek settled himself comfortably in his velvet pew.

He was a solid shortish man of about fifty-five with dark hair worn *en brosse*, a rather fleshy and pale face, and small, intelligent eyes.

"It was founded by Garnette two years ago. I first heard of it from an old patient of mine who lives near-by. She was always raving about the ceremonies and begging me to go. I was called in to see her one Sunday evening just before the service began and she made me promise I'd attend it. I've been several times since. I am attracted by curious places and interested in—how shall I put it?—in the incalculable vagaries of human faith. Garnette's doctrine of dramatised pantheism, if that's what it is, amused and intrigued me. So did the man himself. Where he got the money to buy the place—it was originally a nonconformist club-room, I think—and furnish it and keep it going, I've no idea. Probably it was done by subscription. Ogden is Grand Warden or something. He'll be able to tell you. It's all very expensive, as you see. Garnette is the only priest and literally the 'onlie begetter,' the whole show in fact. He undoubtedly practices hypnotism and that, too, interests me. The service you saw to-night, Mr. Bathgate, is only held once a month and is their star turn. The Chosen Vessel—Miss Quayne on this occasion—has to do a month's preparation, which means, I think, intensive instruction and private meditation with Garnette."

"Odin and Frigga," said Alleyn. "I begin to understand. Are you personally acquainted with any of the Initiates?"

"Ogden introduced himself to me some weeks ago and Garnette came and spoke to me the first evening I was here. On the look-out for new material, I suppose."

"None of the others?"

"No. Ogden suggested I should 'get acquainted,' but"—he smiled—"I enjoy being an onlooker and I evaded it. I'm afraid that's all I can tell you."

"It's all extremely suggestive and most useful. Thank you very much, Dr. Kasbek. I won't keep you any longer. Dr. Curtis may want a word with you before you go. I'll send him down here. You'll be subpœnaed for the inquest of course."

"Of course. Are you Chief Detective-Inspector Alleyn?"

"Yes."

"I remembered your face. I saw you at the Theodore Roberts trial."

"Oh, yes."

"The case interested me. You see I'm an alienist."

"Oh, yes," said Alleyn again with his air of polite detachment.

"I was glad they brought in a verdict of insanity. Poor Roberts. I suppose in a case of that sort the police do not push for the—the other thing."

"The police force is merely a machine. I must fly I'm afraid. Good night. Bathgate, will you let Dr. Kasbek out when he has spoken to Curtis?"

Alleyn returned to the top of the hall. The divisional surgeon joined Kasbek and the two doctors walked down the aisle with that consultation manner, heads together, faces very solemn, like small boys in conference. Nigel followed sheepishly at a tactful distance. The word cynide floated at intervals down the aisle. At last Dr. Curtis said: "Yes. All right. Good night." They shook hands. Nigel hurried up to wrestle with the elaborate bolts and lock that secured the double doors.

"Oh, thank you very much," said Kasbek. "You've made yourself quite invaluable this evening, Mr. Bathgate."

"To tell you the truth, sir," said Nigel, "I am surprised at my own initiative. It was the smell that did it."

"Oh, quite. I was just going to say no one must leave when you spoke up. Very glad of your support. Can you manage? Ah—that's done it. I see there's a constable outside. I hope he let's me out! Good night, Mr. Bathgate."

CHAPTER V

A PRIEST AND TWO ACOLYTES

The constable had arrived with the mortuary-van. A stretcher was brought in. Nigel, not wishing to see again that terrible figure, hung back at the entrance, but after all, try as he would, he could not help watching. The group up in the chancel looked curiously theatrical. Alleyn had turned on all the side lamps but they were dull red and insignificant. The torch flickered confusedly. At one moment it threw down a strong glare, and at the next almost failed, so that the figures of the men continually started to life and seemed to move when actually they were still. Alleyn drew the brocaded satin away from the body and stood contemplating it. The body, still in its same contracted, headlong posture, looked as though some force had thrown it down with a sudden violence. Dr. Curtis said something. His voice sounded small and melancholy in the empty building. Nigel caught the words "rigor mortis—rapid." Alleyn nodded and his shadow, starting up on the wall as the torch flared again, made a monstrous exaggeration of the gesture. They bent down and lifted the body on to the whitish strip of the stretcher. One of the men pulled a sheet up. Curtis spoke to them. They lifted the stretcher and came slowly down the aisle, black silhouettes now against the lighted chancel. They passed Nigel heavily and went out of the open door. The constable stayed in the entrance, so Nigel did not relock the doors. He returned to the chancel.

"I'm glad that part is over," he said to Alleyn.

"What? Oh, the body."

"You appear to be lost in the folds of your professional abstraction," remarked Nigel tartly. "Pray, what are you going to do next?"

"Your style is an unconvincing mixture of George Moore and Lewis Carroll, my dear Bathgate. I am about to interview the ladies and gentlemen. I dislike this affair. I dislike it very much. This is a beastly place. Why did you come to it?"

"I really can't tell you. I was bored and I saw the sign swinging in the rain. I came in search of adventure."

"And I suppose, with your habitual naïveté, you consider that you have found it. Fox, have you made your plan?"

"Not quite finished, sir, but I'll carry on quietly."

"Well, give an ear to the conversation. When we get to M. de Ravigne, you may like to conduct the examination in French."

Fox smiled blandly. He had taken a course of gramophone lessons in French and now followed closely an intermediate course on the radio.

"I'm not quite up to it as yet, sir," he said, "but I'd be glad to listen if you feel like doing it yourself."

"Bless you, Fox, I should make a complete ass of myself. Got your prints, Bailey?"

"I've been over the ground," said Detective-Sergeant Bailey guardedly.

"Then call in the first witness. Find out if any of them are particularly anxious to get away, and I'll take them in order of urgency."

"Very good, sir."

Bailey, with an air of mulish indifference, disappeared through the altar door. In a moment he came back.

"Gentleman just fainted," he grumbled.

"Oh, Lord!" apostrophised Alleyn. "Have a look, will you, Curtis? Which is it, Bailey?"

"One of those affairs in purple shirts, the dark one."

"My oath," said Alleyn.

Dr. Curtis uttered a brief "Tsss!" and disappeared. Bailey emerged with Father Garnette.

"I'm extremely sorry to have kept you waiting, sir," said Alleyn, "but you will understand that there were several matters to deal with. Shall we go down into the chairs there?"

Garnette inclined his head and led the way. He seated himself unhurriedly and hid his hands in his wide sleeves. Fox, all bland detachment, strolled to a near-by pew and seemed to be absorbed in his sketch-plan of the chancel and sanctuary. Nigel, at a glance from Alleyn, joined Inspector Fox and took out his notebook. A shorthand report of the interviews would do no harm. Father Garnette did not so much as glance at Nigel and Fox. Alleyn pulled forward a large fald-stool and sat on it with his back to the flickering torch. The priest and the policeman regarded each other steadily.

"I am appalled," said Father Garnette loudly. His voice was mellifluous and impossibly sorrowful. "Ap-PALL-ed."

"Unpleasant business, isn't it?" remarked Alleyn.

"I am bewildered. I do not understand, as yet, what has happened. What unseen power has struck down this dear soul in the very moment of spiritual ecstasah?"

"Cyanide of potassium I *think*," said Alleyn coolly, "but of course that's not official."

The embroidery on the white sleeves quivered slightly.

"But that is a poison," said Father Garnette.

"One of the deadliest," said Alleyn.

"I am appalled," said Father Garnette.

"The possibility of suicide will have to be explored, of course."

"Suicide!"

"It does not seem likely, certainly. Accident is even more improbable, I should say."

"You mean, then, that she—that she—that murder has been done!"

"That will be for a jury to decide. There will be an inquest, of course. In the meantime there are one or two questions I should like to ask you, Mr. Garnette. I need not remind you that you are not obliged to answer them."

"I know nothing of such matters. I simply wish to do my duty."

"That's excellent, sir," said Alleyn politely. "Now as regards the deceased. I've got her name and address, but I should like to learn a little more about her. You knew her personally as well as officially, I expect?"

"All my children are my friends. Cara Quayne was a very dear friend. Hers was a rare soul, Inspector—ah?"

"Alleyn, sir."

"Inspector Alleyn. Hers was a rare soul, singularly fitted for the tremendous spiritual discoverahs to which it was granted I should point the way."

"Oh, yes. For how long has she been a member of your congregation?"

"Let me think. I can well remember the first evening I was aware of her. I felt the presence of something vital, a kind of intensitah, a—how can I put it?—an increased receptivitah. We have our own words for expressing these experiences."

"I hardly think I should understand them," remarked Alleyn dryly. "Can you give me the date of her first visit?"

"I believe I can. It was on the festival of Aeger. December the fifteenth of last year."

"Since then she has been a regular attendant?"

"Yes. She had attained to the highest rank."

"By that you mean she was a Chosen Vessel?"

Father Garnette bent his extraordinary eyes on the inspector.

"Then you know something of our ritual, Inspector Alleyn?"

"Very little, I am afraid."

"Do you know that you yourself are exceedingly receptive?"

"I receive facts," said Alleyn, "as a spider does flies."

"Ah." Father Garnette nodded his head slowly. "This is not the time. But I think it will come. Well, ask what you will, Inspector."

"I gather that you knew Miss Quayne intimately—that in the course of her preparation for to-night's ceremony you saw a great deal of her."

"A great deal."

"I understand she took the name of Frigga in your ceremony?"

"That is so," said Father Garnette uneasily.

"The wife of Odin, I seem to remember."

"In our ritual the relationship is one of the spirit."

"Ah, yes," said Alleyn. "Had you any reason to believe she suffered from depression or was troubled about anything?"

"I am certain of the contrarah. She was in a state of tranquilitah and joy."

"I see. No worries over money?"

"Money? No. She was what the world calls rich."

"What do you call it, sir?"

Father Garnette gave a frank and dreadfully boyish laugh.

"Why, I should call her rich too, Inspector," he cried gaily.

"Any unhappy love affair, do you know?" pursued Alleyn.

Father Garnette did not answer for a moment. Then he said sadly:

"Ah, Inspector Alleyn, we speak in different languages."

"I didn't realise that," said Alleyn. "Can you translate my question into your own language, or would you rather not answer it?"

"You misunderstand me. Cara Quayne was not concerned

with earthly love; she was on the threshold of a new spiritual life."

"And apparently she has crossed it."

"You speak more faithfully than you realise. I earnestly believe she has crossed it."

"No love affair," said Alleyn, and wrote it down in his notebook. "Was she on friendly terms with the other Initiates?"

"There is perfect loving kindness among them. Nay, that does not express my meaning. The Initiates have attained to the third plane where all human relationships merge in an ecstatic indifference. They cannot hate for there is no hatred They realise that hatred is *maya*—illusion."

"And love?"

"If you mean earthlah love, that too is illusion."

"Then," said Alleyn, "if you follow the idea to a logical conclusion, what one does cannot matter as long as one's actions spring from one's emotions for if these are illusion—or am I wrong?"

"Ah," exclaimed Father Garnette, "I knew I was right. We must have a long talk some day, my dear fellow."

"You are very kind," said Alleyn. "What did Miss Wade mean when she said: 'All that sort of thing should have been kept out'?"

"Did Miss Wade say that?"

"Yes."

"I cannot imagine what she meant. The poor soul was very distressed no doubt."

"What do you think Mrs. Candour meant when she said she knew something dreadful would happen and that she had said so to M. de Ravigne?"

"I did not hear her," answered Father Garnette. His manner suggested that Alleyn as well as Mrs. Candour had committed a gross error in taste.

"Another question, Mr. Garnette. In the course of your interviews with Miss Quayne can you remember any incident or remark that would throw any light on this matter?"

"None."

"This is a very well-appointed hall."

"We think it beautiful," said Father Garnette complacently.

"Please do not think me impertinent. I am obliged to ask

these questions. Is it supported and kept up by subscription?"

"My people welcome as a privilege the right to share in the hospitalitah of the Sacred Flame."

"You mean they pay the running expenses?"

"Yes."

"Was Miss Quayne a generous supporter?"

"Dear soul, yes, indeed she was."

"Do you purchase the wine for the ceremony?"

"I do."

"Would you mind giving me the name of this wine and the address of the shop?"

"It comes from Harrods. I think the name is—let me see—'Le Comte's Invalid Port'."

Alleyn repressed a shudder and wrote it down.

"You decant it yourself? I mean you pour it into the silver flagon?"

"On this occasion, no. I believe Claude Wheatley made all the preparations this evening."

"Would you mind telling me exactly what he would have done?"

"Certainly. He would take an unopened bottle of wine from a cupboard in my room, draw the cork and pour the contents into the vessel. He would then make ready the goblet."

"Make ready——?"

Father Garnette's expression changed a little. He looked at once mulish and haughty.

"A certain preparation is necessarah," he said grandly.

"Oh, yes, of course. You mean the flame that appeared. How was that done? Methylated spirit?"

"In tabliod form," confessed Father Garnette.

"I know," cried Alleyn cheerfully. "The things women use for heating curling-tongs."

"Possiblah," said Father Garnette stiffly. "In our ritual, Inspector Alleyn, the goblet itself is holy and blessed. By the very act of pouring in the wine, this too becomes sacred—sacred by contact with the Cup. Our ceremony of the Cup, though it embraces the virtues of various communions in Christian churches, is actually entirely different in essentials and in intention."

"I was not," said Alleyn coldly, "so mistaken as to suspect

any affinity. Having filled the flagon Mr. Wheatley would then put it—where?"

"In that niche over there on our right of the sanctuarah."

"And what is the procedure with the methylated tablet?"

"Prior to the service Claude comes before the altar and after prostrating himself three times, draws the Sacred Cup from its Monstrance. As he does this he repeats a little prayer in Norse. He genuflects thrice and then rising to his feet he—ah—he——"

"Drops in the tablet and puts the cup away again?"

"Yes."

"I see. Mr. Bathgate tells me the flame appeared after you laid your hands over the cup. How is this done?"

"I—ah—I employ a little capsule," said Father Garnette.

"Really? What does it contain?"

"I believe the substance is known as zinc—ah—ethyl."

"Oh, yes. Very ingenious. You turn away for a moment as you use it perhaps?"

"That is so."

"It all seems quite clear now. One more question. Has there, to your knowledge, ever been any form of poison kept on the premises of this building?"

Father Garnette turned as white as his robes and said no, definitely not.

"Thank you very much. I greatly appreciate your courtesy in answering so readily. I hope you will not mind very much if I ask you to wait in the—is that a vestry over there? It is!—in the vestry, while I see these other people. No doubt you will be glad to change into less ceremonial dress."

"I shall avail myself of the opportunitah to regain in meditation my tranquilitah and spiritual at-oneness."

"Do," said Alleyn cordially.

"My sub-conscious mind, impregnated with the word, will flow to you-wards. In all humilitah I believe I may help you in your task. There are more things in Heaven and earth, Inspector Alleyn——"

"There are indeed, sir," agreed the inspector dryly. "Have you any objection to being searched before you go?"

"Searched? No—er—no, certainly not. Certainly not."

"That's very sensible. Pure routine you know. I'll send a man in."

Father Garnette withdrew to the vestry accompanied by a plain-clothes man.

"Damn', sickly, pseudo, bogus, mumbo-jumbo," said Alleyn with great violence. "What do you think of him, Fox?"

"Well, sir," said Fox placidly, "I must say I wondered if the gentleman knew much more about what he seemed to be talking about than I did."

"And well you might, my Foxkin, well you might. Hullo, Bathgate."

"Hullo," said Nigel guardedly.

"Enjoying yourself?"

"I'm taking shorthand notes. I seem to remember that you have a passion for shorthand notes."

"Ain't dat de truff, Lawd! Have you read 'Ole Man Adam'?"

"Yes."

"I wish Garnette had. Fox!"

"Yes, sir?"

"Send someone else into the vestry with Mr. Garnette, will you, and get them to look him over. And any of the others I send in. Where's the wardress?"

"In the porch out there."

"She can deal with the ladies. Tell them to look for a small piece of crumpled paper or anything that could have held powder. I don't think they'll find it. Bailey!"

Detective-Sergeant Bailey moved down from the sanctuary.

"Yes, sir?"

"The next, if you please."

Bailey went through the little door and reappeared with Claude Wheatley and a general air of having taken an unlucky dip in a bran-tub. Fox returned with another plain-clothes man who went into the vestry.

"This gentleman isn't feeling too good, sir. He wants to go home," said Bailey.

"Oh, yes," said Claude. "Oh, yes, please. Oh, yes."

"Sorry you're upset, Mr. Wheatley," said Alleyn.

"Upset! I'm fearfully ill, Inspector. You can't think. Oh, please may I sit down."

"Do."

Claude sank into one of the Initiates' chairs and gazed wide-eyed at the inspector.

"I feel too ghastly," he moaned.

"What upset you?"

"That appalling old woman. She said such frightful things. I do think old women are awful."

"Whom do you mean?"

"The Candour female."

"What did she say to upset you?"

"Oh, I don't know. I do feel shocking."

Dr. Curtis came out of Garnette's room and strolled down.

"Mr. Wheatley felt a bit squeamish," he said cheerfully, "but he'll be all right. He's had a peg of some really excellent brandy. Father Garnette's a lucky man."

"Splendid," rejoined Alleyn. "Would you be a good fellow and go back to them, Curtis? Some of the others may need attention."

"Certainly." Curtis and Alleyn exchanged a glance and the doctor returned.

"Now, Mr. Wheatley," Alleyn began. "I think you look much better. I've a few questions I'd like to put to you. You can refuse to answer if you think it advisable."

"Yes, but that's all very well. Suppose I do refuse, then you'll start thinking things."

"I might, certainly."

"Yes--well—there!"

"Difficult for you," remarked Alleyn.

"Well, anyway," said Claude very peevishly, "you can ask them. I may as well know what they are."

"I have already asked the first. What did Mrs. Candour say to upset you?"

Claude wriggled.

"Jealous old cat. The whole thing is she loathes Father Garnette taking the slightest notice of anybody else. She's always too loathsomely spiteful for words—especially to Lionel and me. How she dared! And anyway everybody knows all about it. I'd hardly be stupid enough to——" Here Claude stopped short.

"To do what, Mr. Wheatley?"

"To do anything like that, even if I wanted to, and anyway I always thought Cara Quayne was a marvellous person—so piercingly decorative."

"What would you hardly be stupid enough to do?" asked Alleyn patiently.

"To—well—well—to do anything to the wine. Everybody knows it was my week to make preparation."

"You mean you poured the wine into the silver flagon and put the methylated tablet into the cup. What did Mrs. Candour suggest?"

"She didn't actually suggest anything. She simply said I did it. She kept on saying so. Old cat."

"I shouldn't let it worry you. Now, Mr. Wheatley, will you think carefully. Did you notice any peculiar, any unusual smell when you poured out the wine?"

"Any smell!" ejaculated Claude opening his eyes very wide. "Any *smell*!"

"Any smell."

"Well, of course I'd just lit all the censers you know. Don't you think our incense is rather divine, Inspector? Father Garnette gets it from India. It's sweet-almond blossom. There's the oil too. We burn a dish of the oil in front of the altar. I lit it just before I got the wine. It's a gorgeous perfume."

"Evidently. You got the bottle of wine from Mr. Garnette's room. Was it unopened?"

"Yes. I drew the cork."

"You put nothing else in the flagon?"

Claude looked profoundly uncomfortable.

"Well—well, anyway I didn't put any poison in, if that's what you're hinting."

"What else did you put?"

"If you must know it's something from a little bottle that Father Garnette keeps. It has a ceremonial significance. It's always done."

"Have you any idea what it is?"

"I don't know."

"Where is this bottle kept?"

"In the little cupboard in Father Garnette's room."

"I see. Now as I understand it you took the wine to each of the Initiates in turn. Did you at any time notice an unusual smell from the cup?"

"I never touched the cup, Inspector. I never touched it. They all handed it round from one to the other. I didn't notice any smell except the incense. Not ever."

"Right. Did you notice Miss Quayne at all when she took the cup?"

" Did I notice her? My God, yes."

" What happened exactly?"

" It was simply appalling. You see I thought she was in Blessed Ecstasy. Well, I mean she was, up to the time she took the cup. She had spoken in ecstasy and everything. And then she drank. And then—oh, it was frightful! She gave a sort of gasp. A fearfully deep gasp and sort of sharp. She made a face. And then she kind of slewed round and she dropped the cup. Her eyes looked like a doll's eyes. Glistening. And then she twitched all over—jerked—ugh! She fell down in a sort of jerk. Oh, I'm going to be sick, I think."

" No, you're not," said the inspector very firmly. " You are going home. Go into the vestry and change your clothes."

" Where's Lionel?"

" He'll join you in a moment. Good night."

" Oh," said Claude rolling a languishing eye at Alleyn, " you are marvellous, Inspector. Oh, I would so very much rather not be sick. Good-bye."

" Good night."

Claude, under escort, walked with small steps into the vestry where they could hear him talking in a sort of feeble scream to the officer who searched him.

" Oh," cried Inspector Fox suddenly in a falsetto voice, " oh, Inspector, I think I'm going to be sick."

" And well you might be," said Nigel, grinning. " What a loathly, what a nauseating, what an unspeakable little dollop."

" Horrid, wasn't it?" agreed Alleyn absently. " Damn that incense," he added crossly. " Sweet almond too, just the very thing——" he paused and stared thoughtfully at Fox. " Let's have Lionel," he said.

Lionel was produced. His manner was a faithful reproduction of Claud's and he added nothing that was material to the evidence. He was sent into the vestry, whence he and Claude presently emerged wearing, the one, a saxe-blue and the other, a pinkish-brown suit. They fussed off down the aisle and disappeared. Alleyn sent for Mrs. Candour.

CHAPTER VI

MRS. CANDOUR AND MR. OGDEN

Mrs. Candour had wept and her tears had blotted her make-up. She had dried them and in doing so had blotted her make-up again. Her face was an unlovely mess of mascara, powder and rouge. It hung in flabby pockets from the bone of her skull. She looked bewildered, frightened and vindictive. Her hands were tremulous. She was a large woman born to be embarrassingly ineffectual. In answer to Alleyn's suggestion that she should sit on one of the chairs, she twitched her loose lips, whispered something, and walked towards them with that precarious gait induced by excessive flesh mounted on French heels. She moved in a thick aura of essence of violet. Alleyn waited until she was seated before he gave her the customary information that she was under no obligation to answer any questions. He paused, but she made no comment. She simply stared in front of her with lacklustre eyes.

"I take it," said Alleyn, "that you have no objection. Was Miss Cara Quayne a personal friend of yours?"

"Not a great friend."

"An acquaintance?"

"Yes. We—we—only met here." Her voice was thin and faintly common. "At least, well, I did go to see her once or twice."

"Have you got any ideas on the subject of this business?"

"Oh my God!" moaned Mrs. Candour. "I believe it was a judgment."

"A judgment?"

Mrs. Candour drew a lace handkerchief from her bosom.

"What had Miss Quayne done," asked Alleyn, "to merit so terrible a punishment?"

"She coveted the vow of Odin."

"I'm afraid I do not know what that implies."

"That is how I feel about it," said Mrs. Candour, exactly as if she had just finished a lucid and explicit statement. "Father Garnette is above all that sort of thing. He is not of this world. He had told us so, often and often. But Cara was a very passionate sort of woman." She dropped her voice and added with an air of illicit relish: "Cara was dreadfully over-sexed. Pardon me."

"Oh," said Alleyn.

"Yes. Of course I know that ecstatic union is blessed, but ecstatic union is one thing and——" Here Mrs. Candour stopped short and looked frightened.

"Do you mean," said Alleyn, "that——?"

"I don't mean anything definite," interrupted Mrs. Candour in a hurry. "Please, please don't attach any importance to what I've just said. It was only my idea. I'm so dreadfully upset. Poor Cara. Poor, poor Cara."

"Mr. Claude Wheatley tells me——"

"Don't you believe anything that little beast says, Mr.—er—Inspector—er——"

"Inspector Alleyn, madam."

"Oh—Inspector Alleyn. Claude's a little pig. Always prying into other people's affairs. I've told Father, but he's so *good* he doesn't *see*."

"I gather you rather upset Mr. Wheatley by referring to his preparations for the service."

"Serves him right if I did. He kept on saying it was murder, he knew it was murder, and that Cara was such a lovely woman and everyone was jealous of her. I just said: 'Well,' I said, 'if she was murdered,' I said, 'who prepared the goblet and the flagon?' And then he fainted. I thought it looked very queer."

"Miss Quayne *was* a very beautiful woman, I believe?" said Alleyn casually.

"I never could see it. Of course, if you admire that type. But just because that M. de Ravigne went silly over her—I mean everyone knows what foreigners are like. If you give them any encouragement, that is. Well, I myself—— I suppose Claude told you that—about her looks, I mean. Or was it Father Garnette? *Was* it?"

"I'm afraid I don't remember," said Alleyn.

Mrs. Candour jerked her chin up. For a second her face was horrible. "Cara doesn't look very pretty now," she said softly.

Alleyn turned away.

"I mustn't keep you any longer," he said. "There's only

one other point. You were the first, after Mr. Garnette, to take the cup. Did you notice any peculiar smell?"

"I don't know. I don't remember. No, I don't think so."

"I see. Thank you. That is all, I think."

"I may go home?"

"Certainly. There is a wardress in the lobby. Would you object to being examined?"

"Searched!"

"Just looked over, you know. It's the usual thing."

"Oh, yes, please—I'd rather—much rather."

"Thank you. You will be given notice of the inquest."

"The inquest! Oh, how dreadful. I don't know how I'm to get over this—I'm so shockingly sensitive. Inspector Alleyn, you've been marvellously kind. I always thought that police methods were brutal." She looked up at him with a general air of feminine helplessness somewhat negatived by a glint of appraisal in her eye. It was a ghastly combination. She held out her hand.

"Good-bye. Inspector Alleyn.

"Good evening, madam," said Alleyn.

She wobbled away on her French heels.

"This is a very unsavoury case," said Nigel.

"It's murder," said Inspector Fox mildly.

"Most foul," added Alleyn, "as at the best it is. But this *most* foul—— Yes, I agree with you, Bathgate. Bailey!"

"Here" said that worthy, rising up from behind the lectern.

"Next please."

"Right, sir."

"What did you make of Mrs. Candour?" asked Alleyn.

"A perfectly appalling old girl," said Nigel fervently.

"Oh, yes. All that. Almost a pathological case, one might imagine. Still, the exhibition of jealousy was interesting, didn't you think, Fox?"

"Yes, I did" agreed Fox. "This Father Garnette seems to be a peculiar sort of man for the ministry."

"Exactly."

"When she made that appalling remark about Cara not looking very pretty now," said Nigel, "she was positively evil. Without a shadow of doubt she loathed the poor woman. I am surprised at your allowing her to escape. She should have been handcuffed immediately, I consider."

"Don't show off," said Alleyn abstractedly.

"I'll be right there, Ahfficer. Where's the Chief?" cried Mr. Ogden from afar. He appeared with Bailey by the altar, saw Alleyn, and made straight for him.

"Well, well, well. Look what's here!" exclaimed Mr. Ogden.

"Yes, look," said Alleyn. "It's a pathetic sight, Mr. Ogden. Here we go grubbing along—however."

"Say, Inspector, what's the big idea? You look kind of world-weary."

"Do I, Mr. Ogden, do I?"

"And just when I was congratulating myself on sitting right next the works for an inside survey of British criminal investigation."

"And now you'll never talk again about our wonderful police."

"Is that so? Well, I'm not saying anything."

"You won't mind if I ask you a few dreary questions, perhaps? We have to do our stuff, you know."

"Go right ahead. My, my!" said Mr. Ogden contemplating Alleyn with an air of the liveliest satisfaction. "You certainly are the goods. I guess you've got British Manufacture stamped some place where it won't wear off. All this quiet deprecation —it's direct from a sure-fire British best-seller. I can't hardly believe it's true."

Nigel, from his unobtrusive seat by Fox, allowed himself an irritating grin. Alleyn saw it and looked furious.

"That sounds a very damning description, Mr. Ogden," he said, and hurried on. He asked Ogden if he had noticed a peculiar smell and got the now customary reply that the reek of incense was so strong that it would drown any other smell.

"Though, now I get to thinking about it," added Mr. Ogden, "I do seem to remember it was uncommon powerful to-night. Yes, sir, I believe I thought those two he-he boys were certainly hitting up the atmosphere."

"Can you remember at what precise moment you thought this?"

Mr. Ogden's face became very pink. For the first time since Alleyn met him he hesitated.

"Well, Mr. Ogden?"

"Well now, Inspector, I can't remember. Isn't that just too bad?"

"Miss Jenkins was next to you in the circle, wasn't she?"

"That is correct," said Mr. Ogden tonelessly.

"Yes. Now look here, sir. You're a business man I take it?"

"Surely."

"Thank God for that. I don't know how much this organisation means to you, and I don't want to say anything that will be offensive, but I'm longing for a sensible man's view of the whole situation. An intelligent and knowledgeable view."

"Inside dope," said Mr. Ogden.

"Exactly."

"Go right ahead. Maybe I'll talk and maybe not. Maybe I don't know anything."

"I gather you are an officer of the executive?"

"That's so. A Warden."

"You know all these people quite well, I suppose?"

"Why, yes. We are all enthusiastic about uplift. The spirit of comradeship pervades our relationship. You Britishers are weaned on starch, I guess, but I hand myself out a whole lot of roses for the way I've got this bunch started. Right at the commencement of the movement they used to sit round looking at each other like they all suffered from frostbite. Now they've got together like regular fellows. They're a great little crowd."

"You've been interested in the organisation since its foundation?"

"That's so. That was way back in—why, it must be two years ago. I met up with Father Garnette coming across to England. I move about some, Inspector. That's my job. That trip it was the Brightwater Creek Gold Mining Company. Yes, that's what it would be. I recollect I had Father Garnette accept a small nugget as a souvenir. That would be May two years ago. I was very, very much impressed with Father Garnette's personality."

"Really," said Alleyn.

"Yes, sir. I'm a self-made man, Chief I was raised in a ten-cent fish joint, and my education simply forgot to occur, but when I meet culture I respect it. I like it handed out good and peppy, and that's the way Father Garnette let me have it. By the time we hit Southampton we'd doped out a scheme for this church, and before six months had passed we were drawing congregations of three hundred."

"Remarkable," said Alleyn.

"It was swell."

"Where did the money come from?"

"Why, from the flock. Father Garnette had a small hall

'way down Great Holland Road. Compared with this it was a bum show, but say, did we work it? The Father had a service every night for a month. He got right down to it. A small bunch of very influential people came along. Just one or two, but they roped in more. When he'd got them all enthusiastic he had an appeal week and loosed a line of high-voltage oratory. Sob-stuff. I gave five grand and I'm proud to spill the beans."

"Who were the other subscribers?"

"Why, Dagmar Candour was in on the plush seats with a thousand pounds and poor Cara checked in at the same level. Each of those ladies seemed ambitious to carry off the generosity stakes. Then there was M. de Ravigne and—and all the bunch of Initiates. I guess I'd hold up operations some if I recited all the subscribers."

"Miss Quayne must have been a very wealthy woman?"

"She was very, very wealthy, and she had a lovely nature. Why, only last month she deposited five thousand in bearer bonds in the safe back there beyond the altar. They are waiting there until another five is raised among the rest of us and then it's to form a building fund for a new church. That's how generous she was."

Nigel had paused, pen in air, to gape at Mr. Ogden's enthusiastic countenance, and to reflect a little childishly on the gullibility of average men and women. None of these people was particularly stupid, he would say, except perhaps Mrs. Candour. Miss Quayne had looked interesting. Mr. Ogden was obviously an intelligent business man. Janey Jenkins, Maurice Pringle, M. de Ravigne were none of them idiots. He forgot all about Miss Wade. Yet all these apparently sensible individuals had been duped by Garnette into parting with sums of money. Extraordinary! At this moment he remembered his own reaction to Father Garnette's oratory and felt less superior.

"That's how generous she was," repeated Mr. Ogden.

"What was the relationship between M. de Ravigne and the deceased?"

"Crazy about her," answered Mr. Ogden succinctly.

"Yet I rather gathered that the Initiates were a cut above earthly love," ventured Alleyn.

"I guess M. de Ravigne has not altogether cast off the shackles of the body," said Mr. Ogden dryly. "But get this:

Cara was not interested. No, sir. Her soul was yearning after the inner mysteries of the spirit."

"Did you hear what Mr. Pringle and Mrs. Candour said immediately after the tragedy?"

Mr. Ogden looked uncomfortable.

"Well, I can't say——"

Alleyn consulted his notebook and read aloud the conversation as Nigel had reported it to him.

"Mr. Pringle said: 'The whole thing is a farce.' He talked about retribution. He said to Mrs. Candour: 'You would have taken her place if you could.' What do you think he meant, Mr. Ogden?"

"I don't know, Chief, honest I don't," said Mr. Ogden, looking very worried. "Maybe there was a little competition between the ladies for spiritool honours. Maybe Pringle kind of thought Mrs. Candour would have enjoyed a spell as Chosen Vessel."

"I see."

"You don't want to make too much of it. They were all het up. That boy's three hundred per cent nerves. Garsh!" Mr. Ogden went on fervently, "I wish to hell we could smoke."

"Same here," agreed Alleyn. "I'd give my soul for a pipe. No hope for me, I'm afraid, but I don't think I need keep you much longer, Mr. Ogden."

Mr. Ogden looked astounded.

"Well, say!" he remarked, "that's certainly a surprise to me. I don't get the works this trip?"

"Nor the next, I hope. Unless you can think of anything you feel we ought to know I shan't worry you any more until after the inquest. Of course, if you have any theory I should be extremely glad——"

"For Gard's sake!" ejaculated Mr. Ogden. "Listen. Are they all this way around the Yard?" He looked at Fox and lowered his voice to a penetrating whisper. "He looks more like a regular dick. An' yet if I worded him maybe he'd talk back like a bud's guide to society stuff. Is that so?"

"You must meet Inspector Fox and find out," said Alleyn. "Fox!"

"Hullo, sir?" Fox hoisted himself up and walked solemnly round the pews towards them.

"Mr. Ogden finds our methods a little lacking in colour."

"Indeed, sir?"

" Yes. Can you suggest any improvements? Have you any questions you would like to put to Mr. Ogden, Fox? Something really startling, you know."

" Well, sir, I can't say I have. Unless "—Fox paused a moment and stared at Alleyn—" unless Mr. Ogden can tell us anything about the—er—the ingredients of the cup."

" Can you, Mr. Ogden."

" Surely. It's some sissy dope from a departmental store. I've seen the bottles. Invalid Port. One half per cent alcohol. But——"

" Yes?"

" Well, since you're asking, Chief, I reckon Father Garnette has it pepped up some. A drop of brandy I'd say. Mind, I don't know."

" There you are, Fox. Anything else?"

" I don't think so, sir," said Fox with a smile, " unless the gentleman would like to be searched."

" Would you care to be searched, Mr. Ogden? We do that sort of thing rather neatly."

" Well, for crying out loud!" exclaimed Mr. Ogden. He looked from Alleyn to Fox, cast up his eyes, passed a plump hand over his head and burst out laughing.

" Get to it," he begged, " get to it. For the Lord's sake get to it. Would I care to be searched!"

" Carry on, Fox," said Alleyn.

Fox took out a notebook and Alleyn, with the swift precision of a pick-pocket, explored the inner fastnesses of Mr. Ogden's suit.

" Note-case. One fiver and three singles. Pocket-book. Letter. Typewritten, stamped and sealed. Address ' Hector K. Manville, Ogden-Schultz Gold-refining and Extracting Co., 81, East forty-fifth Street, Boston, Massachusetts.' Letter refers to a new gold refining process. It's rather technical."

Fox read it with difficulty.

" Bill from Harrods. £9 10*s.* 8*d.* To account rendered. Date: November 2nd of this year. Letter beginning ' Dear Sam,' signed Heck. Date——"

Alleyn murmured on. It was all over before Mr. Ogden had left off chuckling.

" No phials of poison," said Alleyn lightly. " That's all, sir."

" It was real smart," declared Mr. Ogden handsomely.

"They don't fan a man neater than that in the States. That's saying some. Well, Inspector, if that's all I guess I'll move off. Say, it seems real callous for me to be standing here talking facetious when Cara Quayne is lying—— See here, Chief, have I got to say murdered?"

"We must wait for the inquest, Mr. Ogden."

The American's genial face had suddenly become preternaturally solemn like that of a clown, or a child who has been reproved for laughing.

"If it is murder," he said quietly, "and the trail's not just all that easy and—aw hell, Chief, I've got the dollars and I ain't paralysed yet."

With which cryptic remark Mr. Ogden took himself off.

"Is he real?" asked Nigel, "or is he a murderer with unbridled histrionic ambitions? Surely no American was ever so American. Surely——"

"Do stop making these exclamatory interjections. You behave for all the world like a journalistic Greek chorus. Fox, what *did* the gentleman mean by his last remark. The one about not suffering from paralysis?"

"I understood him to be offering unlimited sums of money to the police and the prosecution, sir."

"Bribery thinly disguised, depend upon it," said Nigel. "I tell you no American was ever——"

"I don't know. His eyes, at all events, are original. People do run true to type. It's an axiom of police investigation. Next please, Bailey."

Janey Jenkins was next.

CHAPTER VII

JANEY AND MAURICE

Miss Jenkins was one of those women who are instinctively thought of by their Christian names. She looked like a Janey. She was shortish, compact, with straight hair, well brushed, snapping black eyes, snub nose, and an amusing mouth. Without being pretty she was attractive. Her age was about twenty-two. She walked briskly towards Alleyn, sat down composedly and said: "Well, Inspector Alleyn, let's get it over. I'll answer any questions you like, compromising or uncompromising, as long as it's over quickly."

"I thank whatever gods may be," rejoined Alleyn, "and there are enough to begin with on the premises, if you'll excuse my saying so."

"We *are* rather generously endowed, aren't we?" said Janey.

"You must forgive me. I didn't mean to be offensive."

"You weren't. I'm not altogether an ass. This is rather a rum show, I dare say."

"You don't talk like my idea of an Initiate."

"Don't I? Well perhaps I'm not a very good one. I'm thinking of back-sliding, Inspector Alleyn. Oh, not because of this awful business. At least—I don't know. Perhaps it has shown us up in rather an unattractive light." She paused and wrinkled her forehead. "It all seems very bogus to you I expect, but—but—there's something in it—or I thought so."

"When I was an undergraduate I became a Plymouth Brother for two months. It seemed frightfully important at the time. I believe nowadays they go in for Black Magic."

"Yes, Maurice tried that when he was up. Then he switched over to this."

"You speak of Mr. Pringle?"

"Yes."

"Did he introduce you to this church?"

"Clever of you," said Janey. "Yes, he did."

"When was this?"

"Oh, about six months ago."

" You have advanced rather quickly, surely."

" This was my first evening as an Initiate. Maurice has been one for some time. I was to have begun special instruction next week."

" You don't mean to go on with it?"

" I don't," said Janey.

" Would you mind telling me why?"

" I think perhaps I would." She looked thoughtfully at Alleyn. " No, I'll tell you. I've got my doubts about it. I've had my doubts about it for some time, to be quite honest."

" Then why——?"

" Maurice was so terribly keen. You see we're engaged. He could talk of nothing else. He's awfully highly strung—terribly sensitive—and—and sort of vulnerable, and I thought——"

" You thought you would keep an eye on him—that it?"

" Yes. I don't know why I'm telling you this."

" I am sure you will not regret doing so. Miss Jenkins, do you know what Mr. Pringle was driving at when he said that Mr. Garnette was keeping them all quiet, that Mrs. Candour would have taken Miss Quayne's place if she could, and that he was going to tell everybody something?"

" How do you know Maurice said that?"

" You may remember he was in the middle of it when I arrived. He stopped short when he saw me. I heard some of it. Mr. Bathgate has told me the rest. What is the explanation?"

" I don't think I can answer that."

" Can't you? Why not?"

" I don't want to stir it all up. It has got nothing to do with this dreadful thing. I'm sure of that."

" You cannot possibly be sure of that. Listen to me. Mr. Bathgate is prepared to swear that Miss Quayne put nothing into the cup after it was handed to her. She took it by the stem in both hands and drank from it without changing their position. She died two minutes after she drank from the cup. It had gone round the circle of Initiates. No one else, except the acolyte and Mr. Garnette, had handled it. Can you not see that the inter-relationships of those six people are of importance? Can you not see that I must learn all I may of them. I must not try to persuade you to speak against your judgment —if I did this I should grossly exceed my duty. But please, Miss Jenkins, *don't* say: ' It's got nothing to do with the case.'

We don't know what may or may not bear on the case. There is only one person who could tell us that."

"Only one person? You mean—a guilty person?"

"I do. If such a one exists."

There was a long silence.

"I'll tell you this much," said Janey at last. "Maurice hero-worshipped Father Garnette. He went, as Mr. Ogden would say, crazy about him. I think Father Garnette took hold of his imagination. Maurice is very responsive to personal magnetism."

"Yes."

"I fell for it myself. When he preaches—it's rather extraordinary—one feels as though the most terrific revelation is being made. No, that's not quite it. Everything seems to be beautifully dovetailed and balanced."

"A sense of exquisite precision," murmured Alleyn. "I believe opium smokers experience it."

Janey flushed.

"You mean we were drugged with words. I don't think I quite admit that. But where was I? Oh. Well, a little while ago Maurice began to suspect that things were happening all the time in the background. He had put Father Garnette on a pedestal, you see, and the least suggestion of—of worldly interest seemed wrong to Maurice. Some of the women in the congregation, Mrs. Candour and poor Cara too, I'm afraid, were rather blatantly doting. Maurice got all worked up about it. He minded most dreadfully. That's what he meant when he talked like that about Mrs. Candour."

"He meant that Mrs. Candour was jealous of Miss Quayne and that Mr. Garnette had kept it quiet?"

"Yes."

"I see."

"But not that Mrs. Candour was so jealous that—he didn't mean that. Please, please don't think that. It was nothing. Maurice was hysterical. He sees everything in an exaggerated light. You do believe me, don't you? Don't you?"

"I'm not sure," said Alleyn, "I think you are understating things, you know."

"I'm not. Oh, why did I say anything! I won't answer any more questions. Let me go." Janey's voice shook. She stood up, her hands clenched, her pupils dilated.

"Of course you may go, Miss Jenkins," said Alleyn very

quietly. "You have had a wretched experience and it's unnerved you. Believe me, you need not reproach yourself for anything you have told me. Really. If only people would understand that in these cases they are under a moral obligation to help the police, that by keeping things back they may actually place an innocent man or woman in the gravest danger! However, I grow pompous and in a minute I might become facetious. Save yourself, Miss Jenkins, and go home."

Janey managed a smile and brushed her hand across her face.

"Oh dear," she whispered.

"You're done up," said Alleyn quickly. "Bathgate, dodge out and get a taxi for Miss Jenkins, will you?"

"I think I'd better wait for Maurice, please."

"Do you? Would you like some of Mr. Garnette's brandy?"

"No thank you. I'll just wait in the back pews if I may."

"Of course you may. If it wouldn't bother you too much the wardress will run over you. Have you ever been searched?"

"Never. It sounds beastly, but I suppose I must."

"That's very sensible. Inspector Fox will take you to the wardress. I'll see your young man now."

Janey walked firmly down the aisle with Fox and disappeared into the shadows. Fox returned and Bailey produced Maurice Pringle.

Maurice looked quickly about him, and stopped like a pointer when he saw Alleyn. At the inspector's suggestion he came into the hall but refused to sit down. He thrust his hands into his pockets and seemed unable to stand still.

"Now then, Mr. Pringle," began Alleyn cheerfully.

"Where's Janey? Miss Jenkins?" demanded Maurice.

"Waiting for you."

"What do you want to know?"

"Anything you can tell me that's to the purpose."

Maurice was silent. Alleyn asked about the smell and heard about the incense. He read Maurice's previous statements from his notebook.

"What were you going to say when I came in?"

"Nothing."

"Do you usually speak in half-phrases, Mr. Pringle?"

"What d'you mean?"

"You said: 'I'm going to tell them that——' and then you know I walked in and you stopped."

Maurice snatched his left hand out of his pocket and bit at one of his fingers.

"Come. What did you mean by retribution? What would Mrs. Candour have had so willingly from Miss Quayne? What had Mr. Garnette kept quiet? What were you going to tell them?"

"I refuse to answer. It's my affair."

"Very good. Fox!"

"Sir?"

"Will you tell Miss Jenkins that Mr. Pringle does not wish to make any statements at present and that I think she need not wait? See that she gets a taxi, will you? She's a bit done up."

"Very good, sir."

"What do you mean?" said Maurice angrily. "I'm taking her home." Fox paused.

"I'm afraid I'll have to ask you to stay a little longer," said Alleyn.

"My God, how I hate officials! Sadism at its worst."

"Off you go, Fox."

"Stay where you are," said Maurice. "I'll—what's the damn' phrase—I'll talk."

Alleyn smiled and Fox blandly returned to his pew.

"You are interested in psycho-analysis, Mr. Pringle?" asked Alleyn politely.

"What's that got to do with it?" rejoined Maurice, who seemed to have set himself some impossible standard of discourtesy. "I should have thought the British Police Force scarcely knew how to pronounce the word—judging by results."

"Someone must have told me about it," said Alleyn vaguely.

Maurice looked sharply at him and then turned red.

"I'm sorry," he muttered. "This filthy show's got me all jumpy."

"Well it might. I only asked you if you were interested in psycho-analysis because you used that pass-word to the intelligentsia—'sadism.' I don't suppose you know what it means. What are your views on crowd psychology?"

"Look here, what the hell are you driving at?"

"On the psychology of oratory, for instance? What do you think happens to people when they come under the sway of, shall we say, a magnetic preacher?"

"What happens to them! My God, they are his slaves."

"Strong," said Alleyn. "Would you describe this congregation as Mr. Garnette's slaves?"

"If you must know—yes. Yes. Yes. Yes!"

"Yourself included?"

The boy looked strangely at Alleyn as though he was bringing the inspector into focus. His lips trembled.

"Look," he said.

Alleyn walked up to him, looked steadily in his face, and then murmured, so quietly that Nigel did not hear, a single word. Maurice nodded.

"How did you guess?"

"You told me to look. It's your eyes, you know. Contracted pupils. Also, if you'll forgive me, your bad manners."

"I can't help it."

"I suppose not. Is this Mr. Garnette's doing?"

"No. I mean somebody gets them for him. He—he gave me special cigarettes. Quite mild really. He said it helped one to become receptive."

"No doubt."

"And it does! It's marvellous. Everything seems so clear. Only—only——"

"It's more than mild cigarettes now, I think."

"Don't be so bloody superior. Oh, God, I'm sorry!"

"Do the other Initiates employ this short cut to spiritual ecstasy?"

"Janey doesn't. Janey doesn't know. Nor does Ogden. Don't tell Janey."

"I won't if I can help it. All the others?"

"No. Cara Quayne had begun. The Candour does. She did before Father Garnette found her. Ogden and de Ravigne don't. At least I'm not sure about de Ravigne. I want him to try. Everyone ought to try and you can always leave off."

"Can you?" said Alleyn.

"Of course. I don't mean to go on with it."

"Did you all meet here in Mr. Garnette's rooms and—smoke his cigarettes."

"At first. But lately those two—Mrs. Candour and Cara—came at separate times." Maurice put his hand to his mouth and pulled shakily at his under lip. "And then—then Cara began to make her preparations for Chosen Vessel and she came alone."

"I see."

"No, you don't. You don't see. You don't know. Only I know." He now spoke rapidly and with great vehemence as though driven by an intolerable urge. "It was one afternoon about three weeks ago when I came in to see him. No one in the church. So I went straight up here—past here—up to the door, his door. I spoke: 'are you there, Father?' They couldn't have heard. I went in—half in—they didn't see me. Oh, God! Oh, God! Frigga and Odin. The Chosen Vessel!" He gave a screech of laughter and flung himself into one of the chairs. He buried his face in his arm and sobbed quite loudly with an utter lack of restraint.

Inspector Fox strolled across the nave and stared with an air of calm appreciation at a small effigy of a most unprepossessing Nordic god. Nigel, acutely embarrassed, bent over his notebook. Detective-Sergeant Bailey emerged from his retreat, cast a glance of weary disparagement at Maurice, and went back again.

"So that is what you meant by retribution," said Alleyn. Pringle made a sort of shuddering movement, an eloquent assent.

A little figure appeared out of the shadows at the end of the hall.

"Have you quite finished, Inspector Alleyn?" asked Janey. She spoke so quietly that it took Nigel a second or two to realise how furiously angry she was.

"I've quite finished," said Alleyn gravely. "You may both go home."

She bent over Pringle.

"Maurice. Maurice darling, let's go."

"Let me alone, Janey."

"Of course I won't. I want you to take me home."

She spoke softly to him for a minute and then he got up. She took his arm. Alleyn stood aside.

"I could murder you for this," said Janey.

"Oh, my child, don't talk like that!" exclaimed Alleyn with so much feeling that Nigel stared.

Janey looked again at the inspector. Perhaps she saw something in his dark face that made her change her mind.

"All right, I won't," said Janey.

CHAPTER VIII

THE TEMPERAMENT OF M. DE RAVIGNE

After Maurice had been searched and sent home Nigel approached Alleyn with a certain air of imbecile fractiousness that he assumed whenever he wished to annoy the inspector.

"Will somebody," asked Nigel plaintively, "be good enough to explain that young man's behaviour to me?"

"What?" asked Alleyn absently.

"I want to know your explanation for Pringalism. Why did Pringle ask you to look at him? Why *did* you look at him? What did you say to Pringle? And why did Pringle cry?"

"Fox," said Alleyn. "will you take Form One for this evening?"

"Very good," said Fox, returning from his god. "What is it you were inquiring about, Mr. Bathgate?"

"Pringalism."

"Meaning the young gentleman's behaviour, sir? Well, it was rather unusual I must say. My idea is he takes something that isn't good for him."

"What do you mean, Inspector Fox? Something dietetically antagonistic? Oysters and whisky?"

"Heroin and hot air," snapped Alleyn. "Oh, Mr. Garnette, Mr. Garnette, it shall go hard if I do not catch you bending."

"I say!" said Nigel. "Do you think *Garnette*——"

"Let us have the French gentleman, please, Bailey," interrupted Alleyn.

Monsieur de Ravigne emerged with an air of sardonic aloofness. He was a good-looking man, tall for a Frenchman and extremely well groomed. He saw Alleyn and walked quickly down towards him.

"You wish to speak to me, Inspector Alleyn?"

"If you please. M. de Ravigne. Will you sit down?"

"After you, monsieur."

"No, no, monsieur, please."

They murmured and skirmished while Fox gazed at them in mild enchantment. At last they both sat down. M. de Ravigne crossed his legs and displayed an elegant foot.

" And now, sir?" he inquired.

" You are very obliging, monsieur. It is the merest formality. A few questions that we are obliged to ask in our official capacity. I am sure you understand."

" Perfectly. Let us discharge this business."

" Immediately. First, were you aware of any unusual or peculiar odour during the ceremony of the cup?"

" You allude, of course, to the odour of prussic acid," said M. de Ravigne.

" Certainly. May I ask how you realise the poison used was a cyanide?"

" I believe you yourself mentioned it, monsieur. If you did not it is no matter. I understood immediately that Cara was poisoned by cyanide. No other poison is so swift, and after she fell——" he broke off, became a little paler and then went on composedly "—after she fell, I bent over her and then—and then—I smelt it."

" I see. But not until then?"

" Not until then—no. The odour of the incense—sweet almond the acolyte tells me—was overpowering and, strangely enough, similar."

De Ravigne turned stiffly towards Alleyn.

" My Cara was murdered. That I know well. Is it possible, Mr. Inspector, that this similarity is a little too strange?"

" It is a point I shall remember, monsieur. You have used the expression ' My Cara.' Am I to understand that between you and Miss Quayne——"

" But yes. I adored her. I asked her many times to do me the honour of becoming my wife. She was, unhappily, indifferent to me. She was devout, you understand, altogether dedicated to the religious life. I see you look fixedly at me, monsieur. You are thinking perhaps that I am too calm. You have the idea of the excitable Frenchman. I should wave my hands and weep and roll about my eyes and even have a hysteric, like that little animal of a Claude."

" No, Monsieur de Ravigne. Those were not my thoughts."

" *N'importe*," murmured de Ravigne.

" *On n'est pas dupe de son cœur*——" began Alleyn.

" I see I misjudged you, M. l'Inspecteur. You have not

the conventional idea of my countrymen. Also you speak with a charming and correct accent."

"You are too kind, monsieur. Has the possibility of suicide occurred to you?"

"Why should she wish to die? She was beautiful and—loved."

"And not poor?"

"I believe, not poor."

"Did you notice her movements when she held the cup?"

"No. I did not watch," said de Ravigne.

"You are religious yourself, of course, or you would not be here?" remarked Alleyn after a pause.

M. de Ravigne delicately moved his shoulders: "I am intrigued with this church and its ceremonial. Also the idea of one godhead embracing all gods appeals to my temperament. One must have a faith, I find. It is not in my temperament to be an atheist."

"When did you first attend the services?"

"It must be—yes, I think about two years ago."

"And you became an Initiate—when?"

"Three months ago, perhaps."

"Are you a subscriber to the organisation? We must ask these questions, as I am sure you understand."

"Certainly, monsieur, one must do one's job. I subscribe a little, yes. Five shillings in the offertory always and at special times a pound. Fifty pounds when I first came. This temple was then recently established. I presented the goblet—an old one in my own family."

"A beautiful piece. Baroque at its best," said Alleyn.

"Yes. It has its history, that cup. Also I gave a statuette. In the shrine on your right, monsieur."

Alleyn looked at the wall and found M. de Ravigne's statuette. It was cast in bronze with a curious plucked technique and represented a nebulous nude figure wearing a winged helmet from which there emerged other and still more nebulous forms.

"Ah yes," said Alleyn, "most interesting. Who is the artist?"

"Myself in ecstasy, monsieur," replied M. de Ravigne coolly.

Alleyn glanced at his shrewd, dark face and murmured politely.

"My temperament," continued M. de Ravigne, "is artistic. I am, I fear, a dilettante. I model a little, *comme çi, comme ça*. I write a little, trifles of elegance. I collect. I am not rich, M. l'Inspecteur, but I amuse myself."

"A delightful existence. I envy you, monsieur. But we must get back to business."

A dim bass rumble from the rear seemed to suggest that Inspector Fox had essayed: "*Revenons à nos moutons*," and had got lost on the way.

"I understand," said Alleyn, "that Miss Quayne has no relations in England. There must be *someone* surely?"

"On the contrary. She has told me that there are none. Cara was an only child and an orphan. She was educated abroad at a convent. Her guardians are both dead."

"You met her abroad perhaps?"

"Yes. In France years ago at the house of a friend."

"Did Miss Quayne introduce you to this hall?"

"No, monsieur. Alas, it was I who introduced her to the ceremonies."

"Returning to her connections, monsieur. Is there no one with whom we should get in touch?"

"Her notary—her solicitor."

"Of course. Do you know who that is?"

"I have heard. One moment. It is—*tiens*!—a name like Rats. No. Rattingtown. No"

"Not Rattisbon by any chance?"

"That is it. You know him?"

"Slightly. Where will the money go, Monsieur de Ravigne?"

M. de Ravigne hitched up his shoulders, elevated his brows, protruded his eyes and pursed his lips.

"I see," said Alleyn.

"This I do know," conceded M. de Ravigne. "Much will go to this church. Five thousand pounds are reposed in the safe here in bearer bonds to await a further subscription. But there will be more for this church. Once Cara told me she had altered her Will for the purpose. It was then I heard the name of this Mr. Rats."

"Oh, yes," said Alleyn politely. "To go to another aspect of the case, do you know anything of the procedure for preparing the cup?"

"Nothing, monsieur. I am not interested in such affairs.

To know the machinery of the service would damage my spiritual poise. Such is my temperament."

"You do not choose to look behind the scenes?"

"Precisely. There must be certain arrangements. A flame does not make itself from nothing, one realises, but I do not wish to inquire into these matters. I enjoy the results."

"Quite so," said Alleyn. "I think that will be all, monsieur. Thank you a thousand times for your courtesy."

"Not at all, monsieur! It is you who have displayed courtesy. If I can be of further use—— It is perhaps a matter of some delicacy, but I assure you that anything I can do to help you—I shall not rest content until this animal is trapped. If there should be a question of expense—you understand?"

"You are very good"

"*Tout au contraire, monsieur.*"

"——but it is for information we ask. Do you object to our searching you, monsieur?"

"I object very much, monsieur, but I submit." Fox searched him and found nothing but money, a cheque-book and a photograph.

"*Mon Dieu!*" said de Ravigne. "Must you paw it over in your large hands? Give it to me."

"Pardon, monsoor," said Fox hastily, and gave it to him.

"It is Cara Quayne," said de Ravigne to Alleyn. "I am sorry if I was too hasty."

"I am sure Inspector Fox understands. Good night, M. de Ravigne."

"Good night, M. l'Inspecteur."

"Well," said Fox when the Frenchman had gone. "Well, that was a fair treat, sir. As soon as you spoke to the gentleman in his own tongue he came along like a lamb. There's the advantage of languages. It puts you on an equal footing, so to speak. I wonder you didn't carry on the rest of the interview in French."

"Fox!" said Alleyn with the oddest look at him. "You make me feel a bloody fool sometimes."

"Me?" exclaimed Fox, looking blandly astonished.

"Yes, you. Tell me, have you any comments to make on the Frenchman?"

Fox wiped his enormous paw slowly down his face.

"Well, no," he said slowly, "except he seemed—well, sir, it's a rum thing two of the gentlemen should offer money for the police investigations. An unheardof idea. But of course they were both foreigners. As far as Mr. Ogden is concerned, well, we have heard of the word 'racket,' haven't we?"

"Exactly," agreed Alleyn dryly. "I imagine his proposal is not unusual in the States."

"Ogden's too good to be true," interrupted Nigel. "You mark my words," he added darkly, "he was trying to bribe you."

"Bribe us to do what, my dear Bathgate? To catch a murderer?"

"Don't be ridiculous," said Nigel loftily.

"And was M. de Ravigne also attempting to undermine the honour of the force?"

"Oh," said Nigel, "de Ravigne's a Frenchman. He is no doubt over-emotionalised and—and—oh, go to the devil."

"It seems to me," rumbled Fox, "that we ought to have a look at that little bottle in the cupboard—the one Mr. Wheatley talked about."

"I agree. We'll move into Mr. Garnette's 'little dwelling.' By the way, where is Mr. Garnette? Is he still in the vestry being searched?"

As if in answer to Alleyn's inquiry, the vestry door opened and the priest came out. He was now dressed in a long garment made of some heavy, dark-green material. The plain-clothes man who had escorted him into the vestry came to the door and stared after the priest with an air of disgusted bewilderment.

"Ah, Inspector!" cried Father Garnette with holy cheeriness. "Still hard at work! Still hard at work!"

"I'm most frightfully sorry," said Alleyn. "There was no need for you to wait in there. You could have returned to your rooms."

"Have I been long? I was engaged in an ecstatic meditation and had passed into the third portal where there is no time."

"You were fortunate."

Bailey came out of Father Garnette's room and approached the inspector.

"That Miss Wade, sir," he said, "is getting kind of resigned. I think she's dropped off to sleep."

Alleyn gazed at Fox and Fox at Alleyn.

" Cripes!" said Inspector Fox.

" Lummie!" said Inspector Alleyn, " I must be in ecstasy myself. I'd quite forgotten her. Lord, I am sorry! Show the lady down, Bailey."

" Right oh, sir."

CHAPTER IX

MISS WADE

Father Garnette showed an inclination to hover, but was most firmly removed to his own rooms. He and Miss Wade met on the chancel steps.

" Ah, you poor soul!" intoned Father Garnette. " Very weary? Very sad?"

Miss Wade looked from Bailey to the priest.

" Father!" she whispered. " They are not—they don't suspect——"

" Courage, dear lady!" interposed Father Garnette very quickly and loudly. " Courage! We are all in good hands. I shall pray for you."

He hurried past and made for his door, followed by Bailey. Miss Wade looked after him for a moment and then turned towards the steps. She peered shortsightedly into the hall. Alleyn went up to her.

" I cannot apologise enough for keeping you so long."

Miss Wade examined him doubtfully. " I am sure you were doing your duty, officer," she said.

" You are very kind, madam. Won't you sit down?"

" Thank you." She sat, very erect, on the edge of one of the chairs.

" There are certain questions that I must ask," began Alleyn, " as a matter of official routine."

" Yes?"

" Yes. I'll be as quick as I can."

" Thank you. It will be nice to get home," said Miss Wade plaintively. " I am distressed by the thought that I have perhaps left my electric heater turned on. I can remember *perfectly* that I *said* to myself: ' Now I must not forget to turn it off,' but——"

Here Miss Wade stopped short and gazed pensively into space for at least seven seconds.

"I recollect," she said at last. "I *did* turn it off. Shall we commence? You were saying?"

"That I should like, if I may, to ask you one or two questions."

"Certainly. I shall be glad to be of any assistance. I am not at all familiar with the methods of the police, although I have a very dear brother who was an officer in the Cape Mounted Police during the Boer War. He suffered great privations and discomforts and his digestion has never quite recovered."

Alleyn stooped abruptly and fastened his shoe.

"The questions, Miss Wade, are these," he began when he had straightened up again. "First: did you notice any unusual smell when you received the cup from M. de Ravigne?"

"Let me think. Any odour? Yes," said Miss Wade triumphantly, "I did. Decidedly. Yes."

"Can you describe it?"

"Indeed I can. Peppermint."

"Peppermint!" ejaculated Alleyn.

"Yes. And onion. You see Claude, the lad who acted as cup-bearer, was bending over me and—and it was rather overwhelming. I have noticed it before and wondered if I should speak to Father about it. Evidently, the lad is passionately fond of these things, and I don't, I really *don't* think it is quite reverent."

"I agree," said Alleyn hurriedly. "Miss Wade, you have said once before this evening that Miss Quayne was not very happy and not very popular. Can you tell me a little more about her? Why was she unpopular?"

"But you were not here when I said that, officer. I am positive of that because when we were in there waiting—no. I'm not telling the truth—that's a fib. It was *before* you came, and it was before that young man went to the telephone and" —Miss Wade again stared fixedly at the inspector for some seconds—"and Father Garnette said to me: 'I implore you not to speak like that to the police,' so you see I know you were not here, so how did you know?"

"Mr. Bathgate remembered and told me. Why was Miss Quayne unhappy?"

"*Because* she was unpopular," said Miss Wade triumphantly.

" And why was she unpopular, do you think?"

" Poor thing! I think there was a certain amount of jealousy. I'm afraid that there was, although perhaps I should not say so. Father Garnette seemed to think I should not say so."

" I am sure you want to help us."

" Oh, yes, of *course* I do. At least—— Would you be good enough to tell me if poor Cara was murdered?"

" I believe so. It looks like it."

" Then if I say that *somebody* was jealous of her you may grow suspicious and begin to think all sorts of things, and I don't believe in capital punishment."

" Jealousy is not invariably followed by homicide."

" Isn't that *precisely* what I was saying! So you see!"

" Mrs. Candour," said Alleyn thoughtfully, " tells me that Miss Quayne was not a particularly striking personality."

" Now that's really naughty of Dagnar. She should try to conquer her feelings. It is not as though Father gave them any encouragement. I am afraid she wilfully misunderstood. He is too noble and too pure even to guess——"

" Guess what, Miss Wade?"

Miss Wade compressed her faded lips and looked acutely uncomfortable.

" Come!" said Alleyn. " I shall jump to some terrible conclusion if you are so mysterious."

" I don't believe what they say," cried Miss Wade. Her voice shook and her thin hands trembled in her lap. " It is wicked—wicked. His thoughts are as pure as a saint's. Cara was a child to him. Dagmar is a wicked woman to speak as she does. Cara was excitable and impulsive, we know that, and generous—generous. Rich people are not always to be envied."

Alleyn was silent for a moment.

" Tell me," he began at last, " were your eyes closed during the ceremony of the cup?"

" Oh, yes. We all must keep our eyes closed, except, of course, when we pour out the wine. One has to open them then."

" You did not notice any of the other Initiates when they poured out the wine?"

" Of course not," said Miss Wade uncomfortably. She became very pink and pursed up her lips.

" I should have thought," pursued Alleyn gently, " that when you took the cup from M. de Ravigne——"

"Oh, *then* of course I had to peep," admitted Miss Wade.

"And when you passed it on to Mr. Pringle?"

"Well, of course. Especially with Mr. Pringle, he has such very tremulous hands. Exceedingly tremulous. It's smoking too many cigarettes. I told him so. I said frankly to him: 'Mr. Pringle, you will undermine your health with this excessive indulgence in nicotine.' My dear brother is also a very prolific smoker, so I *know*."

"Mr. Pringle did not spill any wine, I suppose?"

"No. No, he didn't. But more by good fortune than good management. He took the cup by the stem in one hand and it quivered and, if I may say so reverently, jigged about so much that he was obliged to grasp it by the rim with the other. Then, of course, he had great difficulty in taking the wine-vessel—the silver jug, you know—from Claude, and in pouring out the wine. It wasn't at all nice. Not reverent."

"No. M. de Ravigne?"

"Ah. There, *quite* a different story. Everything very nice and respectful," said Miss Wade. "Dagmar had left a little trickle on the rim and he drew out a *spotless* handkerchief and wiped it. Nothing could be nicer. He might almost be an Englishman."

"In your anxiety—your very natural anxiety about Mr. Pringle—perhaps you just looked to see——"

"When he passed it to dear Janey? Yes, Inspector, I did. Janey must have felt as nervous as I did for she reached out her hands and *took* it as soon as Mr. Pringle had poured in the wine. Well, I say 'poured,' but it is my impression that although he made an attempt he did not actually succeed in doing so. Mr. Ogden is always quite the gentleman, of course," added Miss Wade with one of her magnificent *non sequiturs*. "He receives the cup in *both* hands by the bowl and grasps the vessel firmly by the neck. That sounds a little as though he had three hands, but of course the mere idea is ludicrous."

"And then gives the cup to Mr. Garnette."

"To Father Garnette. Yes. Of course when Father Garnette took it, I did raise my eyes. He does it so beautifully, it is quite uplifting. *One* hand on the stem," described Miss Wade holding up genteel little claws, "and the *other* laid over the cup. Like a benison."

"I suppose you all watch the Chosen Vessel?"

" Oh, yes. As soon as poor Cara took it we all raised our eyes. You see she was speaking in ecstasy. It was a wonderful experience. I thought she was going to dance."

" To dance! " ejaculated the inspector.

" Even," chanted Miss Wade in a pious falsetto, " even as the priests danced before the Stone of Odin. It has happened before. A lady who has since passed through the last portal."

" You mean she has died?"

" Yes."

" What did this lady die of?" asked Alleyn.

" They *called* it epilepsy," replied Miss Wade doubtfully.

" Well, Miss Wade," said Alleyn after a pause, " it has been perfectly charming of you to be so patient with me. I am most grateful. There's only one other thing."

" And that is?" asked Miss Wade with a perky air of being exceedingly businesslike.

" Will you allow the wardress to search you?"

" To *search* me! Oh dear. I—I—must confess. It is such a very cold evening and I did not anticipate——"

" You would not have to—remove anything," said Alleyn hurriedly. " Or rather "—he looked helplessly at Miss Wade's dejected little fur tippet and drab raincoat and, since the raincoat was unbuttoned, at layers of purple and black cardigans—" or rather only your outer things."

" I have no desire," said Miss Wade, " to obstruct the police in the execution of their duty. Where is this woman?"

" In the porch outside."

" But that is very public."

" If you would prefer the vestry."

" I don't think the robing-chamber would be quite nice. Let it be the porch, officer."

" Thank you, madam."

Detective-Sergeant Bailey came down from the chancel and whispered to Inspector Fox. Inspector Fox moved to a strategic position behind Miss Wade and proceeded to raise his eyebrows, wink with extreme deliberation, contort his features into an expression of cunning profundity and finally to hold up a small fragment of paper.

" Eh?" said Alleyn. " Oh! Do you know, Miss Wade, I don't think I need bother you with this business. Just let the wardress see your bag and your pockets if you have any. And your gloves. That will be quite enough."

"More than sufficient," said Miss Wade. "Thank you. Good evening, officer."

"Good evening, madam."

"Have you been through the Police College?"

"Not precisely, madam."

"Indeed?" said Miss Wade, squinting curiously at him. "But you speak nicely."

"You are very kind."

"A superior school perhaps? The advantages——"

"My parents gave me all the advantages they could afford," agreed Alleyn solemnly.

"Chief Detective-Inspector Alleyn, ma'am," began Fox with surprising emphasis, "was——"

"Fox," interrupted Alleyn, "don't be a snob. Get Miss Wade a taxi."

"Oh, thank you, I have my overshoes on."

"My superiors would wish it, madam."

"Then in that case—my grandfather kept his carriage at Dulwich—thank you, I will take a taxi."

CHAPTER X

A PIECE OF PAPER AND A BOTTLE

"Well, Brer Fox," said Alleyn when that gentleman returned, "has the lady been looked at?"

"Mrs. Bekin went through her bag and pockets," replied Fox.

"And what was the trophy you waved at me just now?"

"Bailey found something up in the chancel. It was simply lying on the floor. It had been ground into the carpet by somebody's heel. We thought it was the article you wanted."

"I hope it is. Let's see it."

"It wasn't the same bit I showed you," explained Fox. "That was just, as you might say, a hint. There's the original."

He produced a small box. Nigel drew near. Alleyn opened the box and discovered a tiny piece of very grubby reddish paper. It had been pressed flat and was creased by a heavy indentation.

"M'm," grunted Alleyn, "Wait a bit."

He went to his bag and got a pair of tweezers. Then he carried the paper in the box to one of the side lights and looked closely at it. He lifted it a little with the tweezers, holding it over the box. He smelt it.

"That's it, sure enough," he said. "Look—it's an envelope. A cigarette-paper gummed double. By Jove, Fox, he took a risk. It'd need a bit of sleight-of-hand." He touched it very delicately with the tip of his fingers.

"Wet!" said Alleyn. "So that's how it was done."

"What do you mean?" asked Nigel. "It's red. Is it drenched in somebody's life-blood? Why must you be so tiresomely enigmatic?"

"Nobody's being enigmatic. I'm telling you, as Mr. Ogden would say. Here's a bit of cigarette-paper. It's been doubled over and gummed into a tiny tube. One end has been folded over several times making the tube into an envelope. It has been dyed—I *think* with red ink. It's wet. It smells. It's a clue, damn your eyes, it's a clue."

"It will have to be analysed, won't it, sir?" asked Fox.

"Oh rather, yes. This is the real stuff. 'The Case of the Folded Paper.' 'Inspector Fox sees red.'"

"But, Alleyn," complained Nigel, "if it's wet do you mean it's only recently been dipped in red ink? Oh—wait a bit. Wait a bit."

"Watch our little bud unfolding," said Alleyn.

"It's wet with wine," cried Nigel triumphantly.

"Mr. Bathgate, I do believe you must be right."

"Facetious ass!"

"Sorry. Yes, it floated upon the wine when it was red. Bailey!"

"Hullo, sir?"

"Show us just where you found this. You've done very well." A faint trace of mulish satisfaction appeared on Detective-Sergeant Bailey's face. He crossed over to the chancel steps, stooped, and pointed to a sixpenny piece.

"I left that to mark the place," he said.

"And it is precisely over the spot where the cup lay. There's my chalk mark. That settles it."

"Do you mean," asked Nigel, "that the murderer dropped the paper into the cup?"

"Just that."

"Purposely?"

"I think so. See here, Bathgate. Suppose one of the Initiates had a pinch of cyanide in this little envelope. He—or she—has it concealed about his or her person. In a cigarette-case, perhaps, or an empty lipstick holder. Just before he goes up with the others he takes it out and holds it right end up—wait a moment—like this perhaps."

"No," said Nigel, "like this." He folded his hands like those of a saint in a mediæval drawing. "I noticed they all did that."

"Excellent. The flat open end would be slipped between two fingers, and the thing would be held snug. When he—call it he for the moment—takes the cup, he manages to let the little envelope fall in. Not so difficult as it sounds. We'll experiment later. The paper floats. The folded end uppermost, the open end down. The powder falls out."

"But," objected Fox, "he's running a big risk, sir. Suppose somebody notices the paper floating about on the top of the wine. Suppose, for the sake of argument, Miss Jenkins or Mr. Ogden say they saw it, and Mr. Pringle and the rest don't mention it—well, that won't look too good for Mr. Pringle. If he's the murderer he'll think of that. I mean——"

"I know what you're driving at, Inspector," said Nigel excitedly. "But the gentleman says to himself that if anyone notices the paper he'll notice it too. That will switch it back a place to the one before him."

"Um," rumbled Fox doubtfully.

"I don't think they would see it," Alleyn murmured. "You say, Bathgate, that during the ceremony of the cup the torch was the only light?"

"Yes."

"Quite so. It's nearly burnt out now, but I think you will find that when it's going full blast there will be a shadow immediately beneath it where they knelt, a shadow cast by its own sconce."

"I think there was," agreed Nigel. "I remember that they seemed to be in a sort of pool of gloom."

"Exactly. And in addition, their own heads, bent over the cup, would cast a further shadow. All the same, you're right, Fox. He *is* taking a big risk. Unless——" Alleyn stopped short, stared at his colleague, and then for no apparent reason made a hideous grimace at Nigel.

"What's that for?" demanded Nigel suspiciously.

"This is all pure conjecture," said Alleyn abruptly. "When the analyst finds traces of cyanide we can start talking."

"I can't see why he'd drop the paper in," complained Nigel. "It must have been accidental."

"I don't know, Mr. Bathgate," said Fox in his slow way. "There are points about it. No fingerprints. Nothing to show if he's searched."

"That's right," said Bailey suddenly. "And he'd reckon the lady'd be sure to drop the cup. He'd reckon on it falling out and getting tramped into the carpet like it was."

"Say it stuck to the side?" objected Fox.

"Well, say it did," said Bailey combatively. "What's to stop him getting it out when they're all looking at the lady throwing fancy fits and passing in her checks?"

"Say it slid out on to her lips," continued Fox monotonously.

"Say she drank it! You make me tired, Mr. Fox. It wouldn't slide out, it'd slide back on the top of the wine. Isn't that right?"

"Um," said Fox again.

"What d'yer mean 'Um'! That's fair enough, isn't it, sir?" He appealed to Alleyn.

"Conjecture," said Alleyn. "Surmise and conjecture."

"You started it," remarked Nigel perkily.

"So I did. That's all the thanks I get for thinking aloud. Come on, Fox. It grows beastly late. Shut up your find. We'll know more about it when the analyst has spoken his piece."

Fox took the little box from him, shut it, and put it into the bag.

"What's next, sir?" he asked.

"Why, Mr. Garnette's little bottle. Where is Mr. Garnette?"

"In his rooms. Dr. Curtis is there and one of our men."

"I wonder if he has converted them. Let us join the cosy circle. You can tackle the vestry now, Bailey."

Fox, Alleyn and Nigel went up to Father Garnette's rooms, leaving Bailey and his satellites to continue their prowling.

Father Garnette sat at his desk which, with its collection of *objects de piété,* so closely resembled an altar. Dr. Curtis sat at the table. A uniformed constable with a perfectly expressionless face stood by Father Garnette's prie-dieu, furnishing a most fantastic juxtaposition of opposites. They all had the look of persons who have not spoken for a considerable time. Father Garnette was palid and a little too dignified; Dr. Curtis was wan and puffed with suppressed yawning; the constable was merely pale by nature.

"Ah, Mr. Garnette," said Alleyn cheerfully, "here we are at last. You must long for your bed."

"No, no," said Father Garnette. "No, no."

"We shan't keep you very much longer. I wonder if you will allow me to make an inspection of these rooms? I'm afraid it ought to be done."

"An inspection! But really, Inspector, is that necessarah? I must confess I——" Father Garnette stopped and then added a throaty sound suggestive of sweet reasonableness coupled with distress.

"You object?" said Alleyn briskly. "Then I shall have to leave my men here for the time being. I'm so sorry."

"But—I cannot understand——"

"You see I'm afraid there is little doubt that this is a case of homicide. That means there is a certain routine that we are obliged to follow. A search of the premises is part of this routine. Of course, if you object——"

"I—no—I——"

"You don't?"

"Not if—no. It is merely that this little dwelling is very precious to me. It is filled with the thoughts—the meditations of a specially dedicated life. One shrinks a little from the thought of—ah——"

"Of fools stepping in where—but no, of course this is one of the places where angels tread all over the place. We'll be as quick as we can. You can help us if you will. The bedroom is through there, I suppose."

"Yes."

"Any other rooms?"

"The usual offices," said Father Garnette grandly: "bathroom, etceterah, etceterah."

"Any back door?"

"Ah—yes."

"Is it locked?"

"Invariablah."

"Have a look, will you, Fox? I'll take this room."

Fox dived past a black velvet portière. The constable, at a nod from Alleyn, followed him.

"Would you rather stay here?" asked Alleyn of Father Garnette. Father Garnette cast a somewhat distracted glance round the room and said he thought he would.

"Finished with me, Alleyn?" asked Dr. Curtis.

"Yes, thanks, Curtis. Inquest on Tuesday, I suppose. They'll want a post-mortem, of course."

"Of course. I'll be off."

"Lucky creature. Good night."

"Good night. Good night, Father Garnette."

"Good night, my dear doctor," ejaculated Father Garnette on a sudden gush of geniality.

The little divisional surgeon hurried away. Nigel attempted to make himself inconspicuous by standing in a corner and was at once told to come out of it and give a hand.

"Make a note of anything I tell you about. Now, Mr. Garnette, I understand that in preparing the wine for to-night's ceremony Mr. Wheatley used two ingredients. Where did he find the bottles?"

Father Garnette pointed to a very nice Jacobean cupboard. It was unlocked. Alleyn opened the doors and revealed an extremely representative cellar. All the ingredients for the more elaborate cocktails, some self-respecting port, the brandy that had been recommended by Dr. Curtis, and a dozen bottles of an aristocrat in hocks. On a shelf by themselves stood four bottles of dubious appearance—"Le comte's Invalid Port." One was empty.

"That will be the one broached to-night?" asked Alleyn.

"Ah—yes," said Father Garnette.

Alleyn moved the others to one side and discovered a smaller label-less bottle, half full. He took it out carefully, holding it by the extreme end of the neck. The cork came out easily. Alleyn sniffed at the orifice and raised an eyebrow.

"Big magic, Mr. Garnette," he remarked.

"I beg your pardon?"

"Did this provide the second ingredient in the potion mixed by Mr. Wheatley?"

"Ah—broomp," said Father Garnette, clearing his vocal passage, "yes. That is so."

Alleyn drew a pencil from his pocket, dipped it into the bottle and then sucked it pensively.

"How much of this was used?" he asked.

Father Garnette inclined his head.

"The merest *soupçon*," he said. "It is perfectly pure."

"The best butter," murmured Alleyn. He put the bottle in his bag, which Fox had left on the table.

"You have a complete cellar without it, I see," he said coolly.

"Ah yes. Will you take something, Inspector? This has been a trying evening—for all of us."

"No, thank you so much."

"Mr.—ah—Bathgate?"

Nigel's tongue arched longingly but he too refused a drink.

"I am very much shaken," said Father Garnette. "I feel wretchard. Quite wretchard."

"You had better have a peg yourself, perhaps," suggested Alleyn. Father Garnette passed his hand wearily across his forehead and then let his arm flop on the desk.

"Perhaps I had, perhaps I had," he said with a sort of brave smile. He poured himself out a pretty stiff nip, took a pull at it, and sat down at the table.

Alleyn went on with his investigation of the room. He moved to the desk. Father Garnette watched him.

"I wonder if you would mind moving into the next room, Mr. Garnette," said Alleyn placidly.

"I—but—I—— Surely, Inspector, I may at least watch this distasteful proceeding."

"I think you should spare yourself the pain. I want Inspector Fox to search you."

"I have already been searched."

"That was before you changed, I think. I expect Fox will have almost finished there. I suggest you go to bed."

"I do not want to go to bed," complained Father Garnette. He took another resolute pull at his drink.

"Don't you? It would be simpler. However, I'll get Fox to look you over now. You will have to strip, I'm afraid. Fox."

"Sir?" Inspector Fox thrust a large bland face round the curtain.

Father Garnette suddenly leapt to his feet.

"I refuse," he said very loudly. "This is too much. You exceed your duty. I refuse."

"What's up, sir?" asked Fox.

"Mr. Garnette doesn't want to be searched again, Fox. Did he object the first time?"

"He did not."

"Curious. Ah well!"

"I just thought I'd mention it, sir. The back door is not locked."

"Oh," said Alleyn. "I thought, Mr. Garnette, that you said it was invariably locked."

"So it is, Inspectah. I cannot understand—I locked it myself, this afternoon."

Alleyn took out his notebook and wrote in it. Then he handed it to Fox, who came through the curtain, put on a pair of spectacles, and read solemnly. Father Garnette's eyes were glued on the notebook.

"That's very peculiar, sir," said Fox. "Look here." He swung round with his back to Alleyn and held up a tightly clenched paw. Father Garnette stared at Fox wildly.

"Very peculiar," repeated Fox.

Nigel could have echoed his words, for Alleyn with amazing swiftness whipped the bottle from his bag and, holding it delicately, tipped a handsome proportion of its contents into Father Garnette's glass. He returned the bottle to the bag and strolled over to Fox.

"Ah yes," he said. "Remarkable."

"What d'you mean?" asked Garnette loudly. "What are you talking about?"

"It's of no consequence," murmured Alleyn. "of no consequence whatever."

"I demand——" began Garnette. He glared unhappily at the two detectives, suddenly flopped down into his chair, and drank off the contents of the glass.

"Carry on, Fox," said Alleyn.

CHAPTER XI

CONTENTS OF A DESK, A SAFE, AND A BOOKCASE

The behaviour of Father Garnette underwent a rapid and most perceptible change. This difference was first apparent in his face. It was rather as though a facile modeller in clay had touched the face in several places, leaving subtle but important alterations in its general expression. It became at once bolder and more sly. The resemblance to a purveyor of patent medicines triumphed over the more saintly aspect. Indeed, Father Garnette no longer looked in the least like a saint. He looked both shady and blowsy.

Nigel, fascinated, watched this change into something rich and strange. Alleyn, busy at the desk, had his back to the priest. Inspector Fox had returned to the bedroom where he could be heard humming like a Gargantuan bumble-bee. Presently he burst into song:

"Frerer Jacker, Frerer Jacker,
Dormy-vous, dormy-vous."

It was an earnest attempt to reproduce the intermediate radio French lesson.

The clock on the mantelpiece ticked loudly, cleared its throat, and struck twelve.

"Say, bo!" said Father Garnette suddenly and astonishingly: "Say, bo, why can't we get together?"

Alleyn turned slowly and regarded him.

"That's the way Ogden talks when he talks when he talks," added Father Garnette with an air of great lucidity.

"Oh, yes?" said Alleyn.

"Get together," repeated Father Garnette, "let's get together at the river. The beautiful the beautiful the river. Why can't we gather at the river? I ran a revivalist joint way down in Michitchigan back in '14. It was swell. Boy, it was swell."

"Was Mr. Ogden with you in Michigan?" asked Alleyn.

"That big sap!" said Father Garnette with bitter scorn.

"Why, he thinks I'm the sand-fly's garters." He appeared to regret this last observation and added, with something of his former manner: "Mr. Ogden is sassherated in holy simplicity."

"Oh," said Alleyn. "When *did* you meet Mr. Ogden?"

"Crossing th' 'Tlantic. He gave me a piece of gold. Ogden's all right. Sassherated in simplicity."

"So it would appear."

"Listen," said Father Garnette. "You got me all wrong. I never did a thing to that dame. Is it likely? Little Cara! No, sir."

He looked so obscene as he made this statement that Nigel gave an involuntary exclamation.

"Be quiet, Bathgate," ordered Alleyn very quietly.

"Why can't we get together?" resumed Father Garnette. "I'll talk."

"What with?" asked Alleyn.

"With the right stuff. You lay off this joint and you won't need to ask for the say-so. What's it worth?"

"What's it worth to you?"

"It's your squeak," said Father Garnette obscurely.

"You're bluffing," said Alleyn, "you haven't got tuppence."

Father Garnette was instantly thrown into a violent rage. "Is that so!" he said, so loudly that Fox came back to listen. "Is that so! Listen, you poor simp. In my own line there's no one to touch me. Why? Because I got brains sanimaginasshon and mor'n that—because I got one hundred per cent essay."

"What's that?" asked Alleyn.

"Essay! Ess-shay. 'It.'"

"So you say," grunted Alleyn most offensively.

"So I say and what I say's so I say," said Father Garnette with astounding rapidity. "If you don't believe me—look f'yourself."

He made an effort to rise, fell back in his chair, fumbled in his pocket and produced a ring of keys.

"Little leather box in desk," he said. "And not only that. Safe."

"Thank you," said Alleyn. Father Garnette instantly fell asleep.

Alleyn, without another glance at him, returned to the desk and pulled out the bottom drawer.

"Lor, sir," said Fox, "you've doped the gentleman."

"Not I," Alleyn grunted. "He's merely tight."

"Tight!" ejaculated Nigel. "What was in the bottle?"

"Proof spirit. Over-proof as like as not."

"Pure alcohol?"

"Something of the sort. That or rectified spirit, I imagine. Have to be analysed. This is a very exotic case. Thorndyke stuff. Not my cup of tea at all."

"What," asked Nigel, "did you write on that paper you gave Fox?"

"A suggestion that he should attract Mr. Garnette's attention."

"You bad old Borgia!"

"Stop talking. Can't you see I'm detecting. What's the back door like, Fox?"

"Ordinary key and bolts. Funny it was open."

"Very funny. Go through that waste-paper basket, will you? And the grate."

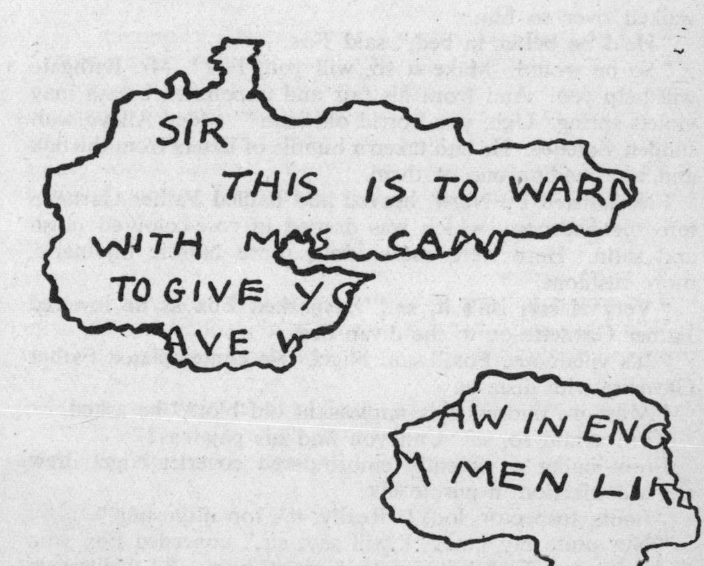

Fox knelt on the hearth-rug. The fire had almost burnt out. For some time the detectives worked in silence. Suddenly Fox grunted.

"How now, brown cow?" asked Alleyn.

"If you mean me, sir, here's a bit of something."

"What?"

Fox, using tweezers, drew two scraps of burnt paper from the ash-tray and laid them before Alleyn. Nigel got up to look. They were the merest fragments of paper, but there were one or two words printed on them in green pencil:

"Oh, Lord!" said Alleyn, "what now! Let's see. Same paper as this stuff on his desk? No. I can't see a green pencil anywhere. We'll have to find out when that thing was last cleaned out. Any more bits?"

"That's the lot," said Fox.

"Put it away tenderly. We'll have to brood over it. I want to get this desk cleaned up. Ah, here we are." He drew out a purple suède case and examined the keys. Father Garnette uttered a stertorous snore. Fox, still looking scandalised, walked over to him.

"He'd be better in bed," said Fox.

"So he would. Make it so, will you, Fox? Mr. Bathgate will help you. And from his fair and unpolluted breath may violets spring. Ugh, you horrid old man!" added Alleyn with sudden violence. He had taken a bundle of letters from the box and was reading one of them.

Fox assisted by Nigel, heaved and hauled Father Garnette into the bedroom, which was draped in rose-coloured plush and satin. Here were more idols, more Nordic bijouterie, more cushions.

"Very classy, isn't it, sir?" remarked Fox as he lowered Father Garnette on to the divan bed.

"It's villainous, Fox," said Nigel. He contemplated Father Garnette with distaste.

"Must we undress this unpleasant old blot?" he asked.

"I'm afraid so, sir. Can you find his pajamas?"

From under a violently embroidered coverlet Nigel drew out a confection in purple silk.

"Look, Inspector, look! Really, it's too disgusting."

"Not quite my fancy, I will say, sir," conceded Fox who had attacked Father Garnette's right boot. "I believe in wool next the skin, summer and winter. I'd feel kind of slippery in that issue."

Nigel tried to picture Inspector Fox in purple satin pyjamas, failed to do so and laughed himself into a good humour. They put Father Garnette to bed. He muttered a little, opened his eyes once, said: "Thank you, my son" in faultless English, showed signs of feeling very ill, but appeared to get over it, and finally sank again into the deepest slumber.

They rejoined Alleyn and found him poring over an array of letters.

"Something doing, sir?" asked Fox.

"Much. Most of it odious. These are all letters from women."

"Any from the deceased?"

"Yes." Alleyn grimaced. "There it is. Read it. A mixture of pseudo-mystic gibberish and hysterical adulation. Garnette seems actually to have persuaded her that the—the union—was blessed, had a spiritual significance—puh!" He made a violent gesture. "Read it. It's important."

Nigel read over Fox's shoulder. The letter was written on mauve paper printed with Cara Quayne's address in Shepherd Market. It was undated. It began:

Beloved Father and Spouse in Ecstasy,

I know you will be out this afternoon, but I feel I must make oblation for the divine, glorious, ecstatic bliss that has been mine ever since last night. I am half frightened, tremulous. Am I worthy? I—the Chosen Vessel? How can I make oblation? With this you will find a parcel. It contains the bonds I told you of. £5,000. Oh, how hateful to speak of money, but—I know you will understand—it is a thank-offering. Tell them about it, and let them give too until we have enough for a new temple. I want you to find it when you come in—after I have gone. Oh, beloved holy——

The letter ran on to eight pages.

"Very peculiar indeed, sir," said Fox who read the whole thing through with a perfectly impassive demeanour. "That will be the money Mr. Ogden and monsieur talked about. In the safe here, they said."

"They did. I'm about to tackle the safe."

Alleyn moved across the room, pulled aside a strip of

Javanese tapestry, and disclosed a small built-in safe. He found the key on the ring Father Garnette had given him, opened the safe and began, with great method, to remove the contents and array them neatly on the table.

"Bank-book. Let's see. He paid in fifty pounds last Monday. I suppose we shan't find much cash. Any offertory to-night, Bathgate?"

"No. I imagine we didn't get so far."

"I suppose not. There's a bag of something. Petty cash, perhaps. What's this? Cheque from Mr. Ogden. Twenty pounds. Dated last Wednesday."

"How he gets it out of the *gentlemen* fairly beats me," said Fox.

"Extraordinary, isn't it? But you know, Fox, there is a kind of simple, shrewd business brain that'll believe any tarradiddle outside its own province."

"Would you say Mr. Ogden's was that sort, sir?" Alleyn flipped the cheque at him.

"Looks like it," he said, and turned again to the safe. "Hullo! This is more the sort of thing."

He pulled out a package and laid it on the table. It was a largish brown-paper parcel tied up with red ribbon. It was addressed to "The Reverend Father Jasper Garnette," and the writing was undoubtedly Cara Quayne's. Alleyn stared fixedly at the ribbon. He turned the parcel over once or twice.

"Aren't you going to open it?" asked Nigel.

"Oh, yes. Yes." But he hesitated a little while longer and at last, laying the parcel on the table, slipped the ribbon very gingerly over one end, cautiously pulled out the folds of paper, and peered into the open end. He held the parcel under a lamp, and examined it even more closely. Then he dropped it back on to the table.

"Well?" asked Nigel.

"Well, Bathgate, I wish Mr. Garnette was not so sound asleep.

"Why on earth?"

"I should like him to have a look at this." Fox lifted the parcel by the open end and looked in.

"Cripes!" he said.

"Here!" Nigel ejaculated. "Let me look."

"Don't pick it up. Look inside."

Nigel did so. Fox flashed his torch into the parcel. Nigel glanced up at the two policemen, peered again into the parcel, grinned, looked doubtful, and at last said:

"But is that all?"

"I think so, oh yes," answered Alleyn.

"But," said Nigel, "it's—it's all newspaper." He thrust a finger in and ferreted round.

"So it is," agreed Alleyn.

"By gum!" ejaculated Nigel. "The motive!"

"Very like, very like."

"Garnette has pinched the bonds."

"Somebody's pinched them. Ask Bailey to come in and get the prints, if any, will you, Bathgate?"

Bailey was grubbing about in the vestry. He returned with Nigel, produced his insufflicator and got to work on the parcel. Alleyn had sat down at the table and was tackling the rest of the material from the safe. Fox embarked on a meticulous search of the sideboard drawers. Nigel, with a sidelong glance at the Chief Detective-Inspector, pulled out his pad, sank into Father Garnette's most spacious arm-chair, lit a cigarette, and began to write.

"Copy?" inquired Alleyn mildly.

"And why not?" said Nigel defiantly.

"No reason at all. Let me see it before you send it in."

"That's a pretty piece of effrontry, that is," said Nigel hotly. "Who was here from the start? Who called you in? I consider I displayed remarkable presence of mind. You've come in on a hot scent. This is a big story and I'm going to make it so. Eye-witness of a murder. That's what I was, and they're going to know it."

"All right. All right. I merely ask to see your story."

"Yes, and you'll blue pencil it out of existence."

"No, I won't. Don't mention the bearer bonds."

"There you go, you see!"

"And pray, Bathgate, don't refer to me as 'The indefatigable Chief Detective-Inspector Alleyn.'"

"But, Alleyn," Nigel protested, "That is altogether unfair. I have never made use of such a phrase. You merely speak for your own amusement."

"What style are you adopting? You have been reading George Moore again, I notice."

"What makes you suppose that?" asked Nigel, turning pink.

"His style has touched your conversation and left it self-conscious."

"Nonsense."

"Nevertheless it is an admirable style, though I shall be interested to see how you apply it to journalism and the mechanics of police investigation."

"That is merely ridiculous," said Nigel. He returned pointedly to his work and after a moment's consideration erased a word or two.

"Any prints on the parcel, Bailey?" asked Alleyn.

"Yes, sir. All one brand. The Reverend, I'll bet. I've got a sample of him off that glass."

"Ah," said Alleyn.

"Ah-ha," said Nigel.

"No, not quite 'Ah-ha' I fancy," murmured the inspector.

"Hullo!" exclaimed Fox suddenly.

"What's up?" asked Alleyn.

"Look here, sir." Fox came to the table and put down a small slip of paper.

"I found it in the cigarette-box," he said. "It's the lady again."

"Yes," agreed Alleyn, "it's the lady. Bless my soul," he added, "the damn' place is choc-a-bloc full of dubious correspondence."

Nigel came across to look. Fox's new find was a very small page of shiny paper. Monday's date was printed in one corner and underneath was scribbled the word: "Sunday." Three edges were gilt, the fourth was torn across at an angle as though it had been wrenched from a book. Cara Quayne had written in pencil: "Must see you. Terrible discovery. After service to-night."

"Where exactly was it?" asked Alleyn.

"In this." Fox displayed an elaborated Benares box almost full of Turkish cigarettes. "It was on the sideboard and the paper lay on top of the cigarettes. Like this." He picked up the paper and put it in the box.

"This is very curious," said Alleyn. He raised an eyebrow and stared fixedly at the little message. "Get the deceased's handbag," he said after a minute. "It's out there."

Fox went out and returned with a morocco handbag. Alleyn

opened it and turned out the contents, and arranged them on the table. They were: A small case containing powder, a lipstick, a handkerchief, a purse, a pair of gloves, and a small pocket-book bound in red leather with a pencil attached.

"That's it," said Alleyn.

He opened the book and laid the note beside it. The paper corresponded exactly. He scribbled a word or two with the pencil.

"That's it," he repeated. "The lead is broken. There's the same double line in each case." He turned the leaves of the book. Cara Quayne had written extensively in it—shopping lists, appointments, memoranda. The notes came to an end about half-way through. Alleyn read the last one and looked up quickly.

"Got an evening paper, either of you?"

"I have," said Fox, producing one, neatly folded, from his pocket.

"Does the new show at the Criterion open to-morrow?"

"You needn't bother to look," interrupted Nigel. "It does."

"You have your uses," grunted the inspector. "That fixes it then. She wrote that note to-day."

"How do you know?" demanded Nigel.

"There's a note on to-day's page: 'Dine and go "Hail Fellow" Criterion, Raoul, to-morrow.' I wanted to be sure she stuck to the printed date. The next page, to-morrow's, is the one she tore out. There's the date. She must have torn it out to-day."

"Things are looking up a bit, aren't they, sir?" ventured Fox.

"Are they, Fox? Perhaps they are. And yet—it's a sticky business, this. Light your pipe, my Foxkin, and do a bit of 'teckery. What's in your mind, you sly old box of tricks?"

Fox lit his pipe, sat down, and gazed solemnly at his superior.

"Come on, now," said Alleyn.

"Well, sir, it's a bit early to speak anything like for sure, but say the lady knew what we know about that parcel there. Say she found it out to-day, when the parson was out—called in to see him perhaps."

"And found the safe open?"

"Might be. Sounds kind of careless, but might be. Anyway, say she found out somehow and wanted to tell him.

Say he came in, read the note, and—well, sir, say he thought something would have to be done about it."

"I don't think he has read the note, Fox."

"Don't you, sir?"

"No. We can see if his prints are on it. If he has read it I don't think he's a murderer."

"Why not?" asked Nigel.

"He'd have destroyed it."

"That's so," admitted Fox.

"But," Alleyn went on, "as I say, I don't think he's read it. There are no cigarette-ends of that brand about, are there?"

They hunted round the room. Alleyn went into the bedroom and came back in a few moments.

"None there," he said, "and dear Mr. Garnette looks very unattractive with his mouth open. But I think we'd better look for prints in there, Bailey. There's that open door. Did you run anything to earth in the bedroom, Fox?"

"A very small trace of a powder in the wash-stand cupboard, sir. That's all."

"Well, what about cigarette-butts?"

"None here," announced Fox, who had examined the grate as well as all the ash-trays in the room. "There are several Virginians—Mr. Bathgate's and Dr. Curtis's I think they are—no Turkish anywhere."

"Then he hasn't opened the box."

"I must say I can't help thinking that note's got a bearing on the case," said Fox.

"I think you're right, Fox. Put it in my bag, box and all. Let's finish off and go home."

"And to-morrow?" asked Nigel.

"To-morrow we'll get Mr. Garnette to open the surprise packet."

"What about the gentleman in question, sir?"

"What about him?"

"Will he be all right? All alone?"

"Good heavens, Fox, what extraordinary solicitude! He'll wake up with a hirsute tongue and a brazen belly And he will be very, very troubled in his mind. There's that back door."

"Yes, sir."

"We'll have to leave a couple of men here. Let's tidy

up. Put all that stuff back in the safe, Fox, will you? I'll tackle the desk."

The two detectives replaced everything with extreme accuracy. Alleyn locked the safe and the desk and pocketed the keys. He strolled over to the bookcase, and as Fox packed up the police bag he murmured titles to himself: *The Koran, Spiritual Experiences of a Fakir, From Wotan to Hitler, The Soul of the Lotus Bud, The Meaning and the Message, Jnana Yoga . . .* "Hullo, here's something of his own invent. As I live, a little book of poems. Purple suède, Heaven help us, purple suède! *Eros on Calvary and Other Poems,* by Jasper Garnette. Old pig!"

He opened the book and read.

The grape and thorn together bind my brows;
Delight and torment is my double mead.

"Oh, Lord, oh, Lord, how inexpressibly beastly!"

He shoved the poems back and then, with a grimace at Nigel, thrust his hand behind the books and, after a little groping, pulled out several dusty volumes, all covered in brown paper.

"Petronius," he said, "and so on. This is his nasty little secret hoard. Notice the disguise, will you! Hullo, what's this?"

He turned to the table and held a very battered old book under the lamp.

"Abberley's *Curiosities of Chemistry.* What a remarkably rum old book! Published by Gasock and Hauptmann, New York, 1865. I've met it before somewhere. Where was it?"

He screwed up his face with an effort to remember and, holding the book lightly in his long, fastidious hands, let it fall open.

"I've got it," said Alleyn. "It was in the Bodleian, twenty years ago."

He opened his eyes and turned to Nigel. That young man was standing with his mouth agape and his eyes bulging.

"What's the matter with you?" asked Alleyn.

Nigel pointed to the book in the inspector's hands. Fox and Alleyn both looked down.

The book had fallen open at a page headed: "A simple but little-known method of making sodium cyanide."

CHAPTER XII

ALLEYN TAKES STOCK

"Dear me!" said Alleyn as he laid the book on the table. "This is a quaint coincidence." He paused a moment and then murmured: "I wonder if coincidence is quite the right word."

"H'm," said Fox, deeply.

"I'd call it the Hand of—of Fate, or Providence, or Nemises or something," said Nigel.

"I dare say you would—on the front page. Not this time, however." But Nigel was reading excitedly.

"Do listen, Alleyn. It says you can make sodium cyanide from wool and washing soda."

"Really? It sounds a most unpalatable mixture."

"You have to heat them terrifically in a retort or something. It says: 'it is, perhaps, a fortunate circumstance that this simple recipe is not generally known. The tyro is advised to avoid the experiment as it is attended by a certain amount of danger, so deadly is the poison thus produced.'"

"Yes. Don't blow down my neck and don't touch the book, there's a good chap. Bailey will have to get to work on it. Not nearly so much dust on this as on the other hidden books, you notice, Fox, and the brown paper cover is newer. The others are strained. Blast! I don't like it at all."

Bailey reappeared and was given the book.

"I don't think the results will be very illuminating," said Alleyn. "Try the open page as well as the cover. What *is* it these books smell of?"

He sniffed at them.

"It's those stains, I seem to imagine. It's very faint. Perhaps I *do* imagine. What about you, Bailey?"

Alleyn examined the *Curiosities* closely.

"It smells faintly. There's no stain on the cover." He slipped the blade of his pocket-knife beneath the brown paper and peered under it: "And there is no stain on the red cover of the book. There you are, Bailey."

"But, Alleyn," interrupted Nigel, "surely it's of the first importance. If the pathologist finds cyanide—sodium cyanide —and Garnette has this book and——"

"I know, I know. Extraordinarily careless of him to leave it there, don't you think? Stupid, what?"

"Do you think it is coincidence?"

"Bless my soul, Bathgate, how on earth am I to know? Your simple faith is most soothing, but I can assure you it's misplaced."

"Well, but what do you *think*? Tell me what you *think*."

"I 'think naught a trifle, though it small appear.'"

"That has the advantage of sounding well and meaning nothing."

"Not altogether. Look here. We know Miss Quayne was probably murdered by cyanide poisoning. We believe that it must have been done by one of eight persons."

Nigel counted beneath his breath.

"Only seven, six Initiates and Garnette."

"Mr. Wheatley, sir," Fox reminded him. "The young fellow that handed round, you know."

"Oh—true. Well?"

"Well," Alleyn went on composedly, "we have reason to suppose the stuff was dropped into the cup in a cigarette-paper. The paper was later found on the place where the cup fell. So much for the actual event. We have learned that Miss Quayne had deposited bearer-bonds, to the tune of five thousand, in the safe. We have found a parcel that appeared to be the original wrapping of these bonds. If so the bonds have been taken and newspaper substituted. We have found a message in Cara Quayne's writing, addressed yesterday, presumably to Garnette. This message says she must see him at once as she had made a terrible discovery. I think the odds are he has not read the message. Whether it referred to the bonds or not we have no idea. We have found an antique work on chemistry hidden among Garnette's books. It falls open at a recipe for home-made cyanide. So much for our tangible data."

"What about motive?" suggested Nigel.

"Motive. You mean Garnette's motive, don't you? I gather you are no longer wedded to Mr. Ogden as the villain of the piece."

"I wasn't really serious about Ogden, but I wouldn't be

surprised if he and Garnette were rogues together in the States."

"What's your view, Fox?" asked Alleyn.

"Well, sir, I must say I don't think so. Father Garnette was very frank under the influence and he said he met Mr. Ogden crossing the Atlantic. That tallies with Mr. Ogden's statement."

"Exactly, Fox."

"And I must say, sir, Mr. Ogden isn't my notion of a Chicago racketeer."

"Nor mine either. Perhaps we are too conservative, Brer Fox. But because two men come from the United States of America and one's a rogue, it doesn't mean they are old associates."

"If you put it like that," said Nigel, "it does sound a bit far-fetched."

"Of course they *are* associates now," ruminated Fox, "but Mr. Ogden seems more like a victim than a crook."

"Well, then—Garnette," urged Nigel.

"If," said Alleyn, "Mr. Garnette stole the bonds and killed Miss Quayne with a jorum of sodium cyanide, he set about it in a most peculiar manner. He chose a moment when he and seven other persons would be equally suspected. He must have known that a search would be made of these rooms, yet he left his recipe book in a place where it was sufficiently concealed to look furtive, and not well enough hidden to escape discovery. He destroyed, so far as we know, none of her letters. He left, inside a cigarette-box, her note, suggesting that she had discovered something very upsetting."

"But you said he never found it," objected Nigel.

"If that's so why did he think it necessary to kill her?"

"She may have rung up or something."

"She may, certainly, but wouldn't she have mentioned the note?"

"Perhaps," said Nigel doubtfully.

"I quite agree it's not cast-iron," Alleyn continued. "I am breaking my own rule and going in heavily for conjecture. So far, I am convinced, we have only scratched the surface of an extremely unsavoury case."

"What about the others?" said Fox. "They are a very strange lot—very strange indeed. There may be motives among them, Chief."

"Oh, yes."

"Such as jealousy," began Nigel eagerly. "Jealousy, you know, and passion, and religious mania."

"*Now* you're talking exactly like the Dormouse. Really, Bathgate, you are a perfect piece of pastiche this evening."

"Don't be ridiculous. Let us take the others in turn."

"Very well," said Alleyn resignedly. "It's hideously late but let us. A. Mrs. Candour."

"There you are!" cried Nigel. "A warped nature if ever there was one. Did you notice how she behaved when you said you supposed Miss Quayne was very beautiful? She fairly writhed. She's even jealous of that little squirt Wheatley. There are those two bits of paper Fox got from the grate. Obviously a letter beginning: 'This is to warn you——' and then later on M—S and CA and what might be the top of an N. Mrs. Candour again. And did you notice her face when she said: 'Cara doesn't look so pretty now?' It was absolutely obscene."

"It was," said Alleyn quietly. "You do see things, Bathgate."

"I suppose you are making mock of me as usual."

"My dear fellow," said Alleyn quickly, "indeed I am not. Please forgive me if I am odiously facetious sometimes. It's a bad habit I've got. I assure you that if I really thought you slow in the uptake I should never dream of ragging you. You're kind enough to let me show off and I take advantage of it. Do forgive me."

He looked so distressed and spoke with such charming formality that Nigel was both embarrassed and delighted.

"Chief Detective-Inspector," he said. "I am your Watson, and your worm. You may both sit and trample on me. I shall continue to offer you the fruits of my inexperience."

"Very nicely put, Mr. Bathgate," said Fox.

Alleyn and Nigel stared at him, but he was perfectly serious.

"Well," said Alleyn hurriedly, "to return to the Candour. She gave, as you say, a very nasty little exhibition. Would she have done so if she'd killed Miss Quayne? It's possible. She certainly tried to ladle out sympathy later on. She was the first to take the cup. That's a naught that may be a trifle. So much for her. B. M. de Ravigne."

"Ah, now, the French gentleman," said Fox. "He was in

love with the deceased and owned up quite frank to it. Well now, it would have come out anyway, so there's not a great deal in his frankness, I must say. There seem to have been some nice goings-on between deceased and the minister. Mr. Pringle evidently was an eye-witness. Now monsieur never hinted at anything of the sort."

"And therefore thought the more," murmured Alleyn. "Yes, Fox, he was very cool, wasn't he?"

"Remarkable," said Fox, "until I handled deceased's photograph and then he blazed up like a rocket. What about this *crime passionel* the French jokers are always dragging in? They let 'em off for that sort of thing over there. Did you notice what Miss Wade said about the handkerchief?"

"I did."

"He's a very cool hand is monsieur," repeated Fox.

"We'll have to trace their friendship back to Paris, I dare say," said Alleyn wearily. "Oh, Lord! C. Miss Wade. I'm taking them in the order in which they knelt. She comes next."

"Nothing there," said Nigel. "She's just a little pagan church-hen with a difference. Rather a nice old girl, I thought."

"She spoke very silly to the chief," pronounced Fox with unexpected heat. "'Have you been through the Police College, officer?' These old ladies! You could write a book on them. She's the sort that makes point-duty what it is."

"I adored the way she said she had her eyes shut all through the cup ceremony, and then told you what each of them did," said Nigel. "Didn't you, Alleyn?"

"Yes," said Alleyn. "It was extremely helpful and rather interesting."

"D. will be Mr. Pringle," observed Fox. "And here we go again To my way of thinking he's the most likely type. Neurotic, excitable young gentleman and dopes, as you found out, sir."

"I agree," said Alleyn. "He is a likely type. He's in a bad way. He's had a violent emotional jolt and he's suffering from the after-effects of unbridled hero-worship. Silly young dolt. I hope it's not Pringle."

"Obviously," ventured Nigel, "he would look on Miss Quayne as Garnette's evil genius."

"Yes," murmured Alleyn. "I don't pretend to speak with

any sort of authority, but I should expect a person in Pringle's condition to turn against the object of his worship rather than against the—what shall I call her?—the temptress. I should expect him in the shock of his discovery to direct his violence against Garnette there and then, not against Miss Quayne some three weeks later. I may be quite wrong about that," he added after a minute or two. "However—there is Pringle. He's neurotic, he's dopey, and he's had a severe emotional shock. He hero-worshipped Garnette and made a hideous discovery. He's probably been living in an ugly little hell of his own for the last three weeks. By the way, we haven't sampled Mr. Garnette's cigarettes, have we? Another little job for the analyst."

"Now Miss Jenkins," said Fox. "She's E."

"She struck me as being a pleasant creature," said Nigel. "Rather amusing I should think. Not a 'lovely' of course, but moderately easy to look at. Intelligent."

"Very intelligent," agreed Alleyn.

"How she got herself mixed up in this show beats me," confessed Fox. "A nice young lady like that."

"She practically said herself," Nigel interrupted. "She's attached to that ass Pringle. Women are——"

"Yes, yes," interrupted Alleyn hastily. "We needn't go into all that, I think. As far as we've got there's no motive apparent in Miss Jenkins's case. We are back at Ogden."

"F. Mr. Ogden," said Fox solemnly. "It seems to me, sir, the only call we've got for suspecting Mr. Ogden more than anybody else is that he's an American, and it seems as if Father Garnette's another. It don't amount to much."

"It don't," said Alleyn. "Personally I fancy the Atlantic meeting was their first one. I agree with you, Fox."

"As regards Father Garnette's later utterances," said Nigel, "we had a clear case of *in vino veritas.*"

"Someone was bound to say *in vino veritas* sooner or later," said Alleyn, "but you are quite right, Bathgate."

"That's the lot, then," said Nigel.

"No. Again you've forgotten Opifex."

"Opifex? What do you mean?"

"Another classical touch. Don't you remember the rhyme in the Latin text-books:

Common are to either sex
Artifex and Opifex.

" Quite good names for Lionel and Claude."

" Really, Inspector!" protested Nigel, grinning broadly.

" Artifex was busy with the censer and seems unlikely. Opifex had, of course, less opportunity than the others. I understand he did not handle the cup?"

" I don't *think* he did," said Nigel. " Of course he was bending over the Initiates while they passed it round."

" Meaning Mr. Wheatley?" asked Fox.

" Yes. Mr. Claude Wheatley."

" Hardly got the guts to kill anybody, would you think, sir?"

" I'd say not," agreed Nigel heartily.

" They call poison a woman's weapon, don't they?" asked Alleyn vaguely. " A dangerous generalisation. Well, let's go home. There's one more point I want to clear up. Any prints of interest, Bailey?"

Detective-Sergeant Bailey had returned from the bedroom and had been at work on the parcel and the book. He had not uttered a word for some time. He now said with an air of disgruntled boredom: " Nothing on the book. Reverend Garnette on the parcel, I think, but I'll take a photograph. There's some prints in the bedroom besides the Reverend's. I think they are Mr. Pringle's. I got a good one of his from that rail out there. Noticed him leaning on it."

" Did you find out how the torch is worked?"

" Yes. Naphtha. Bottle in the vestry."

" Can you ginger it up for a moment, Bailey?"

" Very good, sir."

" Have you got any cigarette-papers on you?"

Bailey, looking completely disinterested, produced a packet and went out. Alleyn got a silver cup from the sideboard, half filled it with some of Father Garnette's Invalid Port, emptied some salt into a cigarette-paper, stuck the margins together, and screwed up the end. Meanwhile, Fox locked the safe and sealed it with tape and wax. Alleyn pocketed the keys.

" Come on out," he said.

They all returned to the sanctuary. Bailey had got the torch flaring again. The hall had taken on a new but rather ghastly lease of life. It looked like a setting for a film in extremely bad taste. The nude gods, the cubistic animals, the velvets and the elaborate ornaments flickered in the torchlight with meretricious theatricality. It was, Nigel told himself, altogether too much of a good thing. And yet, over-emphasised as it was, it did make its gesture. It was not, as it might well have been, merely silly. As the light flared up, the faces of the plaster figures flushed and seemed to move a little. The shadows under the eyes and nostrils of the Wotan wavered and the empty scowl deepened. One god seemed to puff out his cheeks, another to open and close his blank eyes. It was very still; there was no sound at all but for the roar of the naphtha. The men's voices sounded forlorn and small. It had grown very cold.

Alleyn walked down to the chancel steps and peered out into the body of the hall.

" I want you all up here for a moment," he said.

His voice seemed to echo a little. A plain-clothes man came out of the vestry and another appeared in the aisle. A constable came out of the porch.

When they were all assembled under the torch Alleyn asked them to kneel in a circle. They did this, the constable and Fox very stolidly, Bailey with morose detachment, and two plain-clothes men with an air of mild interest. Nigel was unpleasantly moved by this performance. His imagination fashioned out of shadows the figure of Cara Quayne.

Alleyn knelt with them. All their hands were shadowed by the sconce. They held them folded as Nigel showed them. They passed the cup from hand to hand, beginning with Fox who knelt in Mrs. Candour's place. Alleyn made them send it twice round the circle. Then they all stood up.

" Notice anything?" asked Alleyn.

Nobody spoke.

Alleyn suddenly flung the cup from him. It fell with a dull thud and the wine seeped into the carpet. Alleyn bent down and invited them all to look. In the bottom of the cup were the dregs of the wine and a tiny piece of paper.

" You see it's stuck to the side," said Alleyn.

" When did you put it in, sir?" asked Fox.

" The first time round. You see, none of you noticed it. It's much too dark. The little tube tipped up the salt slipped out of the open end, the paper went transparent. I hadn't coloured mine red, but still you didn't see it."

"By Gum," said Fox.

Bailey said: "Cuh!" and bent down again to examine the paper.

"Yes," added Fox suddenly, "but how did the murderer know it would be so safe?"

"That," said Alleyn, "is another matter altogether. I rather think it's the crux of the whole case."

PART II

CHAPTER XIII

NANNIE

When Nigel woke on the morning after his visit to the House of the Sacred Flame, it was with a vague sense of disquietude as though he had been visited by nightmare. As the memory of the night's adventure came back to him it still seemed unreal. He could scarcely believe that, only a few hours ago, he had knelt under a torch among images of Nordic gods, that he had seen a woman, who seemed to be possessed of an evil spirit, drink and die horribly. He closed his eyes and the faces of the Initiates appeared again. There was Miss Wade with prim lips, Pringle talking, talking, Ogden perspiring gently, M. de Ravigne who seemed to bow his head with grotesque courtesy, Janey Jenkins, and Mrs. Candour who opened her mouth wider and wider——

He jerked himself back from sleep, got out of bed, and went to his window. The rain still poured down on the roofs. Wet umbrellas bobbed up and down Chester Terrace. A milkman's cart with a dejected and irritated pony was drawn up at the corner of Knocklatchers Row. Nigel looked down Knocklatchers Row. Perhaps he would not have been very surprised if there had been no Sign of the Sacred Flame, but there it was, swinging backwards and forwards in the wind, and underneath it he could just see the narrow entry.

He bathed, breakfasted, opened his paper and found no reference to the tragedy. So much the better. He rang up his office, got out his notes, sat down to the typewriter and worked solidly for an hour. Then he rang up Scotland Yard. Chief Detective-Inspector Alleyn was in his room and would speak to Mr. Bathgate.

"Hullo!" said Nigel with extreme cordiality.

"What do *you* want?" asked Alleyn guardedly.

"How are you?"

"In excellent health, thank you. What do you want?"

"It's just that matter of my copy——"

"I knew it."

"I want to put it in as soon as possible."

"I'm seeing the A.C. in half an hour, and then I'm going out."

"I'll be with you in ten minutes."

"Come, birdie, come," said Alleyn.

Nigel gathered up his copy and hurried out.

He found Alleyn in his office, writing busily. The inspector grinned at Nigel.

"You persistent devil," he said, "sit down. I won't be five minutes."

Nigel coyly laid the copy before him and subsided into a corner. Alleyn presently turned to the copy, read it, blue-pencilled a word or two, and then handed it back.

"You are learning to behave quite prettily," he said. "I suppose you'll take that straight along to Fleet Street."

"I'd better," agreed Nigel. "It's front-page stuff. They'll pull the old rag to bits for me this time. What are you up to this morning, Inspector?"

"I'm going to Shepherd Market when I've seen the boss-man."

"Cara Quayne's house? I'll meet you there."

"Will you indeed?"

"Don't you want me?"

"I'll be very glad to see you. Don't let any of your brother blood-suckers in."

"I can assure you there is no danger of that. I'll sweep past like a May Queen."

"You'd better have my card. Give it back to me—I remember your previous performances, you see." he flipped a card across to Nigel. "I feel like a form master who goes in for favourites."

"Oh, sir, thanks most horribly, sir. It's frightfully decent of you, sir," bleated Nigel.

"For the honour of the Big Dorm., Bathgate."

"You bet, sir."

"Personally," said Alleyn, "I consider schoolboys were less objectionable when they *did* talk like that."

"When cads were cads and a' that?"

"Yes. They talk like little men of the world nowadays.

They actually take refuge in irony, a commodity that should be reserved for the middle-aged. However, I maunder. Meet me at the Château Quayne in half an hour."

"In half an hour."

Nigel hurried to his office where he made an impressive entry with his copy and had the intense satisfaction of seeing sub-editors tear their hair while the front page was wrecked and rewritten. A photographer was shot off to Knocklatchers Row and another to Shepherd Market. Nigel accompanied the latter expert, and in a few minutes rang the bell at Cara Quayne's front door.

It was opened by a gigantic constable whom he had met before, P.C. Allison.

"I'm afraid you can't come in, sir," began this official very firmly.

"Do you know, you are entirely mistaken?" said Nigel. "I have the entrée. Look."

He produced Alleyn's card.

"Quite correct, Mr. Bathgate," said P.C. Allison. "Now you move off there, sir," he added to a frantic young man who had darted up the steps after Nigel and now endeavoured to follow him in.

"I'm representing——" began the young man.

"Abandon hope," said Nigel over his shoulder. The constable shut the door.

Nigel found Alleyn in Cara Quayne's drawing-room. It was a charming room, temperately, not violently, modern. The walls were a stippled green, the curtains striped in green and cerise, the chairs deep and comfortable and covered in dyed kid. An original Van Gogh hung over the fireplace, vividly and almost disconcertingly alive. A fire crackled in the grate. Alleyn sat at a pleasantly shaped writing-desk. His back was turned towards Nigel, but his face was reflected in a mirror that hung above the desk. He was absorbed in his work and apparently had not heard Nigel come in. Nigel stood in the doorway and looked at him.

"He isn't in the least like a detective," thought Nigel. "He looks like an athletic don with a hint of the army somewhere. No, that's not right: it's too commonplace. He's faunish. And yet he's got all the right things for 'teckery. Dark, thin, long. Deep-set eyes——"

"Are you lost in the pangs of composition, Bathgate?" asked Alleyn suddenly.

"Er—oh—well, as a matter of fact I was," said Nigel. "How are you getting on?"

"Slowly, slowly. Unfortunately Miss Quayne has very efficient servants. I'm just going to see them. Care to do your short-hand stuff? Save calling in the sergeant?"

"Certainly," said Nigel.

"If you sit in that arm-chair they won't notice you are writing."

"Right you are."

He sat down and took out his pad.

"I'll see the staff now, Allison," Alleyn called out.

"Very good, sir."

The first of the staff to appear was an elderly woman dressed in a black material that Nigel thought of as bombazine, but was probably nothing of the kind. She had iron-grey hair, a pale face, heavy eyebrows, and a prim mouth. She had evidently been weeping, but was now quite composed. Alleyn stood up and pushed forward a chair.

"You are Miss Edith Hebborn?" he said.

"Yes, sir."

"I am Inspector Alleyn. We are obliged, as you know, to inquire into Miss Quayne's death. Won't you sit down?"

She seemed to hesitate and then sat rigidly on the edge of the chair.

"I am afraid this has been a great shock to you," said Alleyn.

"It has."

"I hope you will understand that I have to ask you certain questions about Miss Quayne."

He paused for a moment but she did not answer.

"How long have you been with Miss Quayne?" asked Alleyn.

"Thirty-five years."

"Thirty-five years! That must be nearly all her life."

"She was three months old when I took her. I was her Nannie."

She had a curious harsh voice. That comfortable word "Nannie" sounded most incongruous.

"I see," said Alleyn. "Then it is a sorrow as well as a shock. You became her maid after she grew up?"

"Yes, sir."

"Will you tell me a little about her—her childhood and where she lived? Her people?"

She waited for a moment. Nigel wondered if she would refuse to give anything but flat responses to questions, but at last she spoke:

"She was an only child, born after her father died."

"He was Colonel Quayne of Elderbourne Manor, Sevenoaks?"

"Yes. He was in India with the mistress. Killed playing polo. Mrs. Quayne came to England when Miss Cara was a month old. They had a black woman for nurse, an Eh-yah or some such thing. She felt the cold and went back to her own country. I never fancied her. The mistress only lived a year after they came home."

"A tragic entrance into the world," said Alleyn.

"Yes sir."

"Where did you and the baby go?"

"To France," said Nannie and implied "of all places."

"Why was that?"

"There were no relations in England. They had all gone abroad. There were no near relatives at all. A second cousin of the Colonel's in New Zealand or some such place. They had never met. The nearest was an aunt of the mistress. A French lady. The mistress was half French, sir, though you'd never have known it."

Something in Alleyn's manner seemed to have thawed her a little. She went on:

"We settled in a little house near this aunt—Madame Verné, was the name—who had a Shatter, one of those big places, near Antibes. The Shatter Verné it was. We were there for eight years. Then Miss Cara went to a convent school, a Papist place. Madame Verné wished it and so did the other guardian, a gentleman who has since died. I moved to the Shatter, and Miss Cara came home for the holidays."

"That went on for how long?"

"Till she was seventeen. Then Madame died. The Shatter was sold."

"There was always—— There was no difficulty about ways and means?"

"Miss Cara was an heiress, sir. The Colonel, Mrs. Quayne,

and then Madame; they all left something considerable. We were very comfortable as far as that went."

"You stayed on in France?"

"In Paris. Miss Cara liked it. She had formed friendships there."

"Was M. de Ravigne one of these friends?"

"He was," said Miss Hebborn shortly.

"Did you not think this a suitable friendship?"

"I *did*. Until recently."

"Why did you change your opinion?"

"At first I had no fault to find with Mr. Ravigne. He was an old friend of Madame's and often stayed at the Shatter. He seemed a very pleasant gentleman, steady, quiet in his ways, not a lot of high-falutin' nonsense like so many of that nation. A foreigner, of course, but at times you would scarcely have noticed it."

"Miss Wade's very words," murmured Alleyn.

"Her!" said Miss Hebborn. "H'm! Well, sir, it was after we came to London that Mr. Ravigne changed. For the worse. He called soon after we were settled in and said London appealed to his—some expression——"

"His temperament?"

"Yes, sir. Of course it was Miss Cara that did the appealing. He was always very devoted, but she never fancied him. Never. Then he commenced to talk a lot of stuff and nonsense about this new-fangled religion he'd got hold of. A lot of wicked clap-trap."

The pale face flushed angrily. She made a curious gesture with her roughened hand, passing it across her mouth and nose as if to wipe away a cobweb.

"You mean the House of the Sacred Flame and its services?"

"Sacred Flame indeed! Bad, wicked, heathen humbug. And that Mr. Garnette with his smooth ways and silly dangerous talk. I've never forgiven Mr. Ravigne and he knows it. It changed Miss Cara. Changed her whole nature She was always one of the high-strung, nervous sort. Over-excitable as a child and over-excitable as a woman. I recollect the time we went through when she was fourteen. Wanted to turn Papist. I showed her the rights of that. I'd always brought her up strict Anglican. I'm Chapel myself. Primitive Methodist. But it was the parents' wish and I saw it was carried out."

"That was very honourable of you, Nannie. I'm sorry, the 'Nannie' slipped out."

"You're very welcome, sir. I've always been Nannie, ever since—she could talk."

She bit her lip and then went on:

"From the time she went into that wicked place everything went badly. And I couldn't do anything to stop it. I couldn't do anything. I had to stand by and watch my—my—Miss Cara turn her back on the Lord and go down the way of damnation. She took me with her once," added Nannie, ambiguously. "The sight of the place, full of naked heathen idols and all the baubles of Satan—it was worse than Rome. There! And when I found out she was going to be the leader in that lewd mockery of her own Church I wished she had died when she was an innocent baby. I wished——"

She broke off abruptly. She was shaking from head to foot. The whole of her last speech had been reeled off in a high key as though she was giving an oration. Nigel was reminded of a woman he had heard preaching at the Marble Arch. Here was real revivalist fervour, pig-headed, stupid, arrogant. After last night it seemed blessedly straightforward and clean.

"Steady, Nannie," said Alleyn.

"Yes, sir. Thank you. But I don't feel steady when I think of my poor lamb cut off in the midst of her silly wickedness, like as not with heathenish words on her lips. As the Lord's my judge, sir, I'd have rather she'd gone over to Rome that time when she was still an innocent baby, that I would."

"Was it entirely through M. de Ravigne that she became interested in this Church?"

"He started it. He took her off there one evening. Said he thought it would 'amuse' her. Amuse! Not much amusement in any respectable sense of the word. And that Mr. Garnette—Reverend I will not call him—he made what was bad enough, goodness knows, ten thousand times worse. If it had been Satan himself speaking straight out of hell, he couldn't have spoke wickeder. And the goings on! She thought I didn't know. I knew."

"How did you know?"

Nannie looked slightly taken aback at this question.

"I heard remarks passed when that lot came here to see her. That Mrs. Candour. You could tell at a glance. Not a *nice* woman, and not a lady either. And Miss Wade, who ought to know better at her age, always talking, talking, talking about 'Dear Father Garnette.' Father! Father of lies! And I had to stand aside and watch my baby drawing nearer and nearer to hell fire——"

She broke off again. Her lips trembled. She passed her hand over them and fell silent.

"What were Miss Quayne's movements yesterday?" asked Alleyn.

She had spent the morning in her room, it appeared, engaged in meditation. She had not lunched. At about two o'clock she had sent for her car and the chauffeur had told Nannie that he had driven her to the church. He remembered glancing at his watch a second or two before she came out. It was then ten to three. He had said to the other servants that Miss Quayne seemed very upset when she came out. He drove her straight home.

"One more question," said Alleyn. "Where were you last night when we tried to get you on the telephone?"

"I was out for a walk."

"Out for a walk! In that weather?"

"Yes, sir. She'd told me it was her first evening as Chosen Whatever-it-was, and I was that upset and wretched! I tried to talk her out of it but she hardly listened. She just went away as if she didn't hear me. When the door shut and I was left by myself I couldn't endure it. I'd meant to go to chapel but I couldn't. I put on my hat and jacket and I followed her."

"To the hall?"

"Yes, sir. Miss Cara had taken the car, of course, so I knew I wouldn't catch her up, but somehow I felt I'd walk. I was desperate, sir."

"I think I understand. What did you mean to do when you got there?"

"I hardly know. I think I'd have gone in and—and stood up for the Lord in the midst of His enemies. I think I meant to do that, but when I got there the doors were shut and a pimply-faced fellow said I couldn't get in. He said he'd been had once already that evening. I don't know what he meant. So I went away and as I went I heard them caterwauling inside, and it drove me nearly demented. I walked in the rain a long way and it was late when I got in. The others were back and in bed. I waited for her. I was still waiting when the police rang up. Morning it was then."

"Oh, yes. By the way, when did you write to Mr. Garnette to warn him off Miss Cara?"

It would be difficult to say which looked the more astounded at this, Nigel or Nannie. Nannie stared into the mirror over Alleyn's head for some seconds, and then said with a snap:

"Friday night."

"He got it on Saturday?"

"Yes."

"And you went to the hall to see if he had taken heed?"

"Yes."

"I see. Thank you, Nannie."

The old woman hesitated and when she spoke again it was more haltingly.

"There's more to it than that. When I got there and the door was shut in my face, I couldn't rest till I knew—knew if she was doing it. I walked round the block to the back of the building. I came to a sort of a yard, I could still hear the noise inside. There was a door. I stood by it listening. There was one voice, louder than the others. Then I saw the door was not quite shut—and—and——"

"You walked in."

"Yes, sir, I did. I felt I had to. I had to *know*. It was that man's rooms I'd got into. There was a light in the sitting-room. The voice got louder all the time. I—I went in. Miss Cara had told me about him living on the premises in that hole-and-corner fashion, so I knew about the other door—the one into the hall. I opened it a little way. There's a curtain, but I pulled it aside."

A dark flush crept into the pale face. She looked defiantly at Alleyn.

"I tell you I could not help myself."

"I know. What did you see?"

"They were moving. I could see the front row. I saw her—Miss Cara. She came running up the steps towards me. That man was quite close. His back was turned to me. Her face. Her pretty face—it looked dreadful. Then she turned and faced them. She was calling out. Screaming. I tried to go in and stop it. I couldn't. I couldn't move. Only watch. I might have saved her. No, don't say anything—I might. Then I saw that lot coming up after her. Skirmishing round."

"Yes. Go on," said Alleyn quickly. "Tell me exactly——"

"I'll remember to my dying day. First that American gentleman, Ogden. Then one or two of them together, then the young man and Miss Jenkins. The only one of the lot I'd care to have anything to do with. Led astray like my poor child. Mrs. Candour and old Mrs. Wade were trying to get one on each side of that man. I saw Mrs. Candour push in by him. Miss Wade tried to get in on the other side. She was in a great taking-on. In the end she didn't get there. Collided with the American gentleman and nearly fell over. It's my belief he stopped her on purpose, having some sense of decency."

"Oh. What did she do then?"

"He put her next Mr. Ravigne and went next that man himself. Then my poor child began again. Don't ask me. I can't—I couldn't watch. Something seemed to break in me. I turned and—and somehow I got out into the street."

She turned her head aside, gave a harsh sob and then blew her nose defiantly.

Alleyn stood up.

"You must try to get some sleep now."

Nannie was silent.

"At least your Miss Cara is out of it all."

"I thank God for that," said Nannie.

"I won't keep you a moment longer. Do you know if Miss Quayne has left a Will?"

"She made one years ago, sir, when she came of age, but I think she's changed it. She told me she was going to Mr. Rattisbon—that's her lawyer—about it. That lot have been getting money out of her as well I know."

"Much?"

"I don't know, sir, but I have ideas. A great deal, if you ask me. And I dare say she'll have left them the rest." She hesitated and then raised her voice. "And if she's been murdered, sir, it's for her money. Mark my words, it's for her money."

" It often is," said Alleyn. " Thank you. Go and rest somewhere. You need it, you know."

Nannie glared down her nose, muttered: " Very considerate, I'm sure," and tramped to the door. Here she paused and turned.

" May I ask a favour, sir?"

" Certainly."

" Can I—will they let me have her home again before she's put away?"

" Not just yet, Nannie," said Alleyn gently. " To-morrow perhaps—but—I think it would be better not."

She looked fixedly at him and then, without another word, went out of the room.

CHAPTER XIV

NIGEL TAKES STOCK

" Grand old girl, that," agreed Nigel from his arm-chair.

" Wasn't she?" agreed Alleyn. " That doorkeeper in the house of the ungodly will have to be seen."

" To check up on her visit?"

" Just that."

" Look here," said Nigel, " how did you know?"

" Never you mind. Keep quiet. Now I'll have to see the rest of the staff."

The rest of the staff proved to be unproductive of much intelligence. Two housemaids, a parlourmaid, a chauffeur and a cook, who all seemed excited and perturbed as if they had one eye on the tragedy and the other on losing their jobs. The parlourmaid, outwardly a frigid woman, obviously regarded the affair as a personal affront and seemed at the same time to be in a semi-explosive condition. The upper-housemaid was excited, the under-housemaid was incoherent. The cook wept, but absent-mindedly and rather as though she felt it incumbent on her as a fat, comfortable woman to do so. They bore out Nannie's statements as regards their movements on the preceding day. The chauffeur repeated his previous statement that he had driven Miss Quayne to the church at two-thirty and had brought her home at five to three. He had certainly thought she seemed most upset when she came out of the church. "Kind of flabbergasted," was the way he'd describe it. She was very pale and, he thought, out of breath. He had got tired of sitting in the car and had walked up the side entry to the double doors. Miss Quayne had left one door open and he looked into the hall. He saw her come out of the door by the altar. He thought she said something and supposed she was speaking to Father Garnette. One or two people had gone into the church while he waited. Alleyn asked the parlourmaid, who had been with Miss Quayne since she took the house, how many of the Initiates were regular visitors. He gave her a list of their names which she held in genteel fashion with her little finger crooked.

"Most of these neemes are familiar," she said.

"Have all of them visited Miss Quayne?"

"Yes."

"Some more frequently than others?"

"Quayte," said the parlourmaid, whose name was Wilson.

"Which were the most regular visitors?"

"Mr. Ravinje," it appeared, Mr. Ogden and Mrs. Candour.

"Mrs. Candour? When was she last here?"

"I could ascertain," said Wilson, "from the appointment book."

"Please let me see it."

Wilson produced the appointment book. It was a diary, and Alleyn spent some minutes over it.

"I notice," he said at last, "that Mrs. Candour was quite a regular visitor until some three weeks ago. She seems to have lunched or dined pretty well every week. Then her name does not appear again. He raised an eyebrow at Wilson. "Any reason for that, do you know?"

"There was words," said Wilson.

"What about?"

"A certain party."

"Oh. What party? Or don't you know?"

Wilson drew down the corners of her mouth.

"Come on, Wilson," said Alleyn. "Let's know the worst."

"Well, reely, I never am in the habit of repeating the drawing-room in the kitchen," said Wilson.

"This isn't the kitchen and it may be important. Did Mrs. Candour and Miss Quayne have words about Mr. Garnette?"

"Yes, sir," said Wilson who seemed to have weighed Alleyn in the balance and found him quality.

"Tell me about it, Wilson. You'll be speaking in the cause of justice, you know. Think of that and expand. Did this row take place at lunch on Wednesday, November 14th, the last time Mrs. Candour was here?"

"Yes, sir. Or rather it was after lunch. Over the coffee in here."

"You brought the coffee in?"

"Yes. Voices was raised and I heard words as the ladies came out of the dining-room. I was coming into the hall with the tray and I didn't actually know what to do."

"Very awkward for you. What were they saying?"

Wilson suddenly cast off all parlourmaidenly restraint and launched herself into a verbatim account.

"Mrs. Candour said to Miss Quayne: 'You know what I mean, quite well,' sh' said, 'I've been watching you,' sh' said, 'and I was disgusted,' sh' said. That was when they came out of the dining-room and they never noticed me standing there they was so carried away. And Miss Quayne looked at her and said: 'I hope I don't understand you, Dagmar,' sh' said. And the way she said it! 'I hope I don't understand you, Dagmar,' sh' said, 'because I can't believe you would let your soul come down to such an earth-plane,' sh' said, 'as to think of Father Garnette and me in such a way,' sh' said. And Mrs. Candour laughed and she said: 'Earth-plane!' sh' said. 'If you're not revelling on the earth-plane at this very moment I'd like to know who is? Don't pretend, Cara,' sh' said. Then they went into the drawing-room and I waited and I didn't like to go in and they never shut the door and Miss Quayne said very loud: 'It's pathetically clear,' sh' said, 'what's the matter with you. You're devoured by jealousy.' Mrs. Candour gave a kind of—well, a kind of screech, sir, but Miss Quayne said, sh' said: 'Because Father Garnette has chosen me to discover the hidden mysteries of the spirit and the body,' sh' said—or something like that it was, and then Mrs. Candour laughed. And the way she laughed! Well! And she said: 'Cara,' sh' said, 'don't think you can take me in,' sh' said, 'because I know.' And she said: 'I promise you, I'm not going to stand aside and see it,' sh' said. And then I was that upset I kind of quivered if you understand me, sir, and the cups rattled and Miss Quayne said: 'S'ssh!' sh' said, 'Wilson,' sh' said. So I walked in."

"Extraorinarily dramatic!" exclaimed Alleyn. "A princely entrance. And did they drink their coffee?"

"Their hands shook that much they could hardly pour it out, sir."

"And you withdrew?"

"Yes, sir, and closed the door," said Wilson, righteous but regretful. A moment later she followed her own example and Alleyn and Nigel were left alone.

"Could you possibly keep up with all that?" asked Alleyn.

"I may have left out an occasional 'sh' said.' Otherwise it's all here. Do you think Mrs. Candour really talked like that?"

"Wouldn't be surprised. She's a very common woman. She's a liar, what's more. She said she'd only been twice to this house."

"I wonder if she's a murderess," said Nigel.

"Too stupid, I'd have thought," said Alleyn, "but you never know. There's a certain kind of low cunning that comes out very strong on occasion. I wish I had it. I'm scared to death I'll make a fool of myself over this case. The boss-man is very excited about it. It *ought* to be easy—it's so startling. Startling cases are generally easy. The difficult cases are the ones when one drunk heaves a brick at another drunk and leaves him lying in the road. Once they go in for fancy touches it's usually kindergarten stuff. And this is so very fancy, so very extra, so specially Susie. Like to make one of your analyses, Bathgate?"

"What do you mean? My analyses?"

"On paper. All the people and their motives and opportunities with neat little sub-headings. Like a balance-sheet."

"Do you really want me to?"

"Yes, if you will. I shall be able to cast a superior eye over it and then shatter it with a few facetiæ. It will restore my self-respect. No, do make it. You will look at the show from a different point of view. It may easily suggest something. It will be a help. Really."

"I shall be delighted," said Nigel and set to work.

Alleyn returned to Cara Quayne's desk and carried on with the job of sorting her papers. There was a long silence broken only by the rustle of paper, the snap and crackle of the fire, and the sound of Nigel's pen. Presently he looked up and said:

"There. Finished."

"Let me see," said Alleyn.

With a smug but slightly anxious air, Nigel laid his paper before the inspector. This is what he had written:

MURDER OF CARA QUAYNE

Suspects

The Initiates, the priest, and the acolyte.

All of these had the opportunity to slip the cigarette-paper possibly containing cyanide into the cup.

Circumstances

Cara Quayne drank the wine while in a state of great nervous excitement. She seemed to me to be self-hypnotised and scarcely conscious of her actions. I was reminded of a dervish or a negro priestess.

"Have you ever seen one?" asked Alleyn.

"No. That didn't prevent me from being reminded of one."

Alleyn read on:

The other Initiates were also in a highly emotional condition, and it is unlikely that they would notice any hanky-panky with the cup.

Garnette. Probably the only normal person there. He handled the cup twice. He started it off, took it back from Ogden and gave it to Cara Quayne. He had the greatest opportunity. Miss Wade said he covered the cup with one hand so he could have easily dropped the paper into the wine. *Motive*. Deceased had left £5,000 in bearer bonds in his safe. These have been pinched. She had made a 'terrible discovery' and may have told him of it. If he stole the bonds this might induce him to kill her. She may have left him a large sum in her Will. *Note.* A work on poisons was hidden behind his books. It fell open at a recipe for home-made cyanide. Garnette spoke like an American when tight.

Mrs. Candour. First Initiate to take cup. Jealous of Miss Quayne. *Motive.* Quarrelled with her over Garnette. Over-sexed, unattractive, stupid, vindictive. The scrap of paper found in the grate seems to refer to her:——" Sir, this is to warn—with M—s Can," etc. Could this have been a warning against Mrs. Candour? If so, from whom?

M. de Ravigne. Second Initiate to handle cup. Miss Wade says he used handkerchief to wipe rim. Might have palmed poison with this. *Motive.* In love with Miss Quayne, who was evidently Garnette's mistress. A very cool customer. Has known deceased longer than any of the others.

Miss Wade. Third Initiate to handle cup. Unlikely. *motive.* None apparent. She seems unaware of the Quayne-Garnette situation.

Pringle. Fourth to handle cup. Neurotic. Takes drugs. Worships Garnette. *Motive.* He surprised Garnette and Miss Quayne. Possibly shock unhinged him and he was determined to save G. Miss W. says he made a botch of handling cup.

Janey Jenkins. Fifth to handle cup. Engaged to Pringle. Very unlikely. *Motive.* None.

Ogden. Last. American. Met Garnette coming over to England. Very keen on the church. *Seems* straightforward, but you never know. Has given largely to church funds. *Motive.* Possibly he and Garnette were rogues together in the States and are in this together. If so Ogden may have offered to do the killing. Garnette bore out Ogden's statement when he (G.) was tight.

Claude Wheatley. Carried round flagon with wine. Could have dropped cyanide into cup. Horrible youth. Dotes on Garnette. Perhaps the Greeks have a word for him. *Motive.* Jealousy. Unlikely. Wouldn't have the guts. *Note.* If sodium cyanide is found at autopsy it seems certain the book on chemistry is a definite clue. That points to Garnette. Garnette is the obvious man,

I think. The chauffeur's statement about Miss Quayne's afternoon visit to the church seems to suggest that she found something there that upset her and caused her to write the note to Garnette which Fox found in the cigarette-box.

Here Nigel's summary stopped abruptly. He had added a few words and scored them out.

"Excellent," said Alleyn.

"It says nothing new, I'm afraid."

"No, but it raises several disputable points, which is always helpful. By the way, the analyst rang up just before you came. He has found sodium cyanide in the cigarette-paper, but of course the autopsy will take some time yet."

"Then the *Curiosities of Chemistry* is an important clue."

"I don't know," said Alleyn slowly, "but I rather fancy it's not important in quite the way you fancy."

"Whatever does that mean?"

"There were no prints on that book. Bailey has tried all the stock dodges of dactylography."

"What may that be? Oh, wait a bit. Dactyl. Why not say 'fingerprintery'?"

"As you please. He's dabbed nitrate of silver solution on it and developed the pages. Nothing there. It's a glossy paper, so someone must have dealt with the book. If Garnette got his big idea from it he must have wiped his fingerprints off and put it where he knew we would find it. A curious combination of forethought and stupidity, don't you think?"

"Yes, but still—— Oh, I don't know. Go on with Garnette."

"You note that Garnette was probably the only completely self-possessed person present. A very good point to make. Should you say this crime looks more like the work of a calculating, shrewd, unscrupulous individual, or a hysterical monomaniac with a streak of cunning?"

"The latter, I suppose," said Nigel slowly, "which Garnette is not. All the same, he might have meant us to think that."

"Ah," said Alleyn, "that's very subtle, Bathgate."

"Garnette strikes me as being subtlish," said Nigel. "What

do you think about Garnette and Ogden being old partners in infamy?"

"Not a great deal. As I said last night, I think Garnette told the truth when he was tight. If you remember he advanced the colourful suggestion that Ogden looks upon him as the sand-fly's garters. I'm not well up in Americanese, but I had the distinct impression that Mr. Garnette regards Mr. Ogden as fair and easy game."

"Look here," said Nigel suddenly, "let's pretend it's a detective novel. Where would we be by this time? About half-way through, I should think. Well, who's your pick."

"I am invariably gulled by detective novels. No herring so red but I raise my voice and give chase."

"Don't be ridiculous," said Nigel.

"Fact. You see in real detection herrings are so often out of season."

"Well, never mind, who's your pick?"

"It depends on the author. If it's Agatha Christie, Miss Wade's occulted guilt drips from every page. Dorothy Sayers's Lord Peter would plump for Pringle, I fancy. Inspector French would go for Ogden. Of course Ogden, on the face of it, is the first suspect."

"What are you saying! Ogden! Then you *do* think he's a bad hat."

"No. *No!* He seems a perfectly good hat. I merely say that the immediate circumstances—the actual situation at the time of the murder—point to Ogden."

"Why?"

"My dear Bathgate, this is a sad falling-off. Think of his position."

"I'm damned if I know what you are driving at. His position seems to be very comfortable. He's a rich business man."

Alleyn cast his eyes up but said nothing.

"Don't make that maddening grimace, Alleyn. What are you getting at? Do you or do you not suspect Mr. Ogden?"

"I suspect the whole lot of them. Apart from the one point I have noted I don't think he's any likelier than the others."

"Surely he's likelier than Janey Jenkins and Miss Wade."

There was a tap at the door and Inspector Fox came in.

"Another report from Bailey, sir," he said. "Good morning, Mr. Bathgate."

"What's Bailey say?" asked Alleyn.

"Nothing new. He's got to work properly on the prints. Very smart chap, Bailey. He's found Father Garnette's prints on the parcel of newspaper, and he thinks there's a trace of them on the top of the poison book. Nothing on the cyanide page, as you know. Miss Quayne's on the page torn out of the notebook."

"When did he get a pattern to compare them with?"

"That would be from the body, sir."

"Oh, of course."

"There's another print come out on the book," Fox continued, "and he hasn't been able to trace it. He'd like to get impressions from the rest of them."

"He shall have them," said Alleyn, "this afternoon. When's the inquest? To-morrow at eleven?"

"That's right, sir."

"Well, we'd better call it a day here."

"Have you found anything?" Nigel asked. "Any clues?"

"Nothing spectacular. De Ravigne's love letters. A smug and guarded epistle from the Garnette."

"May I see M. de Ravigne's letters, sir?" asked Fox.

"There you are. The one on the top's the most interesting."

Fox seated himself at the table, adjusted a large pair of spectacles and spread out the first of the letters. Nigel strolled up behind him.

"What are *you* up to?" inquired Alleyn.

"Nothing," said Nigel, reading frantically at long range.

M. de Ravigne wrote a large flowing hand. It was dated Friday of last week.

> *My Adored Cara* [the letter began], I distress myself intolerably on your behalf. It is not that you reject me, for that is the fortunes of love which are ever as hazardous as those of war. To accept defeat I can compose myself with dignity and remain, however wounded, your devoted friend. So far have I adopted, at all events outwardly, your English phlegm. It is as your friend I implore you to continue no longer in your design for the rôle of Chosen Vessel. It is a project fraught with danger to yourself. You are blinded with a false glamour. One may amuse oneself and interest oneself in a religion, but there should be a careful

moderation in this as in all things. In becoming the Chosen Vessel you would cast away your moderation and abandon yourself to detestable extremities. I beg, I implore you to refuse this rôle, so injurious to your *amour propre*. You do not comprehend what you undertake. I repeat you are in a danger to lose that which one most prizes. You are in a grave peril. I kiss your hand and entreat again that you take the advice of

Your devoted,

Rauol

I beg that you destroy this as all other of my letters.

"And she didn't," said Nigel.

CHAPTER XV

FATHER GARNETTE EXPLORES THE CONTENTS OF A MARE'S NEST

"No," said Alleyn, "she kept his letters. Women keep love letters for much the same reason as a servant keeps references. They help to preserve, as M. de Ravigne might say, the *amour propre,* and can always be produced upon occasion."

"Angela never shows my letters to anyone," said Nigel hotly. "Never."

"Not to her bosomest friend? No? You are fortunate. Perhaps she hopes they may be found, smelling faintly of orris-root, if she predeceases you."

"That is a remark in bad taste, I consider."

"I agree and apologise. You don't question the taste of reading Miss Quayne's love letters over Fox's shoulder, I notice," said Alleyn mildly.

"That's entirely different," blustered Nigel. "Miss Quayne was murdered."

"Which makes her fair game. I know, I know. Well, what do you think of M. de Ravigne's effusion?"

"It looks monstrous fishy to me," said Nigel. "What does he mean about her putting herself in a position that is fraught with danger? It looks remarkably like a threat.

'Take on the Chosen Vessel job and your life will be in danger.'"

"He doesn't actually say her life, Mr. Bathgate," said Fox, glancing up from another of the letters.

"No," agreed Alleyn. "He may be old-fashioned enough to think there is something a woman values more than her life."

"Well," said Nigel, "what do you think inspired the letter?"

"An interesting point, Bathgate. I don't know. Jealousy perhaps or—yes—it might be fear. He was very agitated when he wrote it."

"How do you make that out?"

"The phraseology betrays him. The English is much less certain than in the other letters. There are several little mistakes."

"I think the postscript looks very shady."

"It does, doesn't it? What do you say, Fox?"

"Well, sir, I'd say the gentleman knew something that he didn't exactly like to mention in black and white. It might be he knew there'd be goings-on with the Reverend, and it might be something he was afraid she'd find out. That postscript to me looks as though he was scared."

"You wise old bird. Well, I've finished here. We'll leave your mates to do the tooth-combing, Fox. They are upstairs at the moment. I've a date with Mr. Rattisbon."

"He was the solicitor in the O'Callighan case, wasn't he?" asked Nigel.

"He was. He's everything that a lawyer ought to be. Desiccated, tittuppy, nice old fuss-pot. Gives one the idea that he is a good actor slightly overdoing his part. I must away, Fox. Meet you at the Garnette apartment, as Mr. Ogden would say."

"Right-oh, sir."

"Anyone else going?" Nigel inquired.

"No doubt you will appear. I expect the Initiates to turn up in full force. Two o'clock."

"Certainly, I shall come," said Nigel. "*Au revoir*."

Nigel returned to his office and Alleyn went down the Strand to the little street where Mr. Rattisbon kept office.

It was one of those offices that look as if they were kept

going as a memorial to Charles Dickens. A dingy entry smelt of cobwebs and old varnish. A dark staircase led to a landing, where a frosted-glass skylight let in enough light to show Mr. Rattisbon's name on the door. Beyond the door Alleyn found Mr. Rattisbon himself in an atmosphere of dust, leather, varnish, dry sherry, and age. The room was not dusty, but it made one think of discreet dust. Mr. Rattisbon was not dressed in Victorian garments, but he conveyed an impression of being so dressed. He was a thin, eager old man with bluish hands and sharp eyes. He spoke rapidly with a sort of stuttering volubility, and had a trick of vibrating the tip of his long tongue between his lips. He dealt, as his father and grandfather had done before him, with the estates of the upper-middle class. He was a very shrewd old gentleman.

"I hope I'm not late, sir," said Alleyn.

"No, no, Chief Inspector, not at all. Quite punctual, quite punctual. Pray sit down. Yes. Let me see. I don't think we have met since that unfortunate affair—um?"

"No. I am sorry to bother you. I expect you have guessed what brought me?"

"Brought you. Yes. Yes. This miserable business of Miss Cara Valerie Quayne. I have received word of it this morning. A most distressing affair, most."

"How did you hear of it, sir?"

"Through the maid, the confidential maid. A Miss—ah—Miss Edith Laura Hebborn. Miss Hebborn felt I should be advised immediately and very properly rang me up. One of the old type of domestic servants. The old type. I suppose there's no doubt about it being a case of homicide. Um? No."

"None, I'm afraid. It's a bizarre case."

"Bizarre!" ejaculated Mr. Rattisbon with distaste. "Tch! Well, Chief Inspector, how can I assist you?"

"By giving me any information you can about Miss Quayne and by letting me see the Will. The inquest is to-morrow. Perhaps it would save time if I told you what I have learned up to date."

Alleyn gave Mr. Rattisbon the gist of the information he had received from Nannie and from the Initiates. The little lawyer listened attentively.

"Precisely," he said when Alleyn had finished. "An excellent account and substantially correct. Accurate."

"Miss Quayne's affairs have always been in your hands, sir?"

"Oh, yes. Yes. Colonel Quayne—her father—old family clients. Charming fellow."

"You have seen Miss Quayne recently?"

"Five weeks ago to-morrow."

"On that occasion did she wish to alter her Will?"

"Um? You heard of that?"

"From M. de Ravigne. I hope you will tell me anything that strikes you as being relevant."

"It is exceedingly distasteful to me to discuss my clients' affairs, Chief Inspector. Of course I quite appreciate the extraordinary nature of the matter. Since you rang up I have considered the advisability of—of—speaking with complete frankness, and—I—in short I have decided to lay the whole matter before you."

Mr. Rattisbon suddenly snatched his pince-nez from his nose and waved them at Alleyn.

"As follows," he said. "Five weeks ago I received a visit from Miss Cara Valerie Quayne. She had advised me first that she wished to make an extensive alteration in her Will, and then that she desired me to draw up a new Will. I therefore had the existing document in readiness for her visit. She arrived." He rubbed his nose violently. "And I may say she astounded me."

Alleyn was silent. After contemplating him with severity for some seconds Mr. Rattisbon leant across the desk and continued:

"She astounded me. The previous Will had been a very proper and sensible disposition of her considerable fortune. Several large sums to various worthy charities. Annuities to her servants. Various legacies. The residuary legatee was a third cousin in New Zealand. A boy whom she has never seen, but he bears her father's name. And so on and so on and so on. Perfectly proper. She now informed me that she wished me completely to revise these terms and—in short to draw up a new document. On these lines: She wished the annuity of two hundred pounds per annum to Miss Edith Laura Hebborn to be increased to three hundred pounds per annum. The lease of her house, its contents, her pictures, jewels and so on to M. Raoul Honoré Christophe de Ravigne. A—a handsome legacy to Father Jasper Garnette. The rest of her very considerable fortune—every penny piece of it—she would leave to the House of the Sacred Flame, 89 Knocklatchers Row, Eaton Place, making Father Garnette the sole trustee."

"Gosh!" said Alleyn.

"You may well say so. I—frankly, Chief Inspector—I was horrified. I had known Miss Quayne from her childhood. Her father was a personal friend as well as a client. In a sense I may say I had considered myself *in loco parentis,* since both guardians were deceased. When I first became aware of Miss Quayne's increasing interest in Mr. Garnette's sect I went so far as to make inquiries about him. What I discovered did not reassure me. On the contrary I became gravely suspicious. Then, to crown everything, she came to me with the request that I should draw up a Will on the lines I have indicated."

"Extraordinary."

"Most extraordinary. As a solicitor I have become accustomed to testamentary—ah—vagaries. I have become accustomed to them. But this caused me the greatest concern. I exceeded the strict limits of propriety by urging her again and again to reconsider. I represented to her that this Father Garnette might not be all she thought him. I strongly urged her to allow me to make further inquiries. When all else failed I begged that she at least left this very considerable sum to be administered by other trustees on behalf of the—the—religious body in which she had become so interested. Not a bit of it!"

"She insisted on leaving Mr. Garnette as sole trustee?"

"Precisely. She was in a most excitable frame of mind and was impatient, I may say intolerant, of any suggestions. I put it to her that her father would have regarded the terms of the new Will with abhorrence. She would not listen. She—in short, she said that if I made any further difficulties she would get a Will form from—from a Smith's bookstall and fill it in herself."

Mr. Rattisbon dropped his pince-nez delicately on his blotting-paper and by this moderate gesture conveyed a sense of overwhelming defeat.

"I drew up the Will," he said. "Three days afterwards, she came here and signed it."

"So that's that," grunted Alleyn. "By how much does the sect benefit?"

"In round figures, twenty-one thousand pounds."

"And may I ask, sir, by how much Mr. Jasper Garnette is to be a richer man?"

"Ten thousand pounds."

"Damn!" said Alleyn.

Mr. Rattisbon shot a shrewd glance at him.

"May I take it as your personal opinion that he will live to—to enjoy it?" he asked.

"He'll need it before I'm done with him."

"That is a cryptic answer, Chief Inspector."

"Yours was a leading question, sir."

Mr. Rattisbon suddenly sucked in his breath three or four times very rapidly and uttered a little whooping noise. He had laughed.

"In any case," Alleyn went on, "couldn't the Will be contested? What about the young Quayne, down under? What about coercion? Or her mental condition? I'm entirely ignorant of the law, sir, but suppose—well, suppose he'd been giving her drugs?"

Mr. Rattisbon stared at the inspector for some seconds.

"If you find evidence of that," he said at last, "I would be greatly obliged if you would call on me again."

"Certainly." Alleyn stood up. "By the way, have you any idea why she increased the bequest to Miss Hebborn?"

"I received an impression that—that it was in the nature of a—how shall I put it?—of a peace-offering. Miss Hebborn had, I believe, expressed herself somewhat warmly on the subject of this sect, which she regarded in a most unfavourable light. There had been a heated argument, hasty words amounting to a quarrel. Miss Quayne was greatly attached to her old nurse, who had given her devoted service. From certain remarks she let fall I gathered that she wished to—in a sense to make reparation."

"And the bequest to M. de Ravigne? It will amount to something pretty considerable, I imagine. The pictures alone are worth a great deal. There's a very fine Van Gogh and I noticed a Famille Verte 'ginger' jar that wouldn't be had for the asking."

"Precisely. M. de Ravigne is an old friend of the family and, I understand, a collector. I have not the pleasure of his acquaintance."

"He has an intriguing temperament. I must go. Good-bye, sir, and thank you a thousand times."

"Good-bye. Yes. Thank-yer. Thank-yer. Don't mention it. Yes," gabbled Mr. Rattisbon with extreme rapidity. He walked out first on to the landing and there leant forward and peered up into Alleyn's face. "And I hope you're going to —eh? By the heels? Eh? Always interested in your work. This time—natural anxiety. Well. Mind the steps."

"I hope so. Of course. Thank you," said Alleyn.

He had a short interview with his Assistant Commissioner, lunched in the Strand and went straight to Knocklatchers Row. Here he found Claude and Lionel and all the Initiates who had been rung up from the Yard grouped in a solid phalanx round Father Garnette's sitting-room under the eye of Detective-Sergeant Bailey. The priest, looking extremely cadaverous and yellow, was seated at the centre table. Nigel, who had hung about the entrance with Inspector Fox, followed the detectives into the room.

"Good afternoon, ladies and gentlemen," said Alleyn cheerfully. "Forgive me if I've kept you waiting."

Janey Jenkins said: "You're punctual. It's just struck two."

Mr. Ogden stood up and said: "Well, well, well, look who's here."

The rest of the ladies and gentlemen uttered self-conscious noises.

"I shan't keep you long," Alleyn went on. "First of all, if you don't mind, we would like to take your fingerprints. It's the usual thing. I could get them on the sly be offering you shiny photos to identify as your third cousins, but there really isn't time. Detective-Sergeant Bailey will fix you up."

Janey looked interested, Maurice disgusted, Ogden solemn and de Ravigne faintly amused, while Mrs. Candour and Miss Wade were obviously terrified. The acolytes turned pale and Father Garnette remained ghastly and rather remote. Bailey took their prints by getting them to roll the cushion of each finger on a little printer's ink and then on a sheet of white paper. He thoughtfully offered them an oiled rag to clean up with. This ceremony ended, Alleyn invited them all to sit round the table.

"First of all," he began, "I should like you all to tell me as far as you can remember what are the contents of the safe. I understand that several of you had access to it."

There was a moment's silence and then Mr. Ogden said bluntly:

"We all know where the key was kept, Chief, but I guess none of us worried."

"Where *was* the key kept."

"On my desk," said Father Garnette, "sometimes."

"In your pocket," said Mr. Ogden. "It wasn't just laying around all the time, Chief. Sometimes there's quite a little bit of coin in that safe."

"How much is there at the moment?" asked Alleyn.

"I—ah—I really forget," said Father Garnette. "Let me see. There should be last Wednesday's offertory. I really don't remembah——"

"It was £61 8*s*. 6*d*.," announced M. de Ravigne.

"You've got it pat!" said Maurice Pringle unpleasantly.

"I am a warden," replied de Ravigne very placidly, "I counted it. Father Garnette and Mr. Ogden were here. It was, I repeat, £61 8*s* 6*d*."

"*And* a cheque for twenty pounds," said Mr. Ogden dryly. "You might remember that."

"Your own offering, Monsieur Ogden. I remember."

"What else?" asked Alleyn.

"There is more importantly, M. l'Inspecteur, a parcel of bearer bonds of which I have told you. They are issued by the Kasternek Oil Company. These were given by Miss Quayne to this church to await the raising of the same amount for a building fund. They are in value five thousand pounds. Since they were here you have always kept the key on your person, is it not so, Father?"

"Quite right, my dear Raoul. You advised me to take this precaution, if you remember."

"Certainly."

"Quite correct," said Mr. Ogden emphatically. "We may all be O.K., but that doesn't say we've got to act crazy." He stopped short, turned bright red, and glanced uneasily at Father Garnette.

"Anything else in the safe?" asked Alleyn.

"The banking-book is there. That, I believe, is all," murmured M. de Ravigne.

"Right. Well, we'll just check it over. I'll ask Mr. Garnette to do that. It's purely a matter of form. You will notice we sealed it last night. The usual procedure under the circumstances. Now, Mr. Garnette, if you please."

He produced the bunch of keys, gave them to Father Garnette and himself broke the police seal. Father Garnette rose, opened the safe and took out the contents one by one, laying them on the table. Nigel noticed that the parcel had been replaced. Bailey must have done that and put a fresh seal on the safe. The cash was counted by Fox who found it correct.

"Have you looked at the parcel of bearer bonds?" asked Alleyn.

Father Garnette glanced at him.

"No," he said. He sounded anxious and surprised. "No, I have not."

"Just open it," suggested Alleyn, "and make sure there has been no theft. We've got to explore every possibility."

Father Garnette undid the red ribbon and pulled open the brown paper.

A neat wad of newspaper lay revealed.

One would have thought it impossible for Father Garnette's face to look more unhealthy than it already was that morning, but it undoubtedly became a shade more livid when the contents of the parcel were displayed. It also became absolutely expressionless. For about three seconds he stood still. Then he raised his eyes and stared inimically at Alleyn. Nigel wondered if, for a moment, the priest had a mad idea that the police had played a practical joke on him. Alleyn returned his glance gravely. Suddenly Father Garnette seized the newspaper and with an ugly fumbling movement clawed it apart, shook the leaves open, and then as abruptly, let them fall again. When he spoke it was in a curiously dead voice, as though his throat had closed.

"Robbed!" he said, "I've been robbed—robbed."

They had watched Father Garnette and Father Garnette only, so that when Mr. Ogden produced his national classic expression of incredulity it made them all jump.

Mr. Ogden placed both hands on the table and leant towards his spiritual leader.

"Oh, yeah?" said Mr. Ogden.

CHAPTER XVI

MR. OGDEN PUTS HIS TRUST IN POLICEMEN

"Is that so?" continued Mr. Ogden; and then, for all the world as though he was an anthology of Quaint American Sayings, he completed the trilogy by adding in a soft undertone:

"Sez you?"

They all turned to watch Mr. Ogden. His good-natured face had settled down into a definitely hard-boiled expression. His lower lip stuck out, his eyes were half-closed. He spoke out of one corner of his mouth. He leant easily on the table, but the very seams of his coat looked tense. He did not remove his gaze from Father Garnette, but he addressed the table at large.

"Folks," he said, "I guess we're the Simps from Simpleton. Cable ad-dress Giggle-Giggle. No flowers by request."

"What the hell do you mean?" asked Maurice Pringle.

De Ravigne swore very softly in French.

"What do you mean?" replied Mr. Ogden, never taking his eyes off Garnette. "What do I mean? Aren't you conscious yet? Who's taken care of the keys ever since Cara parked those bonds in the safe? Didn't we say, right now, Father Garnette had been wearing his keys for safety's sake? Safety is right. I reckon those bonds are so darned safe we'll never see them any more."

"What do you mean, Mr. Ogden?" asked Miss Wade. "I'm afraid I don't quite follow. Has this money been stolen?"

"Nope," answered Mr. Ogden. "It's just kind of disguised itself as the Daily Mail."

"But I don't understand——"

"Cara's bonds have been stolen, Miss Wade," said Janey impatiently, "and newspaper substituted. You can see for yourself."

"Who has done this?" demanded Father Garnette suddenly. He had drawn himself up to his full height. The resonance had come back to his voice, and something of the old dominance to his manner. He was wearing that dark-green garment—a sort of cassock that covered his neck and hung heavily about his feet. In a raffish, theatrical kind of fashion he looked extremely impressive. He puzzled Nigel, who had expected him to crumble up when the theft of the bonds was revealed. He had watched Garnette, and the priest was either dumbfounded or the best actor off the stage that Nigel had ever seen.

"Who has done this?" repeated Garnette. He turned his head and stared round the circle of Initiates.

"I swear I never touched the safe," bleated Claude Wheatley in a hurry.

"I suggest, Father, that you yourself are best situated to answer this question," said de Ravigne softly. "It makes itself apparent. As we have said and you have also agreed—you have kept these keys about your person since our poor Cara made her gift."

"How dare you!" cried Mrs. Candour shrilly. "How dare you suggest such a thing, M. de Ravigne? Father!"

"Quiet, my child," said Father Garnette.

Maurice Pringle burst out laughing. The others stared at him scandalised.

"Look at him," coughed Maurice, "look! To the pure all things are pure."

"Maurice!" cried Janey.

"Just a minute, please," said Alleyn.

They had forgotten all about Alleyn, but now they listened to him.

"Mr. Pringle," he said, "will you be good enough to pull yourself together? You are behaving like a hysterical adolescent. That's better. I gather from what you have all said that no one is prepared to volunteer information about the missing bonds." Father Garnette began to speak, but Alleyn raised a finger. "Very well. I now wish to bring another exhibit to your notice. The book, if you please, Fox."

Inspector Fox loomed forward and put a book into

Alleyn's hand. Alleyn held it up. It was a copy of Abberley's *Curiosities of Chemistry.*

"Quis?" said Alleyn lightly.

Garnette turned and looked calmly at it. Mrs. Candour gape at it with her mouth open. Maurice stared at it as if it were an offensive relic, Janey looked blank, M. de Ravigne curious. Mr. Ogden still glared at Father Garnette. Miss Wade balanced her pince-nez across her nose and leant forward to peer at the book. Claude Wheatley said: "What's that? I can't see."

"It is Abberley's *Curiosities of Chemistry,*" said Alleyn.

"Hey?" exclaimed Mr. Ogden suddenly and wheeled round in his chair. He saw the book and his jaw dropped.

"Why——" he said. "Why——"

"Yes, Mr. Ogden?"

Mr. Ogden looked exceedingly uncomfortable. A dead silence followed.

"What is it?" continued Alleyn patiently.

"Why nothing, Chief. Except that I'm quite curious to know where you located that book."

"Anybody else know anything about it?" asked Alleyn.

"Yes," said Father Garnette, "I do."

He was still on his feet. He stretched out his hand and Alleyn gave him the book.

"This volume," said Father Garnette, "appeared in my shelves some weeks ago. It is not mine and I do not know where it came from. I did not even open it. I simply found it there."

"Next an unexpurgated translation of Petronius?"

"Ah—preciselah!" said Father Garnette.

He still held the book in his hands. Perhaps the habit of the pulpit caused him to let it fall open.

"Who left this book in my room?" he demanded.

"Look at it," said Alleyn.

Garnette hesitated as though he wondered what Alleyn meant. Then he looked at the book. It had again fallen open at the page which gave the formula for sodium cyanide. For a moment Garnette scarcely seemed to take it in. Then with sudden violence he shut the book and dropped it on the table.

"I am the victim of an infamous conspiracy," he said. The baa-ing vowel-sounds had disappeared, and the hint of a nasal inflection had taken their place.

"You tell us," said Alleyn, "that this book was left in your shelves. When did you first discover it?"

"I do not remembah," declared Garnette, rallying slightly.

"Try to remember."

"It was there three Sundays ago, anyway," volunteered Claude.

"Oh?" said Alleyn. "How do you know that, Mr. Wheatley?"

"Because, I mean, I saw it. And I know it was three Sundays ago because you see I do temple service—cleaning the silver, you know—and all that, every fortnight. And it was while I was doing that, I found it, and it wasn't last Sunday, so it must have been three Sundays ago."

"How did you come to find it?"

"Well, I—well, you see—well, I'd finished and Father was out and I thought I'd wait till he came in and so I went into his room to put some things away."

"Where was the book?"

"Well, it was in the shelves."

"Where you could see it?"

"Not quite."

"It was behind the other books?"

"Yes, if you must know, it was," said Claude turning an unattractive crimson. "As a matter of fact I had put all the books there myself"—he stopped and looked nervously from Ogden to Garnette—"about a week before that. I was—I was tidying up in here. I didn't look at them, then. The book on Chemistry wasn't there that day. But it was there on the Sunday—a week later. You see I'd read most of the other books and I thought I'd try and find something else, and so——"

"Did you handle it?"

"I—I—just glanced at it."

"You touched it. You're sure of that?"

"Yes, I am. Because I remember I had my gloves on. The ones I do the polishing in. I like to keep my hands nice. I wondered if they'd marked it. Then I put it away and—and I read something else, you see."

"Petronius, perhaps."

"Yes, it was. I thought it marvellous."

"Thank you."

"I don't understand," began Miss Wade.

"Nor do I," interrupted Mrs. Candour. "Why is such a fuss being made about this book?"

"It's a treatise on poisons," said Maurice. "Cara was poisoned. Find the owner of the book and there's your murderer. Q.E.D. Our wonderful police!"

"I've got an idea," said Mr. Ogden with a curious inflection in his voice, "that it's not just as simple as all that."

"Really?" jeered Maurice. "You seem to know a damn' sight too much to be healthy."

"Maurice, please!" said Janey.

"Oh, God, I'm sorry, Jane."

"The interesting thing about the book," said Alleyn in his quietest voice, "is that if you handle it as Mr. Garnette did, it falls open at a discourse on cyanide." He took the book and handed it to de Ravigne. "Like to try?" he asked.

De Ravigne took the book, but he must have handled it differently. It fell open at another place. He examined it closely, a curiously puzzled expression in his eyes.

"Let me see," said Lionel. "Do, please." With him the experiment worked successfully.

"How too marvellous!" said Claude.

"Here," shouted Mr. Ogden suddenly, "lemme see."

Lionel handed him the book and he experimented with it while they all watched him. The book fell open repeatedly and each time at the same page.

"Well, for crying out loud!" said Mr. Ogden, and slammed it down on the table.

"Now," Alleyn went on, "there's one more exhibit. This box of cigarettes. Yours, isn't it, Mr. Garnette?" He laid the Benares Box on the table.

"Ah, yes."

"Will you open it?"

"Is this a sleight of hand act?" asked Maurice Pringle. "no deception practised."

"None, on my part," replied Alleyn good-humouredly, "as I think you will agree, Mr. Garnette."

Garnette had opened the box. Cara Quayne's note lay on the top of the cigarettes.

"What is this?" asked Garnette. And then: "My God, it's her writing."

"Will you read it aloud?"

Garnette read slowly. The habit of the pulpit was so strong

in him that he pitched his voice and read deliberately with round vowels and stressed final consonants.

"Must see you. Terrible discovery. After service to-night."

He put the paper down on the table and again looked at Alleyn. His lips twitched, but he did not speak. He moved his hands uncertainly. He looked neither guilty nor innocent, but simply puzzled.

"Where did this come from?" he said at last.

"It was found last night in that box," Alleyn said.

"But—I did not know. I did not see it there."

"Does anyone," asked Alleyn, "know anything of this note?" Nobody spoke.

"Had Miss Quayne spoken to any of you of this terrible discovery she had made?"

"When was it written?" asked Maurice suddenly.

"Yesterday."

"How do you know?"

"Because it is dated," answered Alleyn politely.

"Oh, Maurice, my poor pet!" said Janey, and for the first time that morning somebody laughed.

"Shut up!" exclaimed Maurice.

"You did not open this box yesterday, Mr. Garnette?" Alleyn went on.

"No."

"When did Miss Quayne call?"

"I do not know. I did not see her. I was out from midday until about three o'clock."

"Where were you?"

"Father Garnette was my guest at luncheon," said de Ravigne. "I had invited Cara also, but she desired, she said, to spend the day in meditation in her own house."

"She changed her mind, it seems. How would she get in here?"

"The key to the front door of the church is always left in the porch, monsieur. It is concealed behind the porch there. We all use it."

"Did any of you come here yesterday between two-thirty and three o'clock while Miss Quayne was in the hall?"

No one had come, it seemed. Alleyn asked them all in turn where they had been. Maurice had lunched with Janey in her flat and had stayed there till four. Mrs. Candour had been at home for lunch, and so had Miss Wade. Miss Wade to everybody's surprise said she had been in the hall when Cara went through and into Garnette's flat. Miss Wade had been engaged in a little meditation, it appeared. She had seen Cara come out again and had thought she seemed "rather put out."

"Why did you say nothing of this before?" asked Alleyn.

"Because you did not ask me, officer," said Miss Wade.

"*Touché*," said Alleyn, and turned to the others.

Mr. Ogden had lunched at his club and afterwards taken a "carnstitootional" in the park, arriving home at tea-time. Garnette and de Ravigne had remained in the latter's house until two-forty, when de Ravigne had asked Garnette the time in order to set his clock right. About ten minutes later, Garnette left. He had a Neophytes' class at three-thirty, and it seemed that two selected advanced Neophytes always stayed on for what Father Garnette called a little repast in his flat, and then went to the evening instruction. This was a regular routine. That would account, Nigel reflected, for Cara Quayne leaving the note in the cigarette-box. Whatever her terrible discovery was, she would know she had no chance of a private conversation before the evening ceremony. After he left de Ravigne's house Father Garnette had gone straight to the hall. There he found one or two people who had come in early for the ceremony. He had not looked at the safe, but he felt sure he would have noticed if it had been open. De Ravigne lived in Lowndes Square, so it would not have taken many minutes for the priest to walk back to Knocklatchers Row. He probably arrived at about three o'clock. De Ravigne said he had remained at home until it was time to go to the evening ceremony. Claude and Lionel, it transpired, had not got up until half-past three in the afternoon.

"Ah, well," said Alleyn, with the ghost of a sigh, "I shall not keep you here any longer, ladies and gentlemen. The meeting is adjourned."

One by one the Initiates got to their feet. Garnette remained seated at the table, his face buried in his hands. Evidently most of them felt desperately uncomfortable at the thought of Father Garnette. They eyed him surreptitiously and made uneasy noises in their throats. Ogden still glared at him and, alone of the Initiates, seemed disinclined to leave.

M. de Ravigne clicked his heels, made a formal bow which included Alleyn and Garnette, said " Gentlemen "; made a rather more willowy bow, said " Ladies," and walked out with an air of knowing how to deal with the stiffest social contretemps.

Miss Wade, after some hesitation, made a sudden dart at Garnette, extended a black kid claw and said:

" Father! Faithful! Last ditch! Trust!"

Whereupon Mrs. Candour, who had been waiting for a cue from somebody, uttered a lamentable bellow and surged forward, saying: " Yes—yes—yes."

Garnette pulled himself together and cast upon both ladies a sort of languishing glare.

He said: " Faithful! Faithful unto——" and then, disliking the sound of the phrase, hurriedly abandoned it.

Ogden let them all go and then walked up to Alleyn.

" Can I have a word with you, Chief?" he asked.

" Certainly, Mr. Ogden."

" What are you going to say?" demanded Garnette.

" That's nobody's business, Garnette," said Ogden. " C'm on, Chief!"

He led the way out into the hall, followed by Alleyn, Nigel and Fox. When they were down in the aisle, he jerked his thumb at Nigel.

" I ain't giving interviews this trip, Mr. Bathgate," he said, " and something seems to tell me you're a Pressman."

" Mr. Bathgate is not here in his official capacity," said Alleyn. " I think we can trust him."

" Seems like I'm doing a helluva lot of trusting. Well—if you say so, Chief, that's O.K. by me."

Nigel returned to his old perch in the front pews, and Mr. Ogden paid no further attention to him. He addressed himself to Alleyn.

" Listen, Chief. I've spent quite a lot of my time in this little old island, but right now is the first occasion I've come into contact with the Law. Back home in God's Own Country I'd say a guy was crazy to do what I'm doing. But listen, Chief. I guess you're on the level, and I guess you ain't so darned polite you can't do your stuff."

Here Mr. Ogden paused, drew out a large silk handkerchief and wiped his neck with it.

" Hell," he said. " This has got me all shot to bits."

"What's on your mind, Mr. Ogden?" asked Alleyn.

"Hell," repeated Mr. Ogden. "Well, listen. They opine that in this country you don't get the hot squat, not without you earn it good and plenty."

"I beg your pardon?" said Alleyn, gazing at him. "Oh! I see. I think you're quite right. There are no miscarriages of justice in capital charges on the conviction side. Only, we hang them over here, you know."

"That's so," agreed Mr. Ogden, "but the principle's the same."

"True," said Alleyn.

Mr. Ogden seemed to find extreme difficulty in coming to the point. He rolled his eyes and goggled solemnly at Alleyn.

"Listen, Chief," he said again, "I guess that you've got it figured out that whoever owns the book of the words and songs did the murder."

"You mean the book on chemistry?"

"Yup."

"It certainly looks rather like that."

"Then it looks all cock-eyed," said Mr. Ogden violently. "It looks all to—— Hell! Do you know why?"

"I think I can guess," said Alleyn, smiling.

"You can! Well I'd be——"

"I rather fancied the book belonged to you."

"Chief, you said it," said Mr. Ogden.

CHAPTER XVII

MR. OGDEN GROWS LESS TRUSTFUL

"You said it," repeated Mr. Ogden and collapsed into a pew.

"Cheer up, Mr. Ogden," said Alleyn.

Mr. Ogden passed his handkerchief across his brow and contemplated the inspector with a certain expression of low cunning that reminded Nigel of a precocious baby.

"Maybe I seemed a mite too eager about that book," he said. "Maybe I kinda gave you the works."

"My inspiration dates a little further back than that," said Alleyn. "You told us last night that you were interested in gold-refining. A letter which we found in your pockets referred rather fully to a new process. It assumed a certain knowledge of chemistry on your part. The book is an American publication. It was a little suggestive, you see."

"Yup," said Mr. Ogden, "I see. Now listen. I bought that book years ago, way back in the pre-war period when I first began to sit up and take notice. I was a junior clurk at the time in the offices of a gold-refining company. Junior clurk is a swell name for office-boy. I lit on that book laying out in the rain on a five-cent stall, and I was ambitious to educate myself. It's kinda stayed around ever since. The book, I mean. When I came over here it was laying in one of my grips, and I let it lay. I know a bit more than I useter, and some of them antique recipes tickled me. Well, anyhow, it stuck and, and when I got fixed where I am now I packed it in the bookshelves along with the Van Dines and the National Geographics and the *Saturday Evening Posts*. I never opened it. And get this, chief, I never missed it till last night."

"Last night? At what time?"

"After I got home. I got to thinking about Cara, and I figured it out that she passed in her checks very, very sudden, and that the suddenest poison I knew was prussic acid.

Hydrocyanic acid if you want to talk Ritzy. I thought maybe I'd refresh my memory and I looked for the old book. Nothing doing. It was gone. What do you know about that?"

"What do *you* know about it?" rejoined Alleyn.

"Listen," said Mr. Ogden for about the twentieth time that afternoon. "I know this far. It was there four weeks back. Four weeks back from to-night I threw a party. All the Sacred Flame crowd was there. Garnette was there. And Raveenje. And Cara Quayne. All the gang, even Miss Wade, who has a habit of getting mislaid or overlooked: she was there and cracking hardy. Well, Raveenje, he's enthusiastic about literature. First editions are all published by Pep and Kick as he sees it. I saw him looking along the shelves and I yanked down the old *Curiosities* for him to have a slant at. Well, maybe it hadn't enough whiskers on it, but it seemed to excite him about as much as a raspberry drink at a departmental store. He gave a polite once-over and lost interest. But that's how I remember it was there. From that night till last evening I never gave it a thought."

"Did anyone take it away that night?"

"How should I know? I never missed the blamed thing."

"You can't remember anything that would help? The next time you looked at your bookshelves?"

"Nope. Wait a while. Wait a while."

Mr. Ogden clapped a plump hand on top of his head as if to prevent an elusive thought from escaping him.

"The next day or maybe the day after—it was around that time—Claude stopped in and he took Garnette's books away with him. I was out at the time."

"Mr. Garnette's books? What books?"

Mr. Ogden looked remarkably sheepish.

"Aw Gee!" he said. "Just something for a rainy day. He loaned 'em to me. He said they were classics. Classics. And how? Boy, they were central-heated."

"Are they among the lot in brown paper covers, behind the others?"

"You said it."

"And Claude Wheatley took them away?"

"Sure. He told the maid Garnette had sent him for them. He wanted to keep hold of them because they were rare. I'll say they were rare! Anyhow, that's when I last remember anything about books. I suppose Garnette told Claude where they were."

"Was the *Curiosities* in your shelves then?"

"Isn't that what I'm aiming to remember!" exclaimed Mr. Ogden desperately. "Lemme think! Next day Claude told me he'd called for Garnette's books and I said: 'Those were the ones in brown-paper overalls,' and he said he'd recognised them by that."

"The *Curiosities* was not in a brown paper, then?"

"No, sir. I'd no call to camouflage it. It was respectable."

Alleyn laughed.

"Can you remember noticing it that day?"

"Nope."

"Would you have noticed if it had already gone?"

"Lordy, no!" said Mr. Ogden.

He stared wildly into space for an appreciable time and then said slowly:

"Not in that way. I wouldn't have definitely missed it. But in another way I seem to remember *not* seeing it if you get me. It's a red book. Seems like I remember *not* seeing a red book. That sounds crazy, I guess."

"On the contrary, this is all extremely interesting," said Alleyn.

"Yeah? Well, here's hoping it doesn't interest you in Sam J. Ogden. Maybe Raveenje will recall me showing him the book. Or maybe one of the rest will. That," added Mr. Ogden with a naïve smile, "is just why I thought I'd better come clean."

"Do you incline to think somebody took the book that evening, Mr. Ogden?"

"What the hell? I haven't a notion when it was lifted."

"Have any of the Initiates been to see you since then?"

"Sure, they have. I gave a little lunch last Wednesday for Cara and Raveenje and Garnette and Dagmar. Lemme see. Maurice and Janey were around last Sunday. That was the night Dr. Kasbek came in. I haven't had Claude and Lionel come in again. Those two queens give me a pain."

"Now look here, Mr. Ogden, you've got your own ideas on the subject, haven't you? You practically stated, just now, that you believed Mr. Garnette had taken these bonds."

Mr. Ogden looked extremely uncomfortable.

"Didn't you?" pressed Alleyn.

"I'm not saying a thing."

"Very well," said Alleyn shortly, "I can't do anything against that."

Ogden gave him a sidelong but not unattractive grin.

"Seems like the British police is kinda helpless," he said.

"Seems like it," agreed Alleyn dryly. "How many of you are in this thing with Garnette?"

"What the hell? In what thing?"

He broke off, got to his feet, and stood glaring down at Alleyn, his face white and his eyes very angry.

"See here," he said. "Just what do you mean? I'm not muscling in on any homicide rackets. I've told you a straight story about that book and I'm sticking to it. If you don't believe me—find out."

"Mr. Ogden, I fully believe your story. But there are more rackets than one, you know."

"Yeah? Just what are you aiming to insinuate?"

"Merely that I have far too high an opinion of your intelligence to suppose that you would allow yourself to become as enamoured of transcendental mumbo-jumbo as you would have me believe."

"Are you telling me the spiritual dope we hand out here is phoney?"

"I'm saying that you aren't so hypnotised by it that you've lost your business man's acumen."

Mr. Ogden looked very hard at the inspector and a slow grin began to dawn on his face.

"And I'm saying," Alleyn continued, "that you don't float anything with big fat cheques unless you've going to get a more tangible return for your money than a dose of over-proof spiritual uplift."

"Maybe," said Mr. Ogden with a fat chuckle.

"In short, Mr. Ogden, I want to know how you stand as regards the finance of this affair. I've got to find out how everybody stands. It's no good mincing matters. All of the Initiates come under suspicion of this crime; yourself as much as anyone. Believe me, you cannot afford to keep back any information when there's a capital charge in the offing."

"Just when did you get your big idea that I'm interested financially?"

"I got it the first time I saw you. I know that there are, if you will forgive me for saying so, many hard-headed

Americans who can be taken in by highly-coloured religious sects. I told myself you might be one of them, but somehow I didn't think you were. You seemed to me to be too shrewd. Your attatude towards Mr. Garnette, when the theft of the bonds was discovered, confirmed my opinion. Of course, if you prefer not to tell me how matters stand, we can ferret round and find out. Mr. Garnette is now so alarmed he will no doubt be ready to give me his version."

"Like hell he will, the dirty what's it," said Mr. Ogden indignantly. "See here, Chief, you win this deal, hands down. Bar one point. Until to-day I was putting my O.K. stamp on the doctrine of the Sacred Flame. I've never backed a phoney deal in my life and I'm not starting in now. No, sir. The Sacred Flame and Jasper Garnette looked like clean peppy uplift to me. When Garnette and me met up on that trip, he outlined his scheme and he slipped me the line of talk. He told me it'd need capital. Well, I heard him address the passengers and the way he had those society dames asking if he'd accept ten dollars as a favour for the Seamen's Fund got me thinking. Before we landed I'd figured it out. I floated the concern on a percentage basis and Garnette couldn't have done it without me. We were in cahoots, and now, the dirty so-and-so, he's pulled out those bonds on me."

"Are there any other shareholders?"

"M. de Raveenje put five hundred pounds into it. All he could find. The slump hit him up some. Say, I reckon he'll want to know the how-so about those bonds. He's white all through, and he saw Cara way up among the gods."

"Did you," asked Alleyn, "have a written agreement?"

"Certainly we did. Drawn up by a lawyer. Each of us got a copy. Want to see it, Chief?"

"Yes, we'd better have a look at it. I wonder where Mr. Garnette keeps his."

"Most likely at his bank. He's a wise coon!"

"You are convinced Garnette took the bonds?"

"I wish to God I wasn't," said Mr. Ogden unexpectedly. "I—I kind of reverenced that guy. Me! Maybe I'll learn sense—next year."

"Did you keep books?"

"Yes, sir. I did the books and Raveenje and Garnette could see them at any time. Raveenje has got them home right now."

"How did it work?"

"Like any regular company. I'm the biggest shareholder —I put up the most dollars. Garnette is paid a salary and he draws twenty per cent of the profits. That was square enough."

"Do you know Mr. Garnette is a fellow-countryman of yours?"

Mr. Ogden looked as if he might be a sign for an inn called *The Incredulous Man*. "Forget it," he said briefly. "Him! No, sir! We certainly breed one brand of polecat, but it ain't called Garnette. Look at his line of talk! Where do you get that stuff, anyway?"

"You might say," said Alleyn with a glance at Fox, "that the gentleman told me himself."

"Then he piled up one more lie on to his total."

"Ah, well," sighed Alleyn, "I think that's all for the moment, Mr. Ogden."

"Good! But listen, Chief, I don't want to get in wrong over the financial side of his joint. Get this. I put up the dollars. I saw it as a commercial proposition and I backed it. I've run my department straight and I've had no more'n my fair share. Same goes for Raveenje. He's on the level all right. I look at it this way. This temple has brought colour and interest into folk's lives. I'd thought it was something more than that, day-before-yesterday, when Garnette looked like a regular guy. But even if Garnette's synthetic, and he certainly is, it's been a great little party." He paused and then repeated as though it was a manufacturer's slogan: "It has brought colour and interest into otherwise drab and grey lives."

"Together with hysteria and heroin, Mr. Ogden."

Nigel, who had managed to make unostentatious shorthand notes throughout this interview, now watched Ogden eagerly. Would this shot go home? He decided that the American's astonishment bore the unmistakable stamp of sincerity.

"What the sweltering hell d'you mean?" asked Ogden. "Heroin? Snow? Who's doping in this crowd? By heck!" he added after a moment's pause, "is that what's wrong with young Pringle? Who's started it?"

"To the best of my belief, Mr. Garnette."

The American swore, heartily, solidly, and with lurid

emphasis. Alleyn listened politely, Fox with a dispassionate air of expert criticism.

"By God," ended Mr. Ogden, "I wish to —— I'd never touched this —— concern. Never no more! It's taken a murder to put me wise, but never no more. Say, listen, Chief, as God's my witness I never—— Aw, what's the use?"

"It's all right," said Alleyn quietly. "We have been told you were not mixed up in it."

"How's that?"

"Pringle told me. Don't worry about it too much, Mr. Ogden. We're not going to pull you in for drug-running."

Ogden looked nervously from Fox to Alleyn.

"Not for *drug-running*," he said. "I'm not raving about the way you said it."

"Now look here," said Alleyn, "don't you go making things more difficult by getting the wind up. I can't go round like a child in a nursery game saying: 'It isn't you! It isn't you!' until I get to the 'he.' I can only repeat my well-worn slogan that the innocent are safe as long as they stick to the truth."

"I hope to hell you're right."

"Of course I'm right. It'll come out what the Australians call 'jakealoo.' Have any of the Initiates ever been to Australia, do you know?"

"I don't know, Chief. I haven't."

"They have a strong way of putting things there. But I wander. Don't worry, Mr. Ogden."

"That blamed book! If only I knew when it went."

"Never mind about the book. I think I can guess when it went and who took it."

"Well, ain't you the clam's cuticle!" said Mr. Ogden.

CHAPTER XVIII

CONTRIBUTION FROM MISS WADE

After Mr. Ogden had gone Alleyn thrust his hands into his trouser pockets and stood staring at Fox.

"What are we to make of all this, Fox?" he asked. "What do *you* make of it? You're looking very blank and innocent, and that means you've got hold of an idea."

"Not to say an idea, sir. I wouldn't go so far as that. I've been trying to string up a sequence as you might say."

"May we hear it? I've got to such a state I hardly know which of these creatures is which."

"Now, then, sir," said Fox good-humouredly, "you know we won't believe that. Well, this is as far as I've got. We know Miss Quayne went out yesterday afternoon. We know she came here between two-thirty and three. We know she got some sort of a shock while she was here. We know the bonds were stolen, but we don't know when. We know she was murdered last night."

"True, every word of it."

"Starting from there," continued Fox in his slow way, "I've wondered. I've wondered whether she discovered the theft yesterday afternoon and whether the thief knew she discovered it. She used the word 'discovery' in her note. Now if Garnette pinched the bonds she didn't know it was him or she wouldn't have left that note for him. That's if the note *was* meant for him, and I don't see how it could be otherwise. Well, say the safe was open when she got here, and for some reason she wanted to see the bonds and found they were gone. She perhaps hung round waiting for him until the people began to come in for the afternoon show—the chauffeur chap said they did—and then came away leaving the note. I don't quite like this," continued Fox. "It's got some awkward patches in it. Why did she put the bonds away all tidily? Would the safe be unlocked?"

"She might," said Alleyn, "have met somebody who said something to upset her. Something about——"

"I say," interrupted Nigel. "Suppose she met somebody who said they suspected Garnette of foul play and she wanted to warn Garnette against them? How's that?"

"Not a bad idea, sir," said Fox. "Not a bad idea at all. Garnette got wind of it and thought he'd polish the lady off before she had time to alter the Will."

"But how did she get wind of it?" objected Alleyn. "Not through the note. He never read it. And if she wanted to warn him, why should she alter her Will?"

"That's so," sighed Fox. "By the way, sir, what *are* the terms of the Will? Has she left him a fair sum?"

Alleyn told him and Fox looked intensely gratified.

"Ten thousand. And twenty-one thousand for the Church. That's motive enough if you like."

"How much further did you get with your wondering, Brer Fox? Had you fitted in the two scraps of paper we found in the fireplace?"

"Can't say I did, sir. Somebody warning the Reverend about something, and it seems to refer to Mrs. Candour, as Mr. Bathgate pointed out. Judging from their position in the grate they were part of a letter thrown there some time during the evening, or at any rate some time yesterday."

"Certainly, but I don't agree about Mrs. Candour. I've got the thing here. Take another look at it."

Alleyn produced the two scraps of paper.

"I thought at the time," he said slowly, "that they were written by Miss Quayne's old nurse."

"Good Lord!" ejaculated Fox. "How d'you get that out of it?"

"Yes," said Nigel, "how the devil did you? He wouldn't tell me, Inspector Fox."

"Pretty good, isn't it?" said Alleyn complacently. "Not so good, however, when the first glory wears off. It's written in green pencil and there was a green pencil on Miss Quayne's desk. The M—S is the remains of 'Miss' and the CA the beginnings of 'Cara.' That's the top of an R, not an N. The old girl wrote to Garnette warning him off. I fancy it read something like this: 'Sir: this is to warn you that if you [something or other] with Miss Cara, I am determined to give you in charge. There's a law in England to save women from men like you." Something like that."

"Yes," said Fox, "that fits."

"She made that trip here last night to see if the letter had borne any fruit and watched the show from Garnette's room. Don't be cross, Fox! I haven't had time to tell you before. I'll let you see the notes of my interview with Nannie Hebborn. The old lady came clean and was very helpful. But that disposes of the note. Garnette must have chucked it in the grate some time yesterday. Now, Fox, what about the book?"

"I reckon Garnette heard Ogden showing it to M. de Ravigne at the party and pinched it," said Fox. "After all, sir, his prints are on the top of the book and on the wrappings of the parcel. He might have missed wiping them off that part of the book."

"What about that little drip Claude?" demanded Nigel. "You heard Ogden say he was out when he came for the books. And you remember Claude said that a week before he saw the *Curiosities* here he had put the other books at the back of the shelf. He looked mighty uncomfortable over that. Of course that was when he brought them back from Ogden's. Suppose *he* pinched it and didn't want to say so?"

"That's got to be considered too," said Alleyn. "I think the stray prints on the top of the leaves are possibly Claude's, and not Garnette's. Bailey hasn't had much success with them."

"You think *Mr. Wheatley* took the book?" said Fox.

"But," said Nigel, flushed with triumph, "it hadn't got a brown-paper cover on, so if Claude took it he did so deliberately."

"Don't overdo it, Bathgate," said Alleyn kindly. "This is the pace that kills."

"Garnette told him to take it," continued Nigel. "Depend upon it, Garnette told him to take it."

"He'd never do that, Mr. Bathgate," objected Fox. "Not if he meant to make use of it. No, I still think Garnette pinched the book himself."

"Here we go round the mulberry bush for about the millionth time," said Alleyn wearily, "and why the devil we're hanging about this beastly place is more than I can tell. Let's get back to the Yard, Fox. There's an unconscionable lot of drudgery ahead. Have they tackled the fingerprint game?"

"They're at it now," said Fox, as they all walked down the aisle. "And by the way, sir, we've checked Dr. Kasbek's story. He seems to be all right."

"Good. I rang New York early this morning. They were very polite and will try to find us something about Garnette and Ogden. They can check up Ogden through the address on that letter we found on him. Come on."

But they were not quite finished with the House of the Sacred Flame. In the closed entry, watched over by an enormous constable, was Miss Wade.

"Oh, officer," said Miss Wade. She peered up at Alleyn and pitched her voice in a genteel falsetto. "I would like to speak to you for a moment."

"Certainly," said Alleyn politely. "I'll see you in the car, Fox."

Nigel and Fox walked on, and the constable, with massive tact, withdrew to the outer end of the alley.

"What can I do for you, Miss Wade?" asked Alleyn.

"It is a little matter that has rather troubled me. I am afraid I cannot keep pace with all the dreadful things that have happened since yesterday afternoon. Dear Janey says someone has stolen the money that dear Cara so generously gave to the temple. When did they do this?"

"We don't know, unfortunately. The bonds were deposited in the safe last month. They had disappeared last night."

"Were they stolen yesterday afternoon?"

"Why do you ask that, Miss Wade?" said Alleyn quickly.

"I only thought that perhaps that was what poor Cara meant when she said she would tell Father Garnette about it."

Alleyn gazed at Miss Wade rather as though she had suddenly produced a rabbit from somewhere behind her back teeth.

"Would you mind saying that again?" he asked.

Miss Wade repeated her last remark in a somewhat louder voice but with perfect equanimity.

"When," said Alleyn, "did Miss Quayne say this, and to whom?"

"Yesterday afternoon, to be sure. When else?"

"When else, of course," repeated Alleyn with some difficulty. "How do you know she said it, if I may ask?"

"Really, officer! Because I overheard her. Naturally."

"Naturally. In the—the temple?"

"In the temple. Naturally, in the temple."

"Naturally."

"It quite upset my meditation. I had come down early before the Neophytes' instruction to make my preparation for the evening ceremony. I had chosen the word 'bliss' and had just reached the Outer Portal of the Soul when this interruption occurred. It was provoking. I wished, afterwards, that I had chosen a back pew instead of my Initiate's throne."

"I am extremely glad you didn't," Alleyn managed to say.

"Shall I continue?"

"Please do."

"I had held my breath up to forty-five and exhaled slowly while inwardly repeating the word and, as I say, was about to enter the Outer Portal when she opened the door."

"Miss Quayne did?"

"Who else? Before that I had not been aware of her presence in Father Garnette's rooms. She had arrived before I did and had gone through the hall, no doubt. I left my overshoes outside," added Miss Wade with magnificent irrelevancy.

"She opened the door into Mr. Garnette's rooms, and then you heard her?"

"Yes. The curtain was hiding her, of course, but she raised her voice and, being in the front, I heard her. Indeed, I felt a little annoyed with dear Cara. The altar door should never be used in meditation hours. Except, of course, by Father himself. And it was well after meditation began. I glanced at my watch. A quarter to three it was."

"Miss Wade, can you repeat exactly what you overheard Miss Quayne say?"

"Her very words. 'I don't believe you are speaking the truth' was what dear Cara said, 'and I shall tell Father Garnette what you have done.'"

Here Miss Wade paused and drew herself up with a little quiver.

"To whom did she speak?"

"I haven't a notion," said Miss Wade cosily.

Alleyn stifled a groan.

"No," she went on, "*that* I do *not* know. Not Father, naturally."

"Naturally," repeated poor Alleyn.

"Whoever it was, was *quite* inaudible. And then she came hurrying down into the temple with a great lack of reverence, poor thing. She rushed past me without seeing me, though I remained kneeling and gave her a reproachful glance. There were some neophytes in the back pews. It really *was* naughty of Cara. Such a bad example."

"Did she seem much upset?"

"Dis—tracted," said Miss Wade.

"Did anybody come out after her?"

"On the contrary. Father Garnette came *in* at this door about five minutes later. He had been to lunch with M. de Ravigne. He spoke a few words to me. I had quite given up my meditation."

"Did you mention the incident to him?"

"Now did I?" mused Miss Wade with her head on one side. "No! Definitely not. I would have done so, but he spoke of Higher Things."

"Have you told anybody else?"

"No, I think not."

"Then let me implore you not to do so, Miss Wade. What you have just told me is of the very greatest importance. Please promise me you will not repeat it."

Miss Wade bridled.

"Really, officer," she said, "I am not accustomed——"

"No, no. Never mind all that. Please don't think me overbearing, but unless you will give me your word that you will keep this incident to yourself I—I shall be obliged to take very drastic measures. Miss Wade, it is for your own sake I insist on this silence. Do you understand?"

"That I don't," said Miss Wade with spirit.

Alleyn took one of the little black kid claws in his hand, and he bent his head and smiled at Miss Wade.

"Please," he said, "to oblige a poor policeman. Do promise."

She blinked up at him. Something rather youthful came back into her faded eyes. Her cheeks were pink.

"It is a pity you have come down to this sort of work," said Miss Wade. "You have what my dear Mama used to call quite an air. Very well, I promise."

Alleyn made her a bow. She tossed her head and went off down the alley-way at a brisk trot.

He stood there and looked thoughtfully after her, his hat in his hand. At last, with a shrug, he went out to where Inspector Fox waited for him in a police car.

"What's wrong with the old lady?" asked Fox.

"Nothing much. She just felt chatty."

"Anything of interest?"

"Merely that she overheard Cara Quayne telling her murderer she'd speak to Garnette about him or her as the case may be."

"Lor'!" said Fox. "When, for Gawd's sake?"

"At about a quarter to three yesterday afternoon."

"In the hall?"

"Naturally," said Alleyn promptly. "Listen."

He repeated Miss Wade's statement. Fox stared solemnly out of the window.

"Well, that's very interesting, sir," he said when Alleyn had finished. That's very interesting indeed. Do you think she caught him red-handed with the bonds?"

"I wouldn't be surprised. Or else he (or she, you know, Fox) refused to let her see them. There's been some talk of her adding to those bonds. She may have wanted to do so on the eve of her first innings as Chosen Vessel."

"That's right, sir. D'you think she was poisoned to keep her quiet?"

"I think she was killed, in the end, to keep her quiet. But he meant to do it anyway."

"How do you make that out?"

"If it's sodium cyanide he couldn't make it between three and eight o'clock. He must have had it ready."

"Then what was the motive?"

"Same as before, Fox. Why are we sitting in this car?"

"I dunno, sir."

"Tell him to drive—yes, tell him to drive to M. de Ravigne's house."

Fox gave the order.

"What happened to Mr. Bathgate?" asked Alleyn.

"He went up to his flat, sir. I think he took Miss Jenkins and Mr. Pringle with him."

"He's a great hand at cultivating suspects," said Alleyn.

"It's been useful before now."

"So it has."

They lapsed into silence. At a telephone-box Alleyn stopped for a moment to ring the Yard. A message had come through from Bailey who was at Cara Quayne's house. The blotting-paper in her bedroom desk had proved to be interesting. Lots of writing but in some foreign lingo. Alleyn could hear Bailey's disparagement in this phrase. They had made out yesterday's date and an address: "Madame la Comtesse de Barsac, Château Barsac, La Loupe, E. et L., France." This had been checked up from an address book. They had also found evidence on the blotting-paper and on a crumpled sheet in the waste-paper basket of something that looked very much like a Will. Mr. Rattisbon had rung up and would ring again.

"So put that on your needles and knit it," said Alleyn when he had told Fox.

The car turned into Lowndes Square and drew us by M. de Ravigne's flat.

Branscome Chambers proved to be a set of small bachelor flats, and M. de Ravigne appeared to live in the best of them. This was on the fourth floor. They went up in the lift.

"Any flats vacant here?" asked Alleyn of the liftman.

"Yes, sir. One. Top floor."

"How many rooms."

"Three recep., one bed, one servant's bed, bath and the usual, sir," said the liftman. "These are service flats you know. Food all sent up."

"Ah, yes. Central heating throughout the building, isn't it?"

"Yes, sir."

"I can't do without an open fire," said Alleyn.

"No, sir? These electric grates are very convincing though. There's a blazing log effect in No. 5."

"Really? That's not M. de Ravigne's, is it?"

"No, sir. He's just got the usual heaters. Here you are, sir."

"Oh, yes. Sorry. Thank you."

"Thank you very much, sir."

A discreet dark man with a bluish chin opened the door to them. The voice of a piano came softly from within the flat. Monsieur was at home? He would inquire. He took Alleyn's card and returned in a moment. Monsieur was at home and would they come in? The flat proved to be, if anything, overheated. The little hall where they left their hats was as warm as a conservatory and smelt like one. An enormous bowl of freezias stood on a very beautiful Louis Seize table. From here the servant showed them into a long low drawing-room panelled in cream and very heavily carpeted. It was not over-furnished, indeed, the general effect was one of luxurious restraint. The few pieces were "period" and beautiful. Three T'ang ceramics stood alone in a magnificent lacquer cabinet. The only modern note was struck by the pictures—a Van Gogh, a Paul Nash and a Gerald Brockhurst. Seated at a baby grand piano was M. Raoul de Ravigne.

CHAPTER XIX

ALLEYN LOOKS FOR A FLAT

M. de Ravigne greeted them with a suavity so nicely tempered that it could not be called condescension. He looked very *grand seigneur,* standing with one long white hand on the piano, grave, polite, completely at his ease.

"Will you be seated, messieurs? You come to pursue your inquiries about this tragedy?"

"Yes," said Alleyn in his most official voice, "we followed you here in the hopes that we might have a word or two in private. It is an unfortunate necessity in these affairs that the police must constantly make nuisances of themselves and must continually bring the realisation of an unhappy occurence before those who would prefer to forget it."

"One understands that very readily. For myself I am only too anxious to be of any assistance, however slight, in bringing this animal to justice. What can I do for you, messieurs?"

"You are extremely courteous, M. de Ravigne. First I would like to bring this letter to your notice."

De Ravigne held out his hand. Alleyn gave him his own letter, written to Cara Quayne the preceding Friday. De Ravigne glanced at it, read a word or two and then laid it on the arm of his chair. Fox took out his notebook.

"You are correct," said de Ravigne, "when you say that

much unpleasantness attends the activities of the police. I have a profound distaste for having my correspondence handled by those whom it does not concern."

"Unhappily, the police are concerned in every scrap of evidence, relevant or irrelevant, which comes into their hands. Perhaps you can assure us of the irrelevance of this letter."

"I do so most emphatically. It has no bearing on the case."

Alleyn picked it up and looked through it.

"Against what danger did you warn her so earnestly?" he asked quietly.

"It was a personal matter, M. l'Inspecteur."

"Make that quite clear to us, monsieur, and it will be treated as such. You will see, I am sure, that a letter warning Miss Quayne against some unknown peril cannot be passed over without inquiry."

De Ravigne inclined his head slightly.

"I see your argument, of course. The danger to which I refer had nothing to do with physical injury."

"You did not anticipate this tragedy?"

"A thousand times, no. I? How should I?"

"Then what was threatened?"

"Her virtue, M. l'Inspecteur."

"I see," said Alleyn.

De Ravigne eyed him for a moment and then got up. He moved restlessly about the room, as though he was trying to come to some decision. At last he fetched up in front of Alleyn and began to speak in French rapidly and with a certain suppressed vehemence. Inspector Fox breathed heavily and leant forward slightly in his chair.

"Judge of my position, monsieur. I loved her very much. I have loved her very much for so many years. Even since she was a dark *jeune fille* at a convent with my sister. At one time I thought that she would consent to a betrothal. It was in France when she had first made her *début*. Her guardian, Madame de Verné, approved. It was in every way suitable. My own family, too. Then—I do not know how it came about, but perhaps it was her temperament to change as it was mine to remain constant—but she grew colder and —but this is of no importance. She came to London where we met again after a year. I found myself still her slave. She allowed me to see her. We became, after your English fashion, 'friends.' It was to amuse her, to interest her, that I myself introduced her to this accursed temple. I did not know then what I know now of the character of Father Garnette."

"How long did it take you to find him out?" asked Alleyn.

De Ravigne lifted his shoulders very slightly and returned to English.

"I do not know. I was not interested in his morals. It was the ceremonies, the ritual, the bizarre but intriguing form of paganism, that appealed to me. If I became aware that he amused himself, that he had his mistresses, it did not at all disconcert me. It was not inconsistent with the pagan doctrine. One lives one's own life. I cannot say when I first realised that the rôle of Chosen Vessel held a certain significance for this priest. But I am not blind. Dagmar was elected, and—in short, monsieur, I am a man of the world and I saw, accepted, and disregarded *l'affaire Candour*. It was none of my business."

"Precisely," said Alleyn, "but when Miss Quayne became a candidate——"

"Ah, then, monsieur, I was in agony. Again, judge of my position. I had introduced her to this place, forgetting her temperament, her enthusiasms, her—what is your word?—her whole-heartedness. I myself was responsible. I was revolted, remorseful, distracted. I wrote the letter you hold in your hand."

"And continued," said Alleyn, "to draw your dividends?"

"*Sacré nom!*" said de Ravigne. "So you know of that also?"

"Oh, yes."

"Then it will be difficult to persuade you that it was my intention yesterday and is doubly so to-day, to withdraw my capital from this affair."

"Five hundred, isn't it?" asked Alleyn.

"Yes. If I did not make this gesture before, M. l'Inspecteur, it was because I was unwilling to bring about a fracas which would have involved more persons than Father Garnette himself. When I first attended the little temple in Great Holland Road I found it in need of funds. I could not afford to give this sum, but I could afford to lend it.

Mr. Ogden was also willing, and on a larger scale, to invest money. I left the business arrangements to Father Garnette and Mr. Ogden, who is a man of commerce. Myself, I have not the business temperament. But rest assured I shall withdraw. One cannot suffer oneself to become financially associated with such *canaille*."

"Do you call Mr. Ogden *canaille*, monsieur?"

"Monsieur, I refer rather to the priest. But Ogden, he is very much of the people. His perceptions are not acute. He is not fastidious. No doubt he will not feel any delicacy in accepting his interest from this investment. As for the priest—but I prefer not to discuss the priest."

"Do you know that Mr. Garnette has been giving drugs to Pringle, Mrs. Candour and Miss Quayne?"

De Ravigne did not answer at once. He lit a cigarette and then with an apology offered the box.

"No?" he said. "Then perhaps your pipe?"

"Not just at the moment, thank you very much. About this drug business."

"Ah, yes. Your information does not surprise me."

"You knew, then?"

"Monsieur, I must repeat that the private affairs of the Initiates does not interest me."

"But—Miss Quayne?"

"I cannot believe that she indulged in the vice."

"Nevertheless——"

"I cannot believe it," said de Ravigne violently, "and I will not discuss it."

"Ah, well," said Alleyn, "let us leave it then. Apropos of the letter, monsieur. Why did you emphasise your desire that she should destroy it?"

"I have already told you of my distaste for having my letters read. That old Hebborn! She has her nose in everything and she is antagonistic to me. I could not endure that she should intrude her nose into it."

"Then why not write in French?"

"But I wished to impress her of my calmness and deliberation," said M. de Ravigne smoothly. "If I wrote in French, allowing my emotion full scope, what would she think? She would think: 'Ah, he has shot himself off at the deep ending. This Gallic temperament! To-morrow he will be calm again.' So I write coolly in English and request that she destroys this letter."

"Ah, yes, that explains the postscript." Alleyn got to his feet and then, as if it were an afterthought, he said:

"The book on chemistry. I understand you have seen it before?"

De Ravigne hesitated for the fraction of a moment before he replied: "It is strange you should say that. I myself received the impression that I had encountered the book, but where? I cannot recollect."

"Was it in Mr. Ogden's house?"

"But of course! In his house. He showed it to me. How could I have forgotten? The priest was there and looked at it too. And the others. It was too stupid of me to forget. I remember I upset a glass of whisky and soda near it. Ogden fancied the book might be of value, I think, but it was of no interest to me. That is why I did not remember it. So the book is the good Ogden's book? That is interesting, monsieur, is it not?"

"Any information about the book is interesting. And speaking of books, M. de Ravigne, may I have the books of the Sacred Flame Company? I understand you've got them here."

"The books? Ah, yes. The good Ogden insisted that I glance at them. They seem to be in order. Naturally the theft of the bonds would not appear. Perhaps the good Ogden himself has seen to that. Perhaps he and the priest together have arranged these little matters. You see I am bitter, monsieur. I am not easily made suspicious, but when my suspicions are aroused—— But the books! You shall have them, certainly."

He rang for his servant, who produced the books and gave them to Alleyn.

"There's one other question, M. de Ravigne, and then I shall trouble you no further. Do you know anything of a Madame la Comtesse de Barsac?"

"My sister, monsieur," said de Ravigne very frigidly.

"Forgive me. I really didn't know. She was the confidante of Miss Quayne, I think? A very great friend?"

"That is so."

Alleyn got up.

"A thousand thanks," he said. "Is there anything else, Fox? Perhaps you——"

"No thank you, sir," said Fox cheerfully. "I think you've covered the ground."

"Then we will make our adieux, monsieur. You will have received notice of the inquest to-morrow?"

"At eleven o'clock, yes. It will, I imagine, be purely formal."

"One never knows with inquests, but I expect so. The terms of the Will may come out. You know them, I expect?"

"No, monsieur."

"No? Come along, Fox. Where are those books?"

"You've got them under your arm, sir."

"Have I? So I have. *Au 'voir,* Monsieur de Ravigne. I am afraid we have been a great nuisance."

"Not at all, Monsieur l'Inspecteur. I am only too glad—though I am afraid I have been of little assistance——"

"*Tout au contraire, monsieur.*"

"*Vraiment? Au 'voir,* monsieur. Good afternoon, monsieur."

"Oh reevor, monsieur," said Fox very firmly.

On their way down the liftman extolled the virtues of the flats, and Alleyn warmly agreed with him, but still insisted that he preferred the solace of an open fire. Inspector Fox listened gravely to this conversation, occasionally uttering a profound noise in his throat. As they got into the car his good-natured face wore the nearest approach to a sardonic smile of which it was capable.

"The Yard," said Alleyn to the driver. "You'll be able to improve your French if we see much more of that gentleman," he added with a smile at Fox.

"It's a rum thing," said Inspector Fox, "that I can follow that radio bloke a fair treat, and yet when the monsieur gets under way it sounds like a collection of apostrophes. What do we do when we get back to the office?"

"We send a cable to Australia."

"To Australia?"

"Yes, Brer Fox."

"What's that in aid of?"

"You've never been to Australia?"

"I have not."

"I have. Let me tell you about it."

Alleyn discoursed at some length about Australia. They got back to the Yard at five o'clock. The fingerprint people reported that they had been unable to find any of the Sacred Flame prints in the records. Mr. Rattisbon had sent a letter round for Alleyn. The report from Cara Quayne's house together with the blotting-paper and crumpled sheet from the waste-paper basket awaited him in his room. He went there, accompanied by Fox, and tackled Mr. Rattisbon's letter first.

"Let's smoke a pipe apiece," he said. "I'm longing for one."

They lit up, and Fox watched him gravely while he opened the long envelope. Alleyn's eyebrows rose as he read the enclosures. Without a word he handed them across to his subordinate. Mr. Rattisbon wrote to say that the morning mail had brought a new Will from Miss Quayne. She had evidently written it some time yesterday afternoon. It was witnessed by Ethel Parker and May Simes. As regards the bequests to de Ravigne and Laura Hebborn it was a repetition of the old Will. For the rest it was startlingly changed. The entire residue was left to Mr. Jasper Garnette of Knock-latchers Row, Eaton Place. Miss Quayne had written to say she hoped that the new Will was in order, and that if it was not, would Mr. Rattisbon please draw up a fresh document to the same effect. The alteration was so straight-forward that she believed this to be unnecessary. She had urgent reasons for making the alteration, reasons connected with a "terrible discovery." She would call and explain. Her dear Father Garnette, she said, was the victim of an unholy plot. In his covering letter Mr. Rattisbon explained that at the time Alleyn called he had not looked at his morning post. He added that he found the whole affair extremely dis-tressing; an unexpectedly human touch.

"By gum!" said Fox, putting the papers down, "it looks as if you're right, sir."

"Gratifying, isn't it? But how the devil are we going to ram it home? And what about our Jasper? Oh, Garnette, my jewel, my gem above price, you will need your lovely legacy before we've done with you. Where's the report on those cigarettes, Fox? Has it come in? Where's my pad?

F

Here we are. Yes. Oh excellent priest! Perdition catch my soul, but I do love thee. All the top cigarettes as innocent as the wild woodbine, but underneath, in a vicious little mob, ten doped smokes. A fairly high percentage of heroin was found, from one-tenth to as much as one-seventh of a grain per cigarette. It is possible that the cigarette tobacco has been treated with a solution of diamorphine? Oh, Jasper, my dear, my better half, have I caught my heavenly jewel?"

"Come off it, sir," said Fox with a grin.

"How right you are, my Foxkin. Is there any reason why we should not prise the jewel from its setting?"

"Do you mean you'd like to arrest Garnette?"

"Would I like to? And how! as Mr. Ogden would say. And how, my old foxglove, my noxious weed. Has anyone ever written a poem to you, Fox?"

"Never, sir."

"I wish I had the art:

> '*Hercules or Hector? Ah, no!*
> *This is our Inspector Fox,*
> *Mens sana in corpore sano,*
> *Standing in the witness-box.*

"Very feeble, I'm afraid. What about the analyst? Autopsy on body of Miss Cara Quayne. Here we are. He's been very quick about it. 'External appearances: blue nails, fingers clenched, toes contracted, jaws firmly closed.' We know all that. 'Internally'——This is it. 'On opening the stomach the odour of hydrocyanic acid was clearly distinguishable.' How beastly for him. He found the venous system gorged with liquid blood, bright red and arterial in character. The stomach and intestines appeared to be in their natural state. The mucous membrane of the stomach—— How he does run on, to be sure. Let's see. The silver test was carried out. The precipitate gave the characteristic reactions——"

Alleyn read on in silence. Then he dropped the report on his desk and leant back.

"Yes," he said flatly, "it's sodium cyanide. I do well, don't I, to sit here being funny-man, and not so damn' funny either, while a beautiful woman turns into a cadaver, an analyst's exercise, and her murderer——? Fox, in many ways ours is a degrading job-of-work. Custom makes monsters of us all. Do you ever feel like that about it, Fox? No, I don't think you do. You are too nice-minded. You are always quite sane. And such a wise old bird, too. Damn you, Fox, do you think we're on the right lay?"

"I think so, sir. And I know how you feel about homicide cases. I'd put it down to your imagination. You're a very imaginative man, I'd say. I'm not at all fanciful myself, but it does seem queer to me sometimes, how calm-like we get to work, grousing about the routine, put out because our meals don't come regular, and all the time there's a trap and a rope and a broken neck at the end if we do our job properly. Well, there it is. It's got to be done."

"With which comfortable reflection," said Alleyn, "let us consult Mr. Abberley on the subject of sodium cyanide."

He picked the book out of his bag which had been brought back from the church, and once again it opened at the discourse on sodium cyanide.

"You see, Fox, it's quite an elaborate business. List, list, oh list. You take equal weights of wool and dried washing-soda and iron filings. Sounds like Mrs. Beaton gone homicidal. Cook at red heat for three or four hours. Allow to cool. Add water and boil for several more hours. Tedious! Pour off clear solution and evaporate same to small volume. When cool, yellow crystals separate out. And are these sodium cyanide? They are not. To the crystals add a third of their weight of dried washing-soda. Heat as before for an hour or two. While still hot, pour off molten substance from black residue. It will solidify, on cooling, to a white cake. *Alley Houp!* Sodium cyanide as ordered. Serve *à la Garnette* with Invalid Port to taste. *Loud* cheers and *much* laughter. This man is clever."

He re-read the passage and then shut the book.

"As far as one can see this could all be done without the aid of laboratory apparatus. That makes it more difficult, of course. A house-to-house campaign is indicated, and then we may not get much further. Still it will have to be done. I think this is an occasion for Mr. Bathgate, Fox. You tell me he went off with Pringle and Miss Jenkins."

"That's right. I saw them walk down Knocklatchers Row and go into his flat in Chester Terrace."

"I wonder if I'd be justified—— He can't get into trouble over this. It's so much better than going ourselves. He's an observant youth, and if they've got all matey—— What d'you think, Fox?"

"What are you driving at, sir?"

"Wait and see."

He thought for a moment and then reached for his telephone. He dialled a number and waited, staring abstractedly at Fox. A small tinny quack came from the telephone. Alleyn spoke quietly.

"Is that you, Bathgate? Don't say my name. Say 'Hullo, darling.' That's right. Now just answer yes and no in a loving voice if your guests are still with you. Are they? Good. It's Angela speaking."

"Hullo, darling," quacked the little voice.

"Is your telephone the sort that shouts or whispers? Does it shout?"

"No, my sweet. It's too marvellous to hear your voice," said Nigel in Chester Terrace. Without covering the receiver he addressed somebody in the room: "It's Angela—my—I'm engaged to her. Excuse the raptures."

"Are you sure it's all right for me to talk?" continued Alleyn.

"Angela, darling, I can heardly hear you. This telephone is almost dumb."

"That's all right then. Now attend to me. Have you got very friendly?"

"Of *course* I have," said Nigel rapturously.

"Well. Get yourself invited to either or both of their flats. Can you do that?"

"But Angel, I did all that ages ago. When am I going to see you?"

"Do you mean you have already been to their flats?"

"No, no. Of course not. How are you?"

"Getting bloody irritable. "What *do* you mean?"

"Well, at the moment I am sitting looking at your photograph. As a matter of fact I've been showing it to somebody else."

"Blast your eyes."

"No, my sweet, nobody you know. I hope you will soon. They're engaged like us. We're all going to a show. Angela, where are you?"

"At the Yard."

"Darling, how expensive! Yarborough! A toll call. Never mind. When are you coming to London? Is there anything I can do for you?"

"Yes, there is. If you're going to a show, can you engineer a round trip to their flats afterwards?"

"Rather! As a matter of fact I'd rather thought of doing that. Darling——"

"Shut up. Listen carefully now."

"At Harrods? Must it be pink, my sweet?"

"Now don't you be too clever. Miss Angela would cast you off for ever if you mooed at her like that. Pay attention. When you are there I want you to observe certain things."

"All right, darling, I was only being facetious. Let me know the worst."

"I will. This is what I want you to look for——" Alleyn talked on. Fox listened solemnly. Nigel, over in Chester Terrace, blew kisses into the receiver and smiled apologetically at Janey Jenkins and Maurice Pringle.

CHAPTER XX

FOOLS STEP IN

"It annoys Angela beyond endurance if I hold modern conversations with her on the telephone," said Nigel hanging up the receiver on a final oath from Alleyn.

"If that was a sample, I'm not surprised," said Janey Jenkins. "I absolutely forbid Maurice to call me his sweet. Don't I, Blot?"

"Yes," said Maurice unresponsively. He got up and moved restlessly about the room, fetching up at the window where he stood and stared out into the street, biting his fingers.

"What is your Angela's other name?" asked Janey.

"North. She's darkish with a big mouth and thin."

"When are you going to be married?"

"In April. When are you?"

Janey looked at Maurice's back. "It's not settled yet."

"I'd better do something about getting seats for a show,"

said Nigel. "Where shall we go? It's such fun your coming here like this. We must make it a proper party. Have you seen 'Fools Step In' at the Palace?"

"No. We'd love to, but look here, we're not dressed for a party."

"Oh. No, you're not, are you? Wait a moment. Let's make it a real gala. I'll change now and then we'll take a taxi and go to your flat and then to Pringle's. We'll have a drink here first. Pringle, would you make drinks while I change? The things are all in that cupboard there. It's only half-past five. I'll have a quick bath—won't be ten minutes. Do you mind? Will it amuse you? Not my bath, but everything else?"

"Of course it will," said Janey.

Maurice swung round from the window and faced Nigel.

"Look here," he said, "aren't you rather rash to rush into parties with people that are suspected of murder?"

"Don't, Maurice!" whispered Janey.

"My good ass," said Nigel, "you embarrass me. You may of course be a homicidal maniac, but personally I imagine Alleyn has definitely ruled you out."

"I suppose he's told you to say that. You seem to be very thick with him."

"Maurice, please!"

"My dear Jane, it's not impossible."

"No," said Nigel calmly, "of course it's not. Alleyn is by way of being a friend. I think you're suspicions are perfectly reasonable, Pringle."

"Oh, God, you are a little gentleman. I suppose you think I'm bloody unpleasant."

"As a matter of fact I do, at the moment, but you'll be better when you've had a cocktail. Get to work, there's a good chap. And you might ring up the Palace for seats."

"Look here, I'd damned sorry. I'm not myself. My nerves are all to hell. Janey, tell him I'm not entirely bogus. I can't be if you say so."

Janey went to him and held him firmly by one ear.

"Not entirely bogus," she told Nigel.

"That's all right then," said Nigel hurriedly. "Look after yourselves."

As he bathed he thought carefully about his instructions.

In effect Alleyn had told him to cultivate these two with a view to spying on them. Nigel winced. Stated baldly it sounded unpleasant. He had had this sort of thing out with Alleyn on former occasions. The Chief Inspector had told him roundly that his scruples had merely pointed to a wish to have the ha'pence without the kicks, to follow round with the police, write special articles from first-hand experience, and turn squeamish when it came to taking a hand. Alleyn was right of course. If Maurice and Janey were innocent he would help to prove it. If they were guilty—— But Nigel was quite sure neither Janey nor Maurice, for all his peculiar behaviour, was guilty of Cara Quayne's death. He dressed hurriedly and went out into the little hall to get his overcoat. He dived into the cupboard. It was built in to the drawing-room wall and the partition was thin. He heard Janey Jenkin's voice, muffled and flat but distinct:

"But *why* can't you tell me? I know quite well there's something. Maurice, this *can't* go on."

"What do you mean? Are you going to turn me down? I don't blame you."

"You know I won't turn you down. But why can't you trust me?"

"I do trust you. I trust you to stick to what we've said."

"About yesterday afternoon——?"

"Sst!"

"Maurice, is it anything to do with—with your cigarettes? You're smoking one of them now, aren't you? Aren't you?"

"Oh, for God's sake don't start nagging."

"But——"

"When this is over I'll give it up."

"'When.' 'When.' It's always 'when.'"

"Will you shut up, Jane! I tell you I can't stand it."

"Ssh! He'll hear you."

Silence. Nigel stole out and back to his bedroom. In three minutes he rejoined them in the drawing-room. Maurice had mixed their drinks, and Janey had turned on the radio. With an effort Nigel managed to sustain his rôle of cheerful host. Maurice suddenly became more friendly, mixed a second cocktail and began to talk loudly of modern novelists. It appeared that he was himself engaged on a first novel. Nigel was not surprised to learn that it was to be a satire on the upper middle classes. At six o'clock they took a taxi to Janey's studio flat in Yeoman's Row, and while she changed Maurice made more cocktails. Janey, it seemed, was at the Slade. Nigel found the studio very cold though they had put a match to the gas-heater. Shouting at them from the curtained-off recess that served as bedroom Janey explained that she meant to seek warmer quarters. Even the kitchenette-bathroom was cold, she said. She did her cooking over a gas-ring, and you couldn't warm yourself at the bath-geyser. Some of her drawings were pinned up on the walls. She used an austere and wiry line, defined everything with uncompromising boundaries, and went in extensively for simplified form. The drawing had quality. Nigel wandered round the studio and into the kitchen. Everything was very tidy, and rather like Janey herself.

"What are you doing?" called Janey. "You're both very silent."

"I'm looking at your bathkitchenry," said Nigel. "You haven't got nearly enough saucepans."

"I only have breakfast here. There's a restaurant down below. One of ye olde brasse potte kind—all orange curtains and nut salads. Yes," said Janey emerging in evening dress, "I must leave this place. The problem is, where to go."

"Come to Chester Terrace and be neighbours. Angela and I are going to take a bigger flat in my building. It's rather nice. You could have mine."

"Your Angela might hate me at first sight."

"Not she. Are we ready?"

"Yes. Come on, Blot."

"I'm finishing my drink," said Maurice. "You're right, Jane, this is an appalling place. I should go mad here. Come on."

"We should have gone to you first," said Janey. "He is in Lower Sloane Street, Mr. Bathgate. How silly! Maurice, why didn't we go to you first?"

"You can drop me there now. I don't think I'll join the party."

"Maurice! Why ever not?"

"I'm hopelessly inadequate," he muttered. He looked childishly obstinate, staring straight in front of him and smiling sardonically. Nigel could have kicked him.

"Your boy-friend has a talent for quick changes," he said to Janey and hailed a taxi. Janey spoke to Maurice in an urgent undertone. Out of the corner of his eye Nigel saw him shrug his shoulders and give a gloomy assent. When they were in the taxi Janey said:

"Maurice is afraid he's too much upset by last night to be much use to anybody, but I've decided to pay no attention to him. He's coming."

"Splendid!" cried Nigel.

"Marvellous, isn't it?" said Maurice with a short laugh. He was very restless in the taxi, complained that the man should have gone down Pont Street instead of through Cadogan Square, thought they were going to be run over in Sloane Street, insisted on paying the fare, and had a row with the driver over the change. He lived in a small service flat at the top of Harrow Mansions in Lower Sloane Street—sitting-room, bed-room, bathroom. It was comfortable enough, but characterless.

"At least it's warm," said Maurice, and switched on the heater. He opened a cupboard.

"We don't want more drinks, do we?" ventured Janey.

"Isn't this a party?" asked Maurice loudly, and dragged out half a dozen bottles.

He left them as soon as he had made the cocktails, carrying his own with him. The bathroom door slammed and a tap was turned on. Janey leant forward.

"There's something I must tell you," she said urgently.

Nigel found nothing to say and she went on, speaking nervously and quickly:

"It's about Maurice. I know you must think him too impossible. He's been poisonous"—she caught herself up with a gasp—"perfectly odious ever since you asked us up to your flat. It was nice of you to do that, and to take us out. But I want to tell you. Maurice can't help himself. I suppose you know why?"

"Yes, I think so. It's bad luck."

"It's frightful. Not only the cigarettes, but—worse than that. He's taking it now, I know he is. You'll see. When he comes back he'll be excited and—and dreadfully friendly. He's turning into a horrible stranger. You don't know what the real Maurice is like."

"How did he start?"

"It's Father Garnette. He's responsible. I think he must be the wickedest, foulest beast that ever lived. You can tell your friend Alleyn that if you like. But he knows. Maurice told him last night. Mr. Alleyn could help Maurice if—— He doesn't think Maurice did it, does he? He can't."

"I honestly don't believe he does. Honestly."

"I *know* Maurice is—is innocent. But there's something else. Something he knows and he won't tell Mr. Alleyn. He won't tell. He's made me promise. Oh *what* am I to do?"

"Break your promise."

"I can't, I can't. He'd never trust me again and, you see, I can help him as long as he trusts me." Her voice trembled. "It's a shame to bother you with it."

"Good Heavens, what nonsense. I'd like to help you both but—look here, don't tell me anything unless you want Alleyn to know. I ought not to say that. I'm on his side, you see. But if you are hiding anything for Pringle's sake—don't, don't, don't. And if he's hiding something for anybody else's sake you must *make* him tell Alleyn. Do you remember the Unicorn Theatre case?"

"Yes, vaguely. It's queer how one reads every word of murder trials and then forgets them. I'll never forget this one, will I? We must speak softly. He'll be back in a minute."

"In the Unicorn case a man who knew and didn't tell was —killed."

"I remember now."

"Is it something to do with this drug he's taking?"

"How did you guess?"

"Then it *is* Garnette!" said Nigel.

"Ssh! No, for pity's sake! Oh, what have I done!"

"What are you two burbling about?" called Maurice. He sounded very much more cheerful. Janey looked up sharply and then made a despairing little gesture.

"About you, good-looking," she called out.

Maurice laughed. "I must come out and stop that," he said.

"Oh, God," whispered Janey. She suddenly gripped Nigel's arm. "It's not Garnette, it's not, it's not," she said fiercely. "I must see you again."

" After the show," murmured Nigel hurriedly. " I'll come to the flat."

" But—no—it's impossible."

" To-morrow, then. To-morrow morning. About eleven."

" The inquest is at eleven."

" Earlier, then."

" What can you do, after all?"

" Don't worry. I'll fix it."

Janey got up and went to the gramophone. The theme song from " Fools Step In " blared out.

You're no angel, I'm no saint,
You've a modern body with a super coat of paint.
My acceleration's speedy,
You've broken every rule,
You may say that I am greedy,
You may call me just a fool.
You're no angel and I sometimes lost my head,
But fools step in where angels fear to tread.

" The tune's all right," said Maurice, emerging from the bedroom, " but the words are fatuous, as usual."

Nigel gazed at him in astonishment. His eyes were very bright. He had an air of spurious gaiety. He was like a mechanical figure that had been overwound and might break. He talked loudly and incessantly, and laughed at everything he said. He kept repeating that they had plenty of time.

" Loads of time. Fifty gallons of time. Time, the unknown quantity in the celestial cocktail. Time, like an ever-rolling drunk. Jane, you're looking very seductive, my angel. 'You're no angel and I'm no saint'."

He sat on the arm of her chair and began to stroke her neck. Suddenly he stooped and kissed her shoulder.

" 'And I sometimes lose my head.' Don't move."

She sat quite still, staring miserably at Nigel.

" I think we'd better dine," said Nigel. " It's after seven."

Maurice had slid down behind Janey and now pulled her to him. He slipped his arms round her and pressed his face against her bare shoulder.

" Shall we go with him, Janey? Or shall we stay here and step in where angels fear to tread?"

"Don't do that, Blot. And don't be rude about Mr. Bathgate's party. No, get up, do."

He laughed uproariously and pushed her away from him.

"Come on, then," he said, "come on. I'm all for a party."

They dined at the Hungaria. Maurice was very gay and rather noisy. He drank a good deal of champagne and ate next to nothing. Nigel was thankful when they got away. At the theatre Maurice seemed to quieten down. Towards the end of the second act he suddenly whispered that he had a splitting headache and leant forward in his stall with his head between his hands. The people round about them obviously thought he was drunk. Nigel felt acutely uncomfortable. When the lights went up for the final curtain Maurice was leaning back again, his eyes half-closed and his face lividly white.

"Are you all right?" asked Nigel.

"Perfectly, thank you," he said very clearly. "Is it all over?"

"Yes," said Janey quickly, "stand up, Maurice. They're playing The King."

He got up as though he was exhausted, but he was quiet enough as he followed them out into the street. In the taxi he sat absolutely still, his hands lying palm upwards on the seat. In the reflected light for the streets Nigel saw that his eyes were open. The pupils were the size of pin-points. Nigel looked questioningly at Janey. She nodded slightly.

"I'll see you in, Pringle," said Nigel.

"No, thank you," he said loudly.

"But, Maurice——"

"No, thank you; no, thank you; *no, thank you.* Damn you, for ——'s sake leave me alone, will you."

He had got out and now slammed the door shut, and without another look at them went quickly up the steps to the flats.

"Let him go," said Janey.

Nigel said "99, Yeoman's Row" to the man, and they drove away.

Janey began to laugh.

"Charming guest you've had for your party. Has anyone ever been quite so rude to you before? You must have enjoyed it."

"Don't!" said Nigel. "I didn't mind. I'm only so sorry for you both."

"You are nice about it. I won't have hysterics; don't look so nervous. Your Angela's a lucky wench. Tell her I said so. No, don't. Don't talk to me, please."

They finished the short journey in silence. As he saw her into her door Nigel said:

"I'm coming in the morning. Not early, so don't get up too soon. And please remember you'd much better tell Alleyn."

"Ah, but you don't know," said Janey.

CHAPTER XXI

JANEY BREAKS A PROMISE

When Nigel got home it was half-past eleven. He rang Alleyn up.

"Were you in bed?" asked Nigel.

"In bed! I've just got back from the Yard."

"What have you been doing?"

"Routine work."

"That is merely the name you give to the activities you keep a secret from me."

"Think so? What have you been up to yourself?"

"Cultivating a pair of fools."

"That's your opinion of them, is it?"

"It'll be yours when I reveal all. She's a nice fool and he's inexpressibly unpleasant. Look here, Alleyn, Pringle's keeping something up his sleeve. Yesterday afternoon——"

"Hi! No names over the telephone. Your landlady may be lying on her stomach outside the door."

"Shall I come round to your flat?"

"Certainly not. Go to bed and come to the Yard in the morning."

"You might be grateful. I've endured a frightful party and paid for a lot of champagne, all in the cause of justice. Really, Alleyn, it's been a ghastly evening. Pringle's soaked to the back teeth in drugs and——"

"*No names over the telephone.* I am grateful. What would we do without our Mr. Bathgate? Can you get to my office by nine?"

"I suppose so. But I want you to come with me to Janey Jenkins's flat. I think if you tackle her she may tell you about Mau——"

"*Not over the telephone.*"

"But why not? Who do you think is listening? What about your own conversations? Has Miss Wade swarmed up a telegraph pole and tapped the wires?"

"Good night," said Alleyn.

Nigel wrote an article on the beauty and charm of Cara Quayne. The article was to be illustrated with two photographs he had picked up in her flat. Then he cursed Alleyn and went to bed.

The next morning he went down to the Yard at nine and found Alleyn in his room.

"Hullo," said Alleyn. "Sit down and smoke. I won't be a minute. I've just been talking to New York. Mr. Ogden seems to be as pure as a lily as far as they can tell. We rang them up yesterday and they've been pretty nippy. The Ogden-Schultz Gold Refining Company seems to be a smallish but respectable concern. It did well during the gold fever in '31, but not so well since then. Of Mr. Garnette they know nothing. They are going to have a stab at tracing the revivalist joint that was such a success way down in Michigan in '14. The wretched creature has probably changed his name half a dozen times since then."

He pressed his desk-bell and to the constable who answered he gave an envelope and a telegram form.

"Deferred cable for Australia," he said, "and urgent to France. Read out the telegram, will you?"

The constable, with many strange sounds, spelt out a long message in French to the Comtesse de Barsac. As far as Nigel could make out, it broke the news of Miss Quayne's death, and said that a letter would follow, and gave an earnest assurance that the entire police force of Great Britain would be infinitely grateful if Madame la Comtesse would refrain from destroying any letters she received from Miss Cara Quayne. The constable went out looking baffled but impressed.

"What's all that for?"

Alleyn told him about the letter to Madame de Barsac and also about the new Will.

"I've got it here," said Alleyn. "With the exception of the three hundred pounds a year to Nannie and the house to de Ravigne—everything to the glowing Garnette."

"And it was done on Sunday?"

"Yes. At three-thirty. She actually has put the time."

"That's *very* significant," pronounced Nigel.

"Very," agreed Alleyn dryly.

"She had been back from the mysterious visit to the temple about half an hour," continued Nigel with the utmost importance, "and had evidently made up her mind to alter the Will as a result of whatever had taken place in Garnette's room."

"True for you."

"Had she learned about the commercial basis on which the House of the Sacred Flame was established? Or had she heard something derogatory about Garnette himself and wished to make a gesture that would illustrate her faith in Garnette? Doesn't the note in the cigarette-box seem to point to that?"

"Am I supposed to answer these questions or are they merely rhetorical?"

"What do you think yourself? About the new Will?"

"*If* we are right in supposing the interview with the unknown at two-forty-five on Sunday afternoon has got a definite bearing on the case and *if* the unknown was the murderer, then I think the alteration in the Will is the direct outcome of the interview. *If* this is so, then I believe the case narrows down to one individual. But all this is still in the air. Miss Quayne may have found Cyril swigging invalid port and written the note to let Garnette know about it. She may have altered the will simply because she wished to shower everything on Garnette. The whole of Sunday afternoon may be irrelevant. 'Morning, Fox."

"Good morning, sir," said Inspector Fox, who had come in during his speech. What's this about Sunday afternoon being irrelevant? Good morning, Mr. Bathgate."

"Well, Fox, it's possible, you know. We are still in the detestable realms of conjecture. I hope to Heaven Mme de Barsac has not burned that letter. I wired to her last night and got no answer. I've just sent off another telegram. I could get on to the Sûreté, but I don't want to do it that way. We badly need that letter."

"You've got a certain amount from the blotting-paper, haven't you?" asked Fox.

"Bits and pieces. Luckily for us Miss Quayne used medium-sized sheets of notepaper and a thick nib. The result is lots of wet ink and good impressions on the blotting-paper. Here they are. No translation necessary for you, you old tower of Babel."

"May I see?" said Nigel.

"Yes. But they're not for publication."

Fox took out his spectacles and he and Nigel read the sentences from the blotting-paper.

Raoul est tout-à-fait impitoyable——
Une secousse electrique me bouleversa——
Cette supposition me révoltait, mais que voul——
Alarmé en me voyant——
il pay—a——ses crimes.
——le placèrent en qualité d'administrateur d——'

"What's 'secousse'?" asked Fox.

"A shock, a surprise."

"Does she mean she's had an electric shock, sir?"

"It's a figure of speech, Fox. She means she was much put out. The phraseology suggests a rather exuberant hysterical style. I do not advise you to adopt it."

"What do you make of it, Mr. Bathgate?" asked Fox.

"It's very exciting," said Nigel. "The first bit is clear enough. Raoul—that's de Ravigne—is completely indifferent—pitiless. She had a shock. Then she was horrified at her own—what's the word?"

"This hypothesis revolted me," suggested Alleyn.

"Yes. Then somebody took fright when he saw her. And somebody will—I suppose this was 'payera'—will answer for his crimes. And somebody was made a trustee. That's the last bit. That's Garnette," continued Nigel in high feather. "He's a trustee in the first Will. By gum, it looks as if she was talking about Garnette all along."

"Except when she wrote of de Ravigne?" said Alleyn mildly.

"Oh, of course," said Nigel. "Good Lord! Do you suppose she confided in de Ravigne?"

"I refuse to speculate. But I don't like your very free rendering of the last sentence. And now what's all this about Miss Janey Jenkins?"

Nigel launched into an account of his evening's experiences. The two detectives listened in silence.

"You did very well," said Alleyn when Nigel came to a stop. "Thank you, Bathgate. Now let me be quite sure of what you overheard from the perfumed depths of your clothes cupboard. Pringle asked Miss Jenkins to stick to their story about Sunday afternoon?"

"Yes."

"And she asked if it had anything to do with his cigarettes?"

"Yes. That's it."

"Right! You arranged to visit her this morning?"

"Yes. Before the inquest."

"Would you mind if I took your place?"

"Not if you swear you'll tell me what happens."

"What's the time?"

"Half-past nine," said Fox.

"I'll be off. See you at the inquest."

Alleyn took a taxi to Yeoman's Row. Janey's studio was at the far end. It was a sort of liaison office between Bohemia and slumland. Five very grubby little boys and a baby were seated on the steps.

"Hullo," said Alleyn. "What's the game?"

"Ain't no game. Just talkun," said the grubbiest and smallest of the little boys.

"I know," said Alleyn. "Who's going to ring this bell for me?"

There was a violent assault upon the bell.

"I done it, Mister," said the largest of the little boys.

The baby rolled off the second step and set up an appalling yell.

"Stan-lee!" screamed a voice from an upper window, "what are you doing to your little bruvver?"

"'Snot me; it's 'im," said Stanley, pointing at Alleyn.

"I'm frightfully sorry," said Alleyn. "Here. Wait a moment. Is he hurt?"

"'E won't leave 'is 'oller not without you picks 'im up," said Stanley.

Alleyn picked the baby up. The baby instantly seized his nose, screamed with ecstasy, and beat with the other hand upon Alleyn's face.

It was on this tableau that Janey opened her door.

The Chief Inspector hurriedly deposited the child on the pavement, gave Stanley a shilling for the party, took off his hat, and said:

"May I come in, Miss Jenkins?"

"Inspector Alleyn?" said Janey. "Yes. Of course."

As she shut the door Stanley was heard to say "Coo! It's a cop," and the baby instantly began to roar again.

Without speaking Janey led the way upstairs to the studio. A solitary chair was drawn up to the gas-fire. The room was scrupulously tidy and rather desolate.

"Won't you sit down?" said Janey without enthusiasm.

"I'll get another chair," offered Alleyn and did so.

"I suppose Mr. Bathgate sent you here?" asked Janey.

"Yes. In effect he did."

"I was a fool."

"Why?"

"To make friends with—your friend."

"On the contrary," said Alleyn, "you were very wise. If I may say so without impertinence you would do well to make friends with me."

Janey laughed unpleasantly.

"Dilly, dilly, dilly," she said.

"No. Not 'dilly, dilly, dilly.' You didn't murder Miss Quayne, did you?"

"You can hardly expect me to answer 'yes.'"

"I expect an answer, however."

"Then," said Janey, "I did not murder Cara Quayne."

"Did Mr. Pringle murder Miss Quayne?"

"No."

"You see," said Alleyn with a smile, "we get on like a house on fire. Where was Mr. Pringle at three o'clock on Sunday afternoon?"

She drew in her breath with a little gasp.

"I've told you."

"But I'm asking you again. Where was he?"

"Here."

"That," said Alleyn harshly, "is your story and you are sticking to it? I wish you wouldn't."

"What do you mean!"

"It's not true, you know. He may have lunched with you but he did not stay here all the afternoon. He went to the temple."

"You knew——"

"Now you give me an opportunity for the detective's favourite cliché. 'I didn't know, but you have just told me.'"

"You're hateful!" she burst out suddenly. "Hateful! Hateful!"

"Don't cry!" said Alleyn more gently. "It's only a cliché and I would have found out anyway."

"To come prying into my house! To find the weak place and go for it! To pretend to make friends and then trap me into breaking faith with—with someone who can't take care of himself."

"Yes," he said, "it's my job to do those sorts of things."

"You call it a smart bit of work, I suppose."

"The other word for it is 'routine.'"

"I've broken faith," said Janey. "I'll never be able to help him again. We're done for now."

"Nonsense!" said Alleyn crisply. "Don't dramatise yourself."

Something in his manner brought her up sharply. For a second or two she looked at him and then she said very earnestly:

"Do you suspect Maurice?"

"I shall be forced to if you both insist on lying lavishly and badly. Come now. Do you know why he went to the temple on Sunday afternoon?"

"Yes," said Janey, "I think I know. He hasn't told me."

"Is it something to do with the habit he has contracted?"

"He told you himself about that, didn't he?"

"He did. We have analysed Mr. Garnette's cigarettes and found heroin. I believe, however, that Mr. Pringle has gone further than an indulgence in drugged cigarettes. Am I right?"

"Yes," whispered Janey.

"Mr. Garnette is responsible for all this, I suppose."

"Yes." She hesitated, oddly, and then with a lift of her chin repeated: "Yes."

"Now," Alleyn continued, "please will you tell me when Mr. Pringle left here on Sunday afternoon?"

She still looked very earnestly at him. Suddenly she knelt on the rug and held her hands to the heater, her head turned towards him. The movement was singularly expressive. It was as though she had come to a definite decision and had relaxed.

"I will tell you," she said. "He went away from here at about half-past two. I'm not sure of the exact time. He was very restless and—and difficult. He had smoked three of those cigarettes and had got no more with him. We had a scene."

"May I know what it was about?"

"I'll tell you. Mr. Alleyn, I'm sorry I was so rude just now. I must have caught my poor Maurice's manners, I think. I do trust you. Perhaps that's not the right word because you haven't said you think him innocent. But I know he's innocent and I trust you to find out."

"You are very brave," said Alleyn.

"The scene was about—me. When he's had much of that stuff he wants to make love. Not as if it's me, but simply because I'm there. I'm not posing as an ingenue of eighteen—and they're not so 'ingenue' nowadays either. I'm not frightened of passion and I can look after myself, but there's something about him then that horrifies me. It's like a nightmare. Sometimes he seems to focus his—his senses on one tiny little thing—my wrist or just one spot on my arm. It's morbid and rather terrifying."

She spoke rapidly now as though it was a relief to speak and without any embarrassment or hesitation.

"It was like that on Sunday. He held my arm tight and kissed the inside. Just one place over and over again. When I told him to stop he wouldn't. It was horrible. I can give you no idea. I struggled and when he still went on, I hit his face. Then there was the real scene. I told him he was ruining himself and degrading me and all because of the drugs. Then we quarrelled about Father Garnette, desperately. I said he was to blame and that he was rotten all through. I spoke about Cara." She stopped short.

"That made him very angry?"

"Terribly angry. Hatefully angry. For a moment I was

frightened. He said if that was what *they* did—— You understand?"

"Yes," said Alleyn.

"Then he suddenly let me go. He had been almost screaming, but now he began to speak very quietly. He simply told me he would go to the church flat and get more of—more heroin. 'A damn' big shot of it,' he said. He told me quite slowly and distinctly that Father Garnette had some in the bedroom and that he would take it. Then he laughed, gently, and went away. And then, in the evening, when he'd had more of that stuff, I suppose, he met me as though nothing had happened. That's a pretty good sample of the happy wooing we enjoy together."

She still knelt on the rug at Alleyn's feet. She had gone very white and now she began to tremble violently.

"I'm sorry," she stammered. "It's silly. I don't know why —I can't help it."

"Don't mind!" said Alleyn. "It's shock, and thinking about it again."

She laid her hand on his knee and after a second he put his lightly over it.

"Thank you," said Janey. "I didn't see him again until the evening. After you had finished with us I walked back with him to his door. He told me I was to say he had been here all the afternoon. I promised. I promised: that's what is so awful. He said: 'If they go for the wrong man——' and then he stopped. I came on here by myself. That's all."

"I see," said Alleyn. "Have you got any brandy on the premises?"

"There's some—over there."

He got a rug off the couch and dropped it over her shoulders. Then he found the brandy and brought her a stiff nip.

"Down with it," he ordered.

"All right," answered Janey shakily. "Don't bully." She drank the brandy and presently a little colour came back into her face.

"I have made a fool of myself. I suppose it's because I'd kept it all bottled up inside me."

"Another argument in favour of confiding in the police," said Alleyn.

She laughed again and put her hand on his knee.

"——who are only human," Alleyn added and stood up.

"You're a very aloof sort of person to confide in, aren't you?" said Janey abruptly. "Still, I suppose you must be human or I wouldn't have done it. Is it time we went to the inquest?"

"Yes. May I drive you there or do you dislike the idea of arriving in a police car?"

"No, but I think I'd better collect Maurice."

"In that case I shall go. Are you all right?"

"I'm not looking forward to it. Mr. Alleyn, shall I have to repeat all—this—to the coroner?"

"The conduct of an inquest is on the knees of the coroner. Sometimes he has housemaid's knees and then it's all rather trying. This gentleman is not of that type, however. I think we shall have a quick show and a adjournment."

"An adjournment? For what?"

"Oh," said Alleyn vaguely, "for me to earn my wages, you know."

CHAPTER XXII

SIDELIGHT ON MRS. CANDOUR

The inquest was as Alleyn had said it would be. Only the barest bones of the case were exhibited to the jury. Owing, no doubt, to Nigel's handling of a "scoop" the public interest was terrific. Alleyn himself had by this time become a big draw. It would be a diverting pastime to discuss how far homicide cases have gone to cater for the public that used to patronise stock "blood-and-thunder" at Drury Lane. In the days when women of breeding did not stand in queues to get a front seat at a coroner's inquest or a murder trial, melodrama provided an authentic thrill. Nowadays melodrama is not good enough when with a little inconvenience one can watch a real murderer turn green round the gills, while an old gentleman in a black cap, himself rather pale, mumbles actor-proof lines about hanging by the neck until you are dead and may God have mercy on your soul. No curtain ever came down on a better tag. The inquest is a sort of curtain-raiser to the murder-trial, and, in cases such as that of Cara Quayne, provides an additional kick. Which of these people did it? Which of these men or women will hang by the neck until he or she is dead? That priest, Jasper Garnette. Darling, such an incredible name, but rather compelling, don't you think? A definite thrill? Or don't you? He seems to have been. . . . Can *anyone* go to the temple? . . . Chosen Vessel . . . My sweet, you *have* got a mind like a sink, haven't you! The American? . . . *too* hearty and wholesome. . . . Still, one never knows. I must say . . . De Ravigne? My dear, I *know* him. Not frightfully well. His cousin. . . . No, it was his sister. . . . Of course one never knows. That Candour female . . . God, what a mess! The boy? Pringle? Wasn't he one of the Essterhaugh, Browne-White lot? Of course one knows what they're like. He looks as if he might be rather fun. Darling, *did* you ever see anything to *approach* Claude and Lionel? Still, one never knows. One never knows until the big show comes on. One never knows.

In all this undercurrent of conjecture Alleyn, little as he heeded it, played a star part. His was as popular a name as that of the learned pathologist, or the famous counsel who would be briefed if Alleyn did his bit and produced an accused to stand trial. Chief Inspector Alleyn himself, as he assembled the bare bones of the case before the coroner, glanced once round the court and thought vaguely: "All the harpies, as usual."

Nigel Bathgate, Dr. Kasbek, Dr. Curtis and the pathologist were the first witnesses. Dr. Kasbek was asked by a very small juryman why he had not thought it worth while to send for remedies. He said dryly that there was no remedy for death. The ceremony of the cup was outlined and the finding of sodium cyanide described. Alleyn then gave a brief account of his subsequent investigations in the House of the Sacred Flame.

Father Jasper Garnette was called and gave a beautiful rendering of a saint among thieves. He was followed by the rest of the Initiates. Mr. Ogden's deportment was so elaborately respectful that even the coroner seemed suspicious. M. de Ravigne was aloof and looked as if he thought the court smelt insanitary. Mrs. Candour wore black and a stage make-up. Miss Wade wore three cardigans and a cairngorm brooch. She showed a tendency to enlarge on Father Garnette's purity of soul and caused the solicitor who watched the proceedings on Father Garnette's behalf to become very fidgety. Maurice Pringle was called on the strength of his being the first to draw attention to Cara Quayne's condition. He instantly succeeded in antagonising the coroner. Claude Wheatley, who followed him, got very short commons indeed. The coroner stared at him as though he was a monster, asked him precisely what he *did* mean, and then said it seemed to be so entirely irrelevant that Mr. Wheatley might stand down. Janey merely corroborated the rest of the evidence. It was all over very quickly. The coroner, a crisp man, glanced once at Alleyn and ordered an adjournment.

"He's a specimen piece, that one," said Alleyn to Fox as they walked away. "I only wish there were more like him."

"What are the orders for this afternoon, sir?"

"Well, Fox, we must come all over fashionable and pay a round of calls. There are still two ladies and a gentleman to visit. I propose we have a bite of lunch and begin with Mrs. Candour. She's expecting us."

They had their bite of lunch and then made their way to Queen Charlotte flats, Kensington Square, where, in a setting of mauve and green cushions, long-legged dolls and tucked lampshades, Mrs. Candour received them. She seemed disappointed that Alleyn had not come alone, but invited them both to sit down. She herself was arranged on a low divan and exuded synthetic violets. She explained that she suffered from shock. The inquest had been too much for her. The room was stiflingly heated by two ornate radiators and the hot water pipes gurgled like a dyspeptic mammoth.

Alleyn engulfed himself in a mauve satin tub hard by the divan. Inspector Fox chose the only small chair in the room and made it look foolish.

"My doctor is coming at four o'clock," said Mrs. Candour. "He tells me my nerves are shattered. But shattered!"

She gesticulated clumsily. The emeralds flashed above her knuckles. Alleyn realised that she wished him to see a hot-house flower, enervated, perhaps a little degenerate, but fatal, fatal. With a mental squirm he realised he had better play up. He lowered his deep voice, bent his gaze on her and said:

"I cannot forgive myself. You should rest."

"Perhaps I should. It doesn't matter. I must not think of myself."

"That is wonderful of you," said Alleyn.

She shrugged elaborately and sighed.

"It is all so ugly. I cannot bear ugliness. I have always surrounded myself with decorative things. I must have beauty or I sicken."

"You are sensitive," pronounced Alleyn with a strong man's scowl.

"You feel that?" She looked restively at Inspector Fox. "That is rather clever of you, Mr. Alleyn."

"My consciousness of it brought me here this afternoon. We want your help, Mrs. Candour. It is the sensitive people who see things, who receive impressions that may be invaluable."

"Ah," said Mrs. Candour with a sad sardonic smile.

"Before I ask you for this particular kind of help I just want to confirm your statement about your own movements on Sunday. It's purely a matter of form. You were here all day, I think you said."

"Yes, all day. How I wish it had been all the evening too!"

"I bet you do," thought Alleyn. Aloud he said: "Perhaps your servants would be able to confirm this. No doubt they will remember that you were indoors all day."

"There are only two maids. I—I expect they will remember."

"Perhaps Inspector Fox might have a word with them."

"Of course," said Mrs. Candour very readily indeed. "You would like to see them alone, I expect, Inspector? I'll ring."

"Thank you, ma'am," said Fox. "I won't keep them long." A musical-comedy parlourmaid who had shown them in, showed Fox out. His voice could be heard rumbling distantly in the flat.

"And now," said Mrs. Candour turning intimately to Alleyn, "and now, Mr. Alleyn."

Alleyn leant back in his chair and looked at her until she glanced down and up again. Then he said:

"Do you remember a party at Mr. Ogden's four weeks ago, yesterday?"

"Just a moment. Will you get me a cigarette? On the table over there. No, not those," said Mrs. Candour in a hurry. "The large box. The others are Virginian. I loathe Virginian cigarettes."

Alleyn opened the wrong box.

"Do you?" he said. "What make is this? I don't know the look of them." He took one out and smelt it.

"They are hateful. Someone sent them. I meant to have them thrown away. I think the servants must have upset—— My cigarette, Mr. Alleyn. Mayn't I have it?"

"I'm so sorry," said Alleyn and brought the other box. He lit hers for her, stooping over the divan. She made a great business of it.

"You?" she murmured at last.

"Thank you. I prefer Virginians," he said. "May I have one of these?"

"Oh, please don't. They are disgusting. Quite unsmokable."

"Very well," said Alleyn and took out his case. "Do you remember the party?"

"At Sammy Ogden's? Do I? Yes, I believe I do."

"Do you remember that M. de Ravigne looked at one of the books?"

She closed her eyes and laid the tips of her thick fingers on the lids.

"Let me think. Yes!" She opened her eyes wide. "I remember. M. de Ravigne collects old books. He was browsing along the shelves. I can see it all now. I was talking to Father and poor Cara had joined us. Then Sammy came up. I remember that M. de Ravigne called to him: 'Where did you find this?' And he looked across and said: 'On a bookstall. Is it worth anything?' And Father went across and joined them. He adores books. They draw him like a magnet."

"He has a remarkable collection," said Alleyn. "Was he interested in this particular one?"

"Let me think He went across and—— What was the name of the book?" She gaped stupidly. "It wasn't——! Oh, it was! You mean it was that book you showed us, on poisons. My God, is that what you mean?"

"Don't distress yourself. Don't be alarmed. Yes, that was it. You see we want to trace the book."

"But if that was the one it belongs to Sammy Ogden. It's his. And he never said so. When you showed it to us he simply sat there and——" Her eyes brightened; she was avid. "Don't you see what that means? He didn't own up."

"Oh, yes," said Alleyn. Her excitement was horrible. Oh, yes, he told us it was his book. He hadn't missed it."

"But—— Oh." For a moment she looked disappointed. Then he could see an anticipation of deeper pleasure come into her eyes. Her lips trembled. "Then, of course, it was the Frenchman. Listen. I'll tell you something. Listen."

Alleyn waited. She lowered her voice and hitched herself nearer to him.

"He—Raoul de Ravigne I mean—made a fool of himself over Cara. She encouraged him. You know what foreigners are. If I had chosen to let him——" She laughed shrilly. "But I wasn't having any. There was quite a scene once. I had a lot of bother with him. It was after that he turned to Cara. In pique, I always thought. And then—I hardly like to tell you. But Cara was dreadfully—you know. I've read quite a lot of psycho-analysis, and it was easy to see she was *mad* about Father Garnette. De Ravigne saw it. I watched him. I *knew*. He was furious. And when she got herself elected Chosen Vessel, he realised what *that* meant. You know what I mean?"

Alleyn really couldn't manage more than an inclination of his head.

"Well, perhaps it was too much for him. He's a very passionate sort of man. You know. The Celtic—I mean the Gallic temperament. Why didn't he say he'd seen the book before? That's what I'd like to know. I'm right. Don't you think I am right?"

"Did he take the book away with him?" asked Alleyn.

She looked furtively at him.

"I don't know, but he was very interested in it. You could see. He was very interested. He asked Sammy Ogden where he got it. He fossicked about till he found it."

"Mr. Ogden said that he himself drew M. de Ravigne's attention to the book and that M. de Ravigne showed little interest in it."

"He may have *pretended* not to be interested," she said. "He *would* do that. He makes a pose of being uninterested, the dirty beast."

At this last vindictive descent into devastating vulgarity Alleyn must have shown some sort of distaste. A dull red showed through her make-up and for a moment she looked frightened.

"I expect you think I'm awful," she said, "but you see I I know what he's like."

"You tell me you had an unpleasant encounter with M. de Ravigne. May I hear a little more about that?"

But she would not tell him more. She was very uneasy and began to talk about self-respect. The encounter had no bearing on the case. She would rather not discuss it. She would not discuss it. He pressed a little further and asked when it had happened. She could not remember.

"Was it about the time you discontinued your visits to Miss Quayne?"

That shot went home. She now turned so white that he wondered if she would collapse. She seemed to shrivel back into the cushions as though she was scorched.

"What do you mean! Why are you talking like this? What are you thinking?"

"You mustn't distress yourself in this way," said Alleyn.

"How can I help it when you start—— I'm not well. I told you I was ill. I must ask you to go."

"Certainly," said Alleyn. He got up. "I am sorry. I had no idea my question would have such an unfortunate effect."

"It's not that. It's my nerves, I tell you. I'm a nervous wreck."

She stammered, clenched her hands, and burst into a storm of ungracious tears. With a word of apology Alleyn turned and walked to the door.

"Stop!" cried Mrs. Candour. "Stop! Listen to me." He turned.

"No, no," she said wildly, "I won't say any more. I won't. Leave me alone."

He went out.

Fox waited for him outside.

"Bit of a rumpus in there, seemingly," said Fox.

"Heavens, yes! There's been a loathsome scene. I'll have a bad taste in my mouth for weeks. I'll tell you about it in the car. We go to Ogden's house now."

On the way to York Square he related the details of his interview. " What do you make of all that?" he asked.

" Well, it sounds as if Mrs. Candour had tried to do a line with the French gentleman and failed. Then I suppose she turned round and took a dislike to him like these sort of women do. She wouldn't feel too friendly towards Miss Quayne either, seeing Miss Quayne pinched the monsieur and the Reverend as well. No, she wouldn't feel very friendly in that quarter."

" No."

" The point is," continued Fox with a sort of dogged argumentativeness, " did she tell you anything that supports our theory or sets us off on another lay? That's the point."

" She said that de Ravigne found the book and that nobody drew his attention to it until Ogden asked him what it was worth. She was very emphatic about that."

" Was she telling the truth?"

" I wish I knew," said Alleyn.

" And Father Garnette?"

" He saw it too. For the matter of that they may all have glanced at it afterwards. But the question is——"

" Did any of them see enough of it to put ideas of sodium cyanide into their heads?"

" Exactly, Brer Fox, exactly. How did you get on with that remarkably frisky-looking soubrette who showed us in?"

" Oh, her! Rita's her name. And the cook's a Mrs. Bulsome. A very pleasant, friendly woman, the cook was. Made me quite welcome in the kitchen, and answered everything nice and straightforward. Rita took in the coffee at a quarter to two on Sunday. She went and got the cups about ten minutes later and Mrs. Candour was then stretched out on the sofa, smoking and listening to the radio. She was still there when Rita took tea in at four-thirty and they heard the radio going all the afternoon."

" Not exactly a cast-iron alibi. Did you pick up any gossip about that—that inexpressibly tedious lady?"

" Mrs. Candour? Well, she's not very much liked in the hall, sir. Rita said it was her opinion the mistress was half-dopey most of her time, and Mrs. Bulsome, who's a very plain-spoken woman, said the kitchen cat, a fine female tortoiseshell, had a better sense of decency. That was the way Mrs. Bulsome put it."

"You have all the fun, Fox."

"Rita says Mrs. Candour set her cap at monsieur and was always ringing him up and about three weeks ago she got him there and there was a scene. They heard her voice raised and after he'd gone Rita went in and she found Mrs. C. in a great state. She never rang up after that and monsieur never came back. About that time, they said, she left off visits to Miss Quayne."

"As we saw by Miss Quayne's appointment book. Here we are at the Château Ogden. Don't let me forget any important questions, Fox. I'll have to go carefully with Ogden. He's feeling rather self-conscious about his book."

"That's not to be wondered at," said Fox grimly.

"There's a telephone-box. Pop in and ring up the Yard, Foxkin. I'd like to know if there's an answer from Madame la Comtesse."

Fox was away for some minutes. He returned looking more than usually wooden.

"There's an answer. I've taken it down word for word. It's in French, but as far as I can make it out the Comtesse is in a private hospital and can't be disturbed."

"Hell's boots!" said Alleyn. "I'll disturb her if I have to dress up as a French gynaecologist to do it!"

CHAPTER XXIII

MR. OGDEN AT HOME

Mr. Ogden lived in an old-fashioned maisonette. His sitting-room was on the street level and opened off a small hall from which a break-neck stair led up to his dining-room and kitchen and then on to his bedroom and bathroom. He was served by a family who lived in the basement. He answered his own door and gave Alleyn and Fox a hearty, but slightly nervous, greeting.

"Hello! Hello! Look who's here! Come right in."

"You must be sick of the sight of us," said Alleyn.

"Where d'you get that stuff?" demanded Mr. Ogden

with somewhat forced geniality. "Say, when this darn business is through, maybe we'll be able to get together like regular fellows."

"But until then——?" suggested Alleyn with a smile.

Mr. Ogden grinned uncomfortably.

"Well, I won't say nothing," he admitted, "but I'll try and act like I was a pure young thing. What's new, Chief?"

"Nothing much. We've come to look at your house, Mr. Ogden."

Mr. Ogden paled slightly.

"Sure," he said. "What's the big idea?"

"Don't look so uncomfortable. We're not expecting to find a body in the destructor."

"Aw gee!" protested Mr. Ogden. "You make me nervous when you pull that grim British humour stuff."

He showed them over the maisonette, which had the peculiarly characterless look of the ready-furnished dwelling. Mr. Ogden, however, appeared to like it.

"It's never recovered from the shock it got when Queen Victoria okayed gas-lighting," he said. "It's just kind of forgotten to disappear. Look at that grate. I reckon it would have a big appeal in the States as a museum specimen. Some swell apartment! When I first saw it I thought I'd side-slipped down time's speedway. I asked the real estate agent if it was central heated and the old guy looked so grieved I just hadn't the nerve to come at it again."

"There are plenty of modern flats in London, sir," said Inspector Fox rather huffily, as they went into the kitchen.

"Sure there are. Erected by Rip Van Winkle and Co. You don't want to get sore, Inspector. I'm only kidding. I took this apartment *because* it's old-world and British. I get a kick out of buying coal for this grate and feeling Florida in front and Alaska down the back."

"It's a very cosy little kitchenette, sir," said Fox, still on the defensive. "All those nice modern Fyrexo dishes!"

"I've pepped it up some. There was no ice-chest and a line of genuine antiques for fixing the eats. And will you look at that hot-squat, coal-consuming range? I reckon that got George Whatsit Stevenson thinking about trains."

Fox mumbled impotently.

They completed their tour of the maisonette and returned

to the sitting-room. Mr. Ogden drew arm-chairs up to the hearth and attacked the smouldering coals with a battered stump of a poker.

"How about a drink?" he asked.

"Thank you so much, not for me," said Alleyn.

Mr. Ogden again looked nervous.

"I forgot," he mumbled, "I kinda asked for that."

"Good Heavens," protested Alleyn, "you mustn't jump to conclusions like this, Mr. Ogden. We're on duty. We don't drink when we're on duty. That all there is to it."

"Maybe," said Mr. Ogden eyeing him doubtfully. "What can I do for you, Chief?"

"We're still trying to untangle the business of the book. I think you can help us there, if you will. I take it that this is the room where you held your party?"

"Yup."

"And where are your books," continued Alleyn, pointing to where a dispirited collection of monthly journals and cheap editions propped each other up in an old bookcase.

"That's the library. Looks world-weary, doesn't it? I'm not crazy about literature."

"I notice there are no red backs there, so the *Curiosities* must have showed up rather well."

"That's so. It looked like it was surprised at being there," said Mr. Ogden with one of his imaginative flights.

"Well now, can you show me where it was on the night of your party?"

"Lemme see."

He got up and walked over to the shelves.

"I reckon I can," he said. "M. de Ravigne had parked his drink in that gap along by the stack of *Posts* and spilled it over. I remember that because it marked the shelf and he was very repentant about it. He called me over and apologised and I said: 'What the hell's it matter,' and then I saw the old book. That's how I came to show it to him."

"You showed it to him. You're positive of that? He did not find it for himself, and you didn't see him with it before anything was said about it?"

Mr. Ogden thought that over. The significance of Alleyn's question obviously struck him. He looked worried, but he answered with every appearance of complete frankness.

"No, *sir*. Raoul de Ravigne did no snooping around those books. I showed it to him. And get this, Chief. If I hadn't showed it to him he'd never have seen it. He had turned away from the books and was telling Garnette how thoughtless he'd acted putting his glass down on the shelf."

"But he would have seen it before, when he put his glass down."

"Yeah? Well, that's so. But even if that is so you can bet your suspenders Ravigne is on the level. See here, Chief, I get you with this book stuff and God knows I feel weak under my vest whenever I remember the *Curiosities* belonged to me. But if you're thinking of Raoul de Ravigne for the quick hiccough, forget it. He worshipped Cara. He surely worshipped her."

"I know, I know," said Alleyn abstractly.

Fox, who had examined the shelf, suddenly remarked:

"There's the mark of the stuff there still. Spirit, it's lifted the varnish."

"So it has," said Alleyn. "After you had shown him the book what happened to it?"

"Why, I don't just remember. Wait a while. Yeah, I got it. He looked at it sort of polite but not interested, and handed it to Garnette."

"And then?"

"I can't remember. I guess we walked away or something."

"Previous to the glass incident what had you all been doing?"

"Search me. Talking."

"Had you been talking to Mrs. Candour, Miss Quayne and Mr. Garnette?"

"That's so. Checking up, are you? Well, I reckon that's right. We were here by the fire, I guess."

"And you don't remember seeing the book after that evening?"

"No. But I don't remember *not* seeing it till the day that sissy stopped in for Garnette's books. I'm dead sure it wasn't here then. Dead sure."

"That's a most important point. It seems to show——" Alleyn paused and then said: "Look here, Mr Ogden, as far as I can see there's no reason why I shouldn't be perfectly frank with you. Tell me, is it your opinion the book disappeared on the night of your party?"

"Honest, Chief, I'm not sure. I don't know. I can't go any further except that I'd stake a couple of grand Ravigne doesn't come into the picture."

"Who looks after you here and does the housemaiding?"

"The girl Prescott. The daughter of the janitor."

"Could we speak to her, do you think?"

"Sure! She'll be down in the dungeon they call their apartment. I'll fetch her."

He went out into the little hall and they could hear him shouting:

"Hey! Elsie! Cm' on up here, will you?"

A subterranean squeak answered him. He came back grinning.

"She'll be right up. Her old man does the valeting and butling, her ma cooks, and Elsie hands out the cap and apron dope. The bell doesn't work since they forgot to fix it way back eighteen-twenty-five."

Elsie turned out to be a pleasant-faced young woman. She was neatly dressed, and looked intelligent.

"Listen, Elsie. These gentlemen want to ask you something."

"It's about a book of Mr. Ogden's that was stolen," said Alleyn. "It's a valuable book and he wants us to trace it for him."

Elsie looked alarmed.

"Don't worry," said Alleyn, "we rather think it was taken by a man who tried to sell him a wireless. Do you remember the night Mr. Ogden had a large party here? About three weeks ago?"

"Yes, sir. We helped."

"Splendid. Did you do the tidying next day?"

"Yes, sir."

"I suppose you dusted the book-shelves, didn't you?"

"Oh, yes, sir. They were in a terrible mess. A gentleman had upset a glass. Just there it was, sir."

She pointed to the shelf.

"Were any of the books damaged?"

"The one next the place was, sir. It was stained-like."

"What book was that?"

"I never noticed the name, sir. It had brown paper on it. You couldn't see."

"Was there a red book there?"

"You mean the queer-looking old one. That hasn't been there for a—well, for some time."

"That's the one we are trying to trace, Elsie. You think it was not there that morning?"

"No, sir. I'm sure it wasn't. You see that's where it always stood, and I noticed it wasn't there because I thought it was a pity because it wouldn't have mattered if that old book had been marked because I didn't know it was a valuable book, sir. I just laid the other one down by the fire to dry off and put it back again. I didn't take the cover off because I didn't like. It was put on very neat with nice shiny paper."

Alleyn glanced at Mr. Ogden, who turned bright pink.

"But it wasn't the old book, sir. The old book was bigger and it hadn't got a cover. Now I come to think of it, I remember I says to Mr. Ogden, I says: 'Where's the big red book?' Didn't I, sir? When you was looking through them to see the damage."

"By heck, I believe she did," shouted Mr. Ogden.

"Splendid, Elsie. So one way and another you're absolutely certain there was no big red book?"

"Yes, sir, certain sure. There was just a row of five in brown paper covers and then the ones that are there now. I remember it all so distinct because that was the day before we went for our holidays, and I says I'd like to get things nice for a start off because Mr. Ogden was going to do for himself and get his meals out, and he'd been that kind, and it seemed such a pity like, anything should be missing, so I was quite anxious to make everything nice, so I did and so that's how I remember."

"Thank you very much indeed, Elsie."

She went away in high feather.

"Just as well she didn't look at the book, Mr. Ogden," said Alleyn dryly. "Which was it? *Petronius*?"

"Aw, hell!" said Mr. Ogden.

"Well, Fox, we must go our ways." Alleyn wandered over the shelves. "M. de Ravigne certainly left his mark," he said. "The stuff ran some way along. What was it?"

"A highball."

"Ah, well," said Alleyn, "we'll have to find out what Mr. Garnette did with the *Curiosities*."

"By God," began Mr. Ogden violently, "if Garnette——" He stopped short. "I ain't saying a thing," he added darkly.

"Come along, Fox," said Alleyn. "We've kept Mr. Ogden too long already. I must present Elsie with the wherewithal for a new bonnet. She skipped away before I could do it. I'll find her on the way down."

They said good-bye. Elsie was hovering in the little hall. Alleyn winked at Fox who went on ahead. Alleyn joined him in the car five minutes later.

"Very talkative girl that," said Fox dryly.

"She is. In addition to being swamped with thanks I've heard all about her sister's miscarriage, the mystery of the drawing-room poker (it seems Elsie suspects someone of chewing at the tip), her young man who is a terror for crime stories, how Mr. Ogden broke a fyrexo pot and why Elsie likes policemen. She remembers the day Claude came for the books. She put them in his attaché-case for him. Ogden was out, as he said. Elsie says there were six, which is rum, as she spoke of five before that. What's the time?"

"Five-thirty."

"I made an appointment with young Pringle for six. I expect he'll be in. Look here, Fox, I'll drop you at Knocklatchers Row. If Garnette is in, ask him what he did with the book that night at Ogden's. Go easy with him. It would be lovely to hear the truth for once from those perfect lips. He'll swear he left it behind him, of course, but try and get some means of checking up on it. Then, if you've time, look up the unspeakable Claude. Ask him how many books he collected from Ogden for Garnette. He'll probably say he's forgotten, but ask him. Oh, and ask Garnette if he examined them when they came in. Will you do all that, Fox?"

"Right-oh, sir. What's your view now? Things are a bit more shipshape, aren't they?"

"They are, Fox, they are. It's closing in. I've little doubt in my own mind now. Have you?"

"No. It looks as if you're right."

"We haven't got enough for an arrest, of course. Still, the cable from Australia *may* bring forth fruits, and I'll *have* to get in touch with Madame de Barsac. You were quite right. She's in a nursing home. The telegram was from her housekeeper. I hope to Heaven Cara Quayne's letter has survived. I'll ring up the Sûreté to-night. Old Sapineau is by way of being a pal of mine. Perhaps he can do something tactful for me. Here we are at Knocklatchers Row. In you go, Fox. It's better I should see Pringle alone. I've got to convince him we know he came to this church on Sunday afternoon without giving away the source of information. I'll have to bluff, and I can do that better without your eye on me. It may come to taking an extreme measure. Watkins and Bailey are meeting me there. I'll be back at the Yard some time this evening. What a life, ye screeching kittens, what a life!"

Alleyn drove on to Lower Sloane Street, where he was joined by Detective-Sergeants Bailey and Watkins.

"Stay down opposite the door," said Alleyn, "and try not to look like sleuths, there's good fellows. If you see me come to the window, wander quietly upstairs. Hope it won't be necessary."

He went upstairs to the flat, where he found Maurice Pringle.

Maurice looked a pretty good specimen of a wreck. His face was the colour of wet cement, there were pockets of green plasticine under his eyes, and he had the general appearance of having spent the day on an unmade bed. Alleyn dealt roundly with him.

"Good evening, Mr. Pringle. You're looking ill."

"I'm feeling bloody if it's of any interest," said Maurice. "Sit down, won't you?"

"Thank you." Alleyn sat down and proceeded to look calmly and fixedly at Maurice.

"Well, what's the matter?" demanded Maurice. "I suppose you haven't come here to memorise my face, have you?"

"Partly," said Alleyn coolly.

"What the devil do you mean? See here, Inspector Alleyn, if that's your name, I'm about fed up with your methods. You're one of the new gentlemen-police, aren't you?"

"No," said Alleyn.

"Well, what the hell are you?"

"Just police."

"I'd be obliged," said Maurice loftily, "if you'd get your business done as quickly as possible. I'm busy."

"So am I, rather," said Alleyn. "I should be delighted to get it over. May I be brief, Mr. Pringle?"

"As brief as you like."

"Right. Who supplies you with heroin?"

"None of your cursed business. You've no right to ask questions of that sort. I'll damn well report you."

"Very good," said Alleyn.

Maurice flung himself down in his chair, bit his nails and glowered.

"I wish to God I hadn't told you," he said.

"Your behaviour and your looks told me long before you did," rejoined Alleyn.

Maurice suddenly flung his hands up to his face.

"If my manner is discourteous I must apologise," Alleyn went on, "but this is a serious matter. You have deliberately lied to me. Please let me go on. You informed me that you spent Sunday afternoon with Miss Jenkins in Yeoman's Row. That was a lie. You were seen in Knocklatchers Row on Sunday afternoon. You went into the House of the Sacred Flame. Am I right?"

"I won't answer."

"If you persist in this course I shall arrest you."

"On what charge?"

"On the charge of receiving prohibited drugs."

"You can't prove it."

"Will you risk that?"

"Yes."

"Do you hold to your statement that you did not go to the House of the Sacred Flame on Sunday afternoon?"

"Yes."

"Are you protecting yourself—or someone else?"

Silence.

"Mr. Pringle," said Alleyn gently, "if you are placed under arrest what will you do about your heroin then?"

"Damn your eyes!" said Maurice.

"I am now going to search your flat. Here is my warrant. Unless, of course, you prefer to show me how much dope you have on the premises?"

Maurice stared at him in silence. Suddenly his face twisted like a miserable child's.

"Why can't you leave me alone? I only want to be left alone! I'm not interfering with anyone else. It doesn't matter to anyone else what I do."

"Not to Miss Jenkins?" asked Alleyn.

"Oh, God, they haven't sent you here to preach, have they?"

"Look here," said Alleyn, "you won't believe me, but I don't particularly want to search your flat or to arrest you. I came here hoping that you'd give me a certain amount of help. You went to Knocklatchers Row on Sunday afternoon. I think you went into Garnette's rooms. There you must either have overheard a discussion between Miss Quayne and another individual, or had a discussion with her yourself. For some reason you kept all this a secret. From our point of view that looks remarkably fishy. We must know what happened in Garnette's rooms between two-thirty and three on Sunday afternoon. If you persist in your refusal I shall arrest you on the minor charge, and I warn you that you'll be in a very unpleasant position."

"What do you want to know?"

"To whom did Miss Quayne say: 'I shall tell Father Garnette what you have done?'"

"You know she said that?"

"Yes. Was it to you?"

"No."

"Was it to M. de Ravigne?"

"I won't tell you. It wasn't to me."

"Had you gone there to get heroin?"

"I won't tell you."

Alleyn walked over to the window and looked down into the street.

"Does Mr. Garnette supply you with heroin?" he asked.

"I'll tell you one thing," said Maurice suddenly. "Garnette didn't kill Cara Quayne."

"How do you know that, Mr. Pringle?"

"Never you mind. I do know."

"I am afraid that sort of statement would not be welcomed by learned counsel on either side."

"It's all you'll get from me."

"—— and if you happened to be in the dock, the information would be superfluous."

"I didn't kill her. You can't arrest me for that. I tell you before God I didn't kill her."

"You may be an accessory before the fact. I'm not

bluffing, Mr. Pringle. For the last time will you tell me who supplies you with heroin?"

"No."

"Oh, come in, you two," said Alleyn disgustedly.

Bailey and Watkins came in, their hats in their hands. Alleyn was rather particular on points of etiquette.

"Just look round, will you," he said.

The look-round consisted of a very painstaking search of the flat. It lasted for an hour, but in the first ten minutes they found a little white packet that Alleyn commandeered. No written matter of any importance was discovered. A hypodermic syringe was their second find. Alleyn himself took six cigarettes and added them to the collection. Throughout the search Maurice remained seated by the electric radiator. He smoked continually, and maintained a sulky silence. Alleyn looked at him occasionally with something like pity in his eyes.

When it was all over he sent the two Yard men out into the landing, walked over to where Maurice sat by the heater, and stood there looking down at him.

"I'm going to tell you what I think is at the back of your obstinacy," he said. "I wish I could say I thought you were doing the stupid but noble protection game. I don't believe you are. Very few people go in for that sort of heroism. I think self, self-indulgence if you like, is at the back of your stupid and very churlish behaviour. I'm going to make a guess, a reprehensible thing for any criminal investigator to do. I guess that on Sunday afternoon you went to Garnette's flat to get the packet of heroin we found in your boot-box. I think that Garnette is a receiver and disperser of such drugs, and that you knew he had this packet in his bedroom. I think you went in at the back door, through into the bedroom. While you were there someone came into the sitting-room from the hall. You were not sure who this person was, so you kept quiet, not moving for fear they should hear you and look in at the connecting door. While you stood still, listening, this unknown person came quite close to the door. You heard a faint metallic click and you knew the key had been turned in the lock of the safe. Then there was an interruption. Someone else had come into the sitting-room. It was Cara Quayne. There followed a dialogue between Cara Quayne and the other person. I shall emulate the thrilling example of learned Counsel and call this other person X. Cara Quayne began to make things very awkward for X. She wanted to know about her bonds. I think perhaps she wanted to add to them on the occasion of her initiation as Chosen Vessel. It was all very difficult because the bonds were not there. X tried a line of pacifying reasonable talk, but she wasn't having any. She was very excited and most upset. X had a certain amount of difficulty in keeping her quiet. At last she said loudly: 'I shall tell Father Garnette what you have done,' and a second later you heard the rattle of curtain rings and the slam of the outer door. She had gone. Now your actions after this are not perfectly clear to me. What I think, however, is this: You behaved in rather a curious manner. You did not go in to the sitting-room, strike an attitude in the doorway, and say: 'X, all is discovered,' or: 'X, X, can I believe my ears?' No. You tiptoed out of the bedroom and through the back door which you did not lock and which remained unlocked all through the evening. Then you scuttled back here and proceeded to make a beast of yourself with the contents of the little white packet. Now why did you do this? Either because X was a person who had a very strong hold of some sort over you, or else because X was someone to whom you were deeply attached. There is of course, a third—damn it, why can't one say a third alternative?—a third explanation. You may have drugged yourself into such a pitiable condition that you haven't the nerve to tackle a white louse, much less X."

"God!" said Maurice Pringle. "I'll tackle you if there's much more of this."

"There's very little more. You asked me to be brief. You had to take Miss Jenkins into your confidence over this because you wanted her to tell us you'd been in her flat all the afternoon. Now if you refuse to tell me who X is you're going to force me to do something very nasty about Miss Jenkins. She's a secondary accessory *after* the fact. With you, of course. You're going to force me to arrest you on the dope game. If you persist in your silence after your arrest you will be the direct cause of fixing the suspicion of homicide on the man who you say is innocent. There will be no more heroin. I should imagine your condition is pathological. You should go into a home and be scientifically treated. How you'll stand up to being under lock and key in a police station is best known to yourself. Well, there you are. Is it to be a wholesale sacrifice of yourself, Miss Jenkins and—possibly—an innocent person? Or are you going to clear away the sacrificial smoke at present obscuring the features of Mr. or Madam X?"

Alleyn stopped abruptly, made a curious self-deprecatory grimace, and lit a cigarette. In the silence that followed, Maurice stared at him piteously. His fingers trembled on the arm of the chair. He seemed scarcely to think. Suddenly his face twisted and with the shamefaced abandon of a small boy he turned and buried his eyes in the cushions.

After a moment Alleyn stretched out a thin hand and touched him.

"It's best," he said. "I'm not altogether inhuman, and believe me, in every way, it's best."

He could not hear the answer.

"Do you agree?" asked Alleyn gently.

Without raising his head Maurice spoke again. "—— want to think—to-morrow—give me time."

Alleyn thought for a moment.

"Very well," he said at last, "I'll give you till to-morrow. But don't commit suicide. It would be so very unprincipled, and we should have to arrest Miss Jenkins for perjury or something, and hang Mr. Garnette. Perhaps I'd better leave someone here. You are a nuisance, aren't you? Good evening."

CHAPTER XXIV

MAURICE SPEAKS

On a stormy evening of December last year, five days after the murder of Cara Quayne, Nigel Bathgate stood at the window of his flat in Chester Terrace and looked across the street into Knocklatchers Row. It was blowing a gale and the rain made diagonal streamers of tinsel against the wet black of the houses. The sign of the Sacred Flame swung crazily out and back. A faint light shone from the concealed entry and ran in a gleaming streak down the margin of a policeman's cape. The policeman had just arrived, relieving a man who had been on duty there all the afternoon. As Nigel looked down through the rain Miss Wade's umbrella appeared from the direction of Westbourne Street. He knew it was Miss Wade's umbrella because of its colour, a dejected sap-green, and because Miss Wade's goloshes and parts of herself were revealed as she struggled against the wind. The goloshes turned in at Knocklatchers Row just as a taxi came up from the opposite direction. It stopped at the House of the Sacred Flame. Mr. Ogden got out, paid his fare, threw away his cigar and, nodding to the policeman, disappeared down the entry. Then Maurice Pringle came down Chester Terrace, the collar of his mackintosh turned up and the brim of his hat pulled down over his eyes. Another taxi followed Mr. Ogden's. It overtook and passed Maurice Pringle and a man who came from the same direction as Maurice. There was an interval, and then Lionel and Claude appeared under one umbrella. Then two more taxis and at last a closed car that whisked round the corner and drew up stylishly under the Sign of the Sacred Flame. Two men got out of this car. The first was large and solid, the second tall with a good figure, and a certain air of being well-dressed.

When Nigel saw this last figure he turned from the window, picked up his hat and umbrella, and went out into the rain.

In Chester Terrace the wind blew as violently as it had

done on the night of the murder. The whole scene was a repetition so exact that Nigel had a curious sensation of suspended time, as though everything that had happened since Sunday evening was happening still. Even as he lowered his umbrella to meet the veering wind, Cara Quayne raised the cup to her lips, Garnette drank brandy and rectified spirit in the room behind the altar, his face veiled by the smoke of Maurice Pringle's cigarette. De Ravigne stood with the book in his hand, and Ogden stared at him with his mouth open. Mrs. Candour, Miss Wade and the two acolytes nodded like mandarins in the background, and the doorkeeper repeated incessantly: "I'm afraid you're too late. May I draw your attention to our regulations?"

"It would be fun to write it all up on those lines," thought Nigel, "but not precisely what the Press-lord ordered."

This reflection brought him to the entry and the end of his fancies.

The torch in the wire frame was unlit. A large constable stood in the doorkeeper's place and beside him were Chief Detective-Inspector Alleyn and Detective-Inspector Fox.

"They're all in, sir," said the constable.

"Ah," answered Alleyn. "We'll give them a minute to get comfortably settled and then we shall gate-crash."

"Good evening," said Nigel.

"Hullo. Here's Public Benefactor No. 1. Well, Bathgate, your information was correct and we're all much obliged. How did you find out?"

"Through Janey Jenkins. I rang up to see if she was all right after our ghastly night out with Pringle, and she told me they were meeting at Garnette's flat this afternoon. It's Ogden's idea. He thought they ought to get together like regular fellows and figure things out."

"Americans are a gregarious race," said Alleyn. "Did you get the eavesdropper fixed up, Fox?"

"We did, sir. The Reverend went for a constitutional this afternoon and we fixed it all up nice and quiet while he was away. It's a small room and everything ought to come through very clear."

"What are you talking about?" asked Nigel composedly.

"A cunning device, Bathgate, a cunning device. We shall sit among pagan gods and listen, like a Sforza in a Renaissance palace, to tales of murder. It will probably be inexpressibly tedious, but we may pick up a bit here and there."

"You mean, I suppose, that you have installed a dictaphone."

"Not quite that. We have installed a microphone with wires leading to a small loud-speaker. What a pity Leonardo is not alive to-day. I believe he is the only man of his time who would not be disconcerted by modern contraptions."

"He wouldn't like the women," said Nigel.

"He wouldn't recognise them as such. I think we might go in, Fox, don't you?"

They went quietly into the hall. Alleyn led the way to a recess on the right where Monsieur de Ravigne's statuette stood above a small altar. The whole recess only held six rows of chairs and was like a miniature shrine. The entrance was framed with heavy curtains which Fox drew after them. They were thus completely hidden from the main body of the hall. Fox switched on his torch and pointed it at the far corner by the altar. Nigel saw a glint of metal. They moved forward. Fox stooped down. A tiny metallic sound broke the silence. It was like a minute telephone under a heap of cushions. At a sign from Alleyn they squatted on the ground. Nigel's knees gave two stentorian cracks and Alleyn hissed at him. A Lilliputian Mr. Ogden remarked:

"O.K. by me. Well folks, there's no cops listening in. The plain-clothes guy that's been sticking around the back door came unglued this morning, and the dick at the front's only there for show. I guess we'd better square up and make it a regular meeting. There's no sense in sitting around and handing out hot air. The first thing to do is to appoint a chairman."

"Oh, God!" said Pringle's voice.

"But surely, Mr. Ogden," said Father Garnette, "there is no necessitah——"

"I agree with Mr. Ogden." That was de Ravigne. "It is better to make this affair formal. Let us appoint a chairman. I propose Mr. Ogden should fill this office."

"Aw say, I wasn't putting out feelers——"

"I second that. Hem!" Miss Wade.

"Well, thanks a lot. I certainly appreciate——"

"Good Lord," said Alleyn. "he's going to make a

speech!" And sure enough, make a speech Mr. Ogden did. He used every conceivable American business phrase, but what he said might be summed up as follows: They were all under suspicion of murder, and they all wished to clear themselves. No doubt each of them had his or her own theory. He thought it would be to their mutual benefit to share these theories. After the disaster of Sunday it was unlikely that their ceremonies should or could be continued. The House of the Sacred Flame was a business concern and therefore should be wound up in a businesslike manner. At this juncture there was a confused but energetic protest from Father Garnette, Mrs. Candour and Miss Wade. The word "spiritual" was used repeatedly.

"Sure, I'm alive to the spiritual dope," interrupted Mr. Ogden. "I thought it was sure-fire honest-to-God uplift. Otherwise I'd never have backed it. It looked good-oh to me."

Alleyn gave a curious little exclamation.

"But," the voice went on, "now I think different. And right here is where I hand out the inside stuff. Listen."

He then gave them an account of the financial basis on which the House of the Sacred Flame was built. It agreed in every detail with the statement he had made to Alleyn. Mr. Ogden backed the organisation, paid for the building in which they now sat, and held the bulk of the shares. M. de Ravigne was a much smaller shareholder, Father Garnette received twenty per cent of the profits and a salary.

When Mr. Ogden finished speaking there was a silence so long that Nigel wondered if the microphone had broken down. Suddenly someone began to laugh. It was Maurice Pringle. He sounded as though he would never stop. At last he began to splutter out words.

"All this time—thank-offerings—self-denials—— Oh, God! It's too screechingly funny!"

A babel of voices broke out.

"Quite appalling——"

"Business arrangement——"

"All so sordid and worldly. I never thought——"

"I don't pretend to understand business. My only care is for my flock——"

"If Father says it is——"

"Oh, shut up!"

"Lionel, do be quiet. I must say——"

"Cut it out," shouted Mr. Ogden.

Silence.

"This is no way to act," continued Mr. Ogden firmly, "I said this was to be a regular well-conducted meeting, and by heck, I'm going to have it that way. There's the copies of our agreement. Pass them round. Read them. They're the goods. They've been okayed by a lawyer and they're law. Laugh that off!"

A rustle, a clearing of throats, and then a murmur.

"Now," said Ogden, "get this. The profits of this outfit belong legally to me, Garnette and Monsieur de Ravigne. In that order. Any money coming in is ours. In that order. We kept up the temple and handed out the goods. Cara Quayne's donation of five thousand pounds in bearer bonds was our property——"

"No, it wasn't," interrupted Maurice. "Cara gave that money to a building fund, and it should have been used for nothing else."

"It wouldn't have been used any other way, Pringle, if I'd had the say-so. But it was ours to administer. Yeah, that's so. Well, someone here present got a swell idea about that packet of stuff and lifted it. After that, it was just too bad about Cara."

"You think," de Ravigne spoke for the first time, "that whoever stole this money also murdered my poor Cara. I incline to agree with you."

"Sure. And these Ritzy cops think so too. Something happened in this room around two-thirty on Sunday. Cara came here then. Alleyn may talk queeny, but he's doped that out. Yeah, he seems like he was too refined to get busy. but he's got busy. Too right he has. Well, I guess I know what his idea is. He reckons Cara came here Sunday to add to those bonds and caught the double-crosser red-handed. I don't know just how you folks respond to this idea, but it looks good to me. Find the man or woman who was in this room at two-thirty on Sunday and you've got the killer."

"Certainly," said de Ravigne smoothly.

"But, I don't see——" began Father Garnette.

"Just a moment, Garnette," interrupted Mr. Ogden. "I'm coming to you. Who was in Cara's confidence? Who lifted my book on poisons. Oh, yeah, it was my book."

"Why didn't you say so?" asked Janey.

"Because I thought you all knew. I reckon M. de Ravigne remembered looking at that book the night of my party and was too white to say so. It was swell, and I'm surely grateful."

"It was nothing," said de Ravigne.

"But I reckoned I hadn't a thing to conceal and I came clean about the book to Alleyn. But who lifted that book and put a brown-paper wrapper on it? Who put it way back behind that shelf where it wouldn't be seen? Who got the book that way it opened itself up like it was tired, at the straight dope on sodium cyanide?"

"It does not always open in this manner," said de Ravigne.

"Practically, it does," interrupted either Lionel or Claude. "When I tried it——"

"Wait a moment. Wait a moment. Lemme get on with my whosits. Who had control of the keys after Cara's bonds were parked in the safe? Who lifted the bonds? Who kidded Cara into leaving him enough to re-christen himself Rockefeller?"

"What do you say?" cried Garnette suddenly. "She left the money to the temple not to me."

"How the blazing hell do you know?"

"She told me, poor soul, she told me."

"That's right." Mrs. Candour's voice sounded shrilly. "She told me herself weeks ago—well, about three weeks ago—when she first knew she was chosen. And she left her house and everything in it to Raoul de Ravigne. Ask him! he knows. Ask him! There are pictures worth hundreds. Ask him!"

"I do not wish to discuss it," said de Ravigne. "If she did this, and it is true she spoke of it, I am most grateful. But I will not discuss it."

"Because you know——"

"Quit it, Dagmar. Where do you get that stuff?"

"What stuff?" cried Mrs. Candour in alarm. "What stuff? Do you mean——?"

"He only means: 'What are you talking about'," said Pringle hurriedly.

"I thought you meant *the* stuff. That detective, Alleyn; I'm sure he suspects. Sammy, can they——?"

"Shut up," said Maurice violently.

"Stick to the point," begged Mr. Ogden. "I'm interested in Garnette."

"I, too," said de Ravigne. "It seems to me that you make the argument very clear against this priest, M. Ogden."

"A murderer! Father Garnette, this is infamous." That was Miss Wade.

"It's a fact. Listen, you, Garnette——"

"Stop!"

Maurice Pringle's voice rose above the others. Nigel could picture him on his feet, confronting them.

"Sit down, Pringle," said Mr. Ogden angrily.

"I won't. I'm going to——"

"That's my cue," whispered Alleyn. "Come on."

Nigel followed him out of the little shrine and up the aisle. The voices of the Initiates sounded confusedly from behind the altar. Alleyn led the way up the hall to Father Garnette's door. He motioned to Nigel. They stood one on each side of the door. Very stealthily Alleyn turned the handle and pulled it ajar. The curtain inside was bunched a little towards the centre and by squinting slantways they were able to see into the room beyond. Nigel glued his eye to the crevice beneath the hinge. He was reminded, ridiculously, of Brighton pier. He found himself looking across the top of Miss Wade's purple toque straight into Maurice Pringle's eyes.

Maurice stood on the far side of the table. His face was ashen. A lock of hair had fallen across his forehead. He looked impossibly melodramatic. He seemed to have come to the end of a speech, interrupted perhaps by the hubbub that had broken out among the other Initiates. Miss Wade's hat bobbed and bobbed. A dark object momentarily hid this picture. Someone was standing just on the other side of the door. It was on this person Maurice had fixed his gaze. Whoever it was moved again and the picture reappeared in a flash. Mr. Ogden's voice sounded close to Nigel's ear.

"The kid's crazy. Sit down, Pringle."

"Go on, Maurice," said Janey clearly from somewhere.

"Courage, my dear lad," boomed Father Garnette with something of his old unctuousness.

Maurice jerked his head as though he had been struck.

"For God's sake don't start that stuff again or I'll let them hang you. Don't imagine I still worship at your shrine.

I know what you're like now; I think I've known for a long time. A little bit of bloody Brummagen. I've let myself be ruined æsthetically and, if you like, morally, for a plaster reproduction that wouldn't take in a housemaid. If I let them get you I'd be helping at a bit of spring-cleaning. God knows why I'm doing this. That's not true, either. I'm doing it because I can't help myself."

"What the hell are you talking about, Pringle? You're dopey."

"Dopey!" He turned to stare again at the hidden Ogden. "For the first time in six months I'm not more or less doped. For Christ's sake let's speak the truth. Dope! Half of us are soaked in it. Dagmar, Cara, Me! You two bloody little pansies. You've been experimenting, haven't you? Just trying to see what it's like. Dear Father Garnette's been giving you cigarettes. And where does dear Father Garnette get his heroin? You none of you know. He doesn't know himself. He knows it comes from Paris through an agent in Seven Dials. He doesn't know who the agent is. I do."

"He's mad," screamed Mrs. Candour.

"Sure, he's crazy," said Mr. Ogden soothingly. "You don't want to get this way, Dagmar."

A slight movement beside Nigel caused him to turn. Alleyn had opened the door a little wider and now slid in behind the curtain.

"I'm sane, and there's one of you who knows it. Keep still, all of you. I'm going to tell you what happened here on Sunday afternoon."

"By all means," said de Ravigne softly, "let us hear."

"I came here on Sunday afternoon to pick up a packet of stuff Garnette had arranged to let me have. Cigarettes aren't good enough for me. I need more than the rest of you. This lot cost me ten pounds. Father Garnette has spiritual qualms about handing it over. Haven't you, Father? It makes him feel self-conscious, you know. So he leaves it in his little bedside cupboard and I get it for myself and plant the cash. He says heroin helps to divorce the psyche from the body. I came here some time after half-past two. Jane and I had had a row and I needed the stuff. I came in at the front door and went through here into the bedroom. I just got the stuff and was going when I heard someone come out of the temple into this room. It wasn't our spiritual father. I know his step."

"Oh, for Heaven's sake——"

"Go on, Maurice."

"Yes, Jane. Let me alone. I didn't quite like to reveal myself. It looked a bit queer my being there. I hesitated. Then I heard a click. Then two or three clicks. It dawned on me that someone was monkeying with the safe. The door wasn't quite shut. I looked through and saw who it was. It was——"

"I'm chairman of this meeting and I'm not standing for this. It's out of order. Sit down!"

"No."

"*Sit down!*"

"By God, if you don't shut up yourself I'll make you."

"Yeah? You and who else?"

"Me," said Alleyn. "You've covered, Mr. Ogden."

CHAPTER XXV

ALLEYN SNUFFS THE FLAME

Chief Detective-Inspector Alleyn once confessed to Nigel Bathgate that he enjoyed a dramatic close to a big case. "It casts," he explained, "a spurious but acceptable glamour over the more squalid aspect of my profession." In the case of Cara Quayne this preference must have been gratified. The close could scarcely have been more dramatic.

At the precise moment when Alleyn gripped his arms from behind, Ogden had reached for his gun, whether to shoot Pringle or himself, will never be known. At that same moment Detective-Sergeant Bailey came in from Garnette's bedroom, followed by two other officers. Bailey, looking liverish carried an automatic. Ogden struggled savagely for about a minute. They had to handcuff him. Then Alleyn charged him. Mrs. Candour, seconded by Claude and Lionel, screamed steadily throughout this performance and fainted, unnoticed, at the end of it. The others were silent. Ogden did not speak until they told him to come away. Then he twisted round and confronted Pringle.

"Let him finish," he said. "He's got nothing I can't answer. Let him finish."

Maurice glanced at Alleyn, who nodded. Maurice turned his eyes towards Ogden, and began to speak.

"I saw you at the safe. You had just opened it. You had the bonds in your hand. Or rather you had the faked packet, I suppose. Then Cara came in quietly. She asked you what you were doing with the bonds. You told her Garnette had said you were to look at them. She just stared at you. I think you knew she didn't believe you because almost at once you began to talk about the stuff, heroin."

He paused for a second, moistened his lips, and looked at Alleyn.

"He said he knew she was at it. He asked her if she would miss it very much if she couldn't get any more. He was very genial and friendly and said he felt like taking her into his confidence. Then he told her about the place in Seven Dials where Garnette got the stuff. He said quite calmly that he owned the racket. It would just be a little secret between himself and Cara, he said, and even Garnette himself didn't know he had anything to do with it. Then, when Cara said nothing, he added that it would be just too bad if anyone got curious about him because if he was put in an awkward position he'd have to come across with the whole story and then—— He made it quite clear that if she gave him away he'd drag her name in and Garnette's as well. All of us. He told her that a word from him about her would cut her off from all chance of supply. He had only to suggest she was an agent of the police, and no one would sell it to her. While he was talking he put the packet back into the safe. He said: 'So that's O.K.' His back was turned while he re-locked the safe and I think it was then she wrote that note you found—it was only a few words—and put it in the cigarette-box, because I heard the lid drop and then a match was struck. She took a cigarette and lit it. All that time she said nothing. Just before she went away, he said very softly: 'And if that isn't enough—well, it'd be too bad if we had to look around for another Chosen Vessel.' There was a long silence after that. Then, Cara said loudly: 'I shall tell Father Garnette what you have done.' Ogden said: 'No you won't, Cara.' Without another word she went away.

I realised he might come through into the bedroom and I got out by the back door."

"Why did you say nothing of all this?" demanded de Ravigne.

"Because I'm a bloody skunk," answered Maurice immediately. "Because I hadn't got as much courage as she had, if you want to know. I was in the same boat. I've got to have the stuff. I'll go mad without it. I thought he'd put the bonds back. When I found he hadn't, it didn't make any difference. I've got to have it. God, can't you understand?"

"Then why have you done this?" asked Miss Wade. "I'm afraid I don't quite understand."

"Because he's *not* a bloody skunk," said Janey loudly.

"Janey, dear!"

"It's an admirable explanation, Miss Wade," said Alleyn. "Let us leave it at that. Mr. Garnette, I am afraid I must ask you to come to the police station with us."

"On what charge? This is an infamous conspiracy. I am innocent. This man whom I have taken to my bosom—this viper——"

"Aw, can it, you——!" said Ogden so savagely that Garnette was suddenly silent and suffered himself to be led away without further protest.

"Ready, Mr. Ogden?" asked Alleyn. "Right, Fox!"

Inspector Fox, who had come in immediately after the arrest, approached Ogden with his customary air of placid courtesy.

"We'll just move along now, if you please, sir," he said.

Ogden seemed to come out of a morose trance. He raised his skewbald eyes and looked from Alleyn to Fox.

"You —— Britishers," he said.

"But aren't Australians British?" asked Alleyn. For the first time Ogden looked frightened.

"I was born in Michigan," he said.

"Australia may congratulate herself," answered Alleyn.

"Sez you!"

"Mr. Ogden," said Alleyn, "you are too vulnerable. What are you waiting for, Fox?"

They took Ogden out. One by one the Initiates drifted away. Mrs. Candour, Claude and Lionel, who seemed to have discovered some mysterious affinity, left together. De

Ravigne, who had remained completely unruffled, made ceremonious adieux.

"I imagine, M. l'Inspecteur, that there is something more than hops to the eye in this affair."

"It will be all hop to the eye soon enough, M. de Ravigne," said Alleyn sombrely.

"I can believe it. So long as my poor Cara is revenged I am satisfied. I must confess I myself suspected the priest. Without a doubt he is on an equality with Ogden. He introduced to Cara so many infamies. The drugs—to one of her temperament——"

"Did you never suspect the drug?"

"Certainly. I confronted her with it. Monsieur, I am myself almost as culpable. I introduced her to this accursed place. For this I can never forgive myself."

"There is one question I should like to ask you," said Alleyn. "Did you remember the *Curiosities of Chemistry* when you saw it again in this room?"

"I remembered that I had held it in my hands, but I could not recollect where, or upon what occasion. It had not interested me. Later, in my flat, the whole scene returned to me. I had upset the glass. The book was stained. I cannot conceive why I had forgotten."

"I see," said Alleyn politely. "You discovered the book? Ogden did not show it to you?"

"I discovered it, monsieur. Had I not upset my glass that evening the book would not have been taken from the shelf. I myself called Ogden's attention to it. He was, as I remember, speaking to Mrs. Candour at the time. I called him to me in order to ask about the book."

"Ah," said Alleyn, "that tallies. Thank you very much, monsieur."

"Not at all, monsieur. If you will excuse me——?"

De Ravigne went out, unruffled. Miss Wade approached Alleyn. As usual she had a deceptive air of perspicacity.

"Good evening, officer," she said.

"Good evening, Miss Wade," said Alleyn gravely.

"I am most upset," announced Miss Wade. "Mr. Ogden has always impressed me as being a very gentlemanly fellow, for a foreigner of course. And now you say he is a poisoner."

"He is charged with murder," murmured Alleyn.

"Exactly," said Miss Wade. "My dear brother was once in Michigan. The world is very small, after all."

"Indupitably!"

"Obviously," continued Miss Wade, "Father Garnette has been greatly abused. By whom?"

"Miss Wade," said Alleyn, "if I may make a suggestion, I—I do most earnestly advise that you put this place and all its associations right out of your mind."

"Nonsense, officer. I shall continue to attend the ceremonies."

"There will be no ceremonies."

Miss Wade stared at him. Gradually a look of desolation came into her faded eyes.

"No ceremonies? But what shall I do?"

"I'm so sorry," said Alleyn gently.

She instantly quelled him with a look that seemed to remind him of this place. She tweaked her shabby gloves and turned to the door.

"Good evening," said Miss Wade, and went out into the deserted hall.

"Oh, Mr. Garnette!" swore Alleyn, "and oh, Mr. Ogden!" Maurice and Janey were the last to leave.

"Look here," said Alleyn, "I'm not going to be official with you two people. Miss Wade has snubbed me, poor little thing, and you can too if you think fit. Mr. Pringle, I have to thank you most sincerely for the stand you took just now. It was, of course, an extremely courageous move. You spoke frankly about the habit you have contracted. I shall speak as frankly. I think you should go into a nursing home where such cases are treated. I know of an excellent place. If you will allow me to do so I can write to the doctor-in-charge. He will treat you sympathetically and wisely. It won't be pleasant, but it is, I believe, your only chance. Don't answer now. Think it over and let me know. In the meantime, I have asked Dr. Curtis to have a look at you and he will help you, I am sure. This is an inexcusable bit of cheek on my part, but I hope you will forgive me."

Maurice stood and stared at him.

"Can I come and see you?" he said suddenly.

"Yes, when I'm not too busy," answered Alleyn coolly. "But don't go and distort me into an object for hero-worship.

I seem to see it threatened in your eye. I'm too commonplace and you're too old for these adolescent fervours."

He turned to Janey.

"Good-bye," he said. "I'm afraid you'll both be called as witnesses."

"I suppose so," said Janey. "Am I allowed to do a spot of hero-worship?"

"You reduce me to the status of an insufferable popinjay," replied Alleyn. "Good-bye and God bless you."

"Same to you," said Janey. "Come on, Blot."

"Well, Bathgate," said Alleyn.

"Hullo," said Nigel.

"You were right again, you see."

"Was I? When?"

"You warned me on Sunday that Ogden was too good to be true."

"Good Lord!" said Nigel. "So I did. I'd forgotten. Extraordinarily clever of me. Look here. Could you bear to sit down for ten minutes and—and—confirm my first impression?"

"I knew this was coming. All right. But let it be in your flat."

"Oh, of course."

They locked up Father Garnette's flat and went out into the hall. Only two side lamps were alight and the building was almost full of shadows as it had been when Nigel walked in, unbidden, on Sunday night. It was so still that the sound of rain beating on the roof filled the place with desolation. The statues, grey shapes against the walls, assumed a new significance. The clumsy gesture of the Wotan seemed indeed to threaten. The phœnix rose menacingly from the sacred flame. Alleyn followed Nigel down the centre aisle. At the door he turned and looked back.

"I wonder what will happen to them," he said. "One of Garnette's symbols, at least, is true. The phœnix of quackery rises again and again from its own ashes. To-night we slam the door on this bit of hocus-pocus and to-morrow someone else starts a new side-show for the credulous. Come on."

They went down the outside passage and out into the rain. The constable was still on duty.

"It's all over," said Alleyn. "You can go home to bed."

Up in Nigel's flat they built themselves a roaring fire and mixed drinks.

"Now then," said Nigel.

"What do you want to know?" asked Alleyn a little wearily.

"I don't want to bore you. If you'd rather——"

"No, no. It's only the beastly anti-climax depression. Always sets in after these cases. If I don't talk about it I think about it. Go ahead."

"When did you first suspect him?"

"As soon as I learnt the order in which they had knelt. He was the last to take the cup before it returned to Garnette. That meant that he had least to risk. Except Garnette, of course. Miss Wade told us that the priest always took the cup in one hand and laid the other over the top. That meant he would not see the little tube of paper. Do you remember I said that Ogden's position made him the first suspect?"

"Yes. I thought you meant—— Never mind. Go on."

"Ogden would know that Garnette handled the cup in that way. He would also know that Miss Quayne would spend some time over her hysterical demonstration before she drank the wine. There would be time for the cyanide to dissolve. The point you made about the uncertainty of whether the paper would be seen is a good one. It pointed strongly to Ogden. He is the only one, except Garnette and Claude, who could be sure it would not be noticed. I felt that the others would be unlikely to risk it. Claude had neither the motive nor the guts. Garnette had an overwhelming motive, but he's an astute man and I simply couldn't believe that he would be ass enough to leave the book lying about for us to find."

"Did Ogden plant the book?"

"No. Master Claude did that."

"Claude?"

"Yes, when he called for Garnette's books, three weeks ago, after the party."

"On purpose?"

"No. Accidentally."

"How do you know?"

"The books Garnette lent Ogden were in brown-paper wrappers. There were five of them. Ogden's maid said so and when we saw them in Garnette's flat there were five that were so covered. Six, counting the *Curiosities*. But Claude told Fox he knew he returned six books to Garnette. He took them in an attaché case, and they just fitted it. What happened, I believe, was something like this. For some time Ogden had thought of murdering Cara Quayne. He may even have pondered over the sodium cyanide recipe, but I think that came later. He knew she was leaving her fortune to Sacred Flame Limited, and he was the biggest shareholder. He may have meant to destroy the book and then have thought of a brighter idea, that of planting it in Garnette's flat. When De Ravigne drew everybody's attention to the book at the party, I believe Ogden made up his mind to risk this last plan. As soon as they had gone he covered the *Curiosities* in brown paper. Next morning when the maid cleaned up the mess she had noticed it had gone. It hadn't gone. It was disguised as one of Garnette's bits of hot literature. When Claude called for the books he took the ones with brown-paper wrappers: the *Curiosities* among them. I suppose when Ogden found what had happened he waited for developments, but there were none. The six books had been shoved back behind the others and neither Garnette nor Claude had noticed anything. This was a phenomenal stroke of luck for Ogden. No doubt if it hadn't happened he would have planted the book himself, but Claude had saved him the trouble. He must have waited his chance to find the book and wipe off any prints. He was emphatic about drawing de Ravigne's attention to the *Curiosities*, but the others, questioned independently, said that de Ravigne himself found the book. If he had already laid his plans this chance discovery by de Ravigne must have disconcerted our Samuel, as it brought the book into unwelcome prominence. He may have thought then of the pretty ruse of incriminating Garnette and pulling in his share of the bequest. But I rather fancy that chance finding by de Ravigne put the whole idea into his head. Otherwise the book would not have been on show. Yes. I think the cyanide scheme was born on the night of the party. It sounds risky, but how nearly it succeeded! There was Elsie, the maid, to swear the book had gone the morning after the party. There were the others to say Garnette and de Ravigne had both handled it the night before. Ogden made a great show of defending de Ravigne, but, of course, if I'd gone for de Ravigne it would have suited his book almost as well as if I'd gone for Garnette. Ogden played his cards very neatly. He owned up to the book with just the right amount of honest reluctance. He gave a perfectly true account of the business arrangement with de Ravigne and Garnette. He had to bring that out, of course, in order to collect when the Will was proved. He made a great point of the legality of their contract. He's a fly bird, is our Samuel."

"I'm sure you're right about all this," said Nigel diffidently, "but it seems very much in the air. Without Pringle's evidence could you ever bring the thing home to him? Isn't it altogether too speculative?"

"It's nailed down with one or two tin-tacks. Ogden and Garnette were the only two who could have concocted the sodium cyanide at what house-agents call the Home Fireside."

"Really?"

"Yes. They are the only two who have open fires. The others, if you wash out Miss Jenkins's gas-ring, all live in electrically heated, or central-heated, service flats. The cooking of sodium cyanide is not the sort of thing one would do away from the Home Fireside, and anyway they have, none of them, been out of residence for the last six months. Then Elsie told me that two days after the party the servants all went on their holiday and Mr. Ogden, who was so kind, 'did' for himself. A dazzling chance for him to do for Cara Quayne at the same time. When Elsie returned from the night-life of Marine Parade, Margate, she no doubt found everything in perfect order. A little less washing-soda in the wooden box over the sink, perhaps, one new Fyrexo patent heat-proof crock. Mr. Ogden had unfortunately dropped the old one and it was just too bad, but he had got her another. He didn't say anything about it, but bright little Elsie spotted the difference. While she was away he had made his sodium cyanide."

"Yes, but you don't *know*——"

"Here's another tin-tack."

Alleyn went to his overcoat and took out a thin object wrapped in paper.

"I brought it to show you. I stole it from Ogden's flat."

He unwrapped the paper. A very short and extremely black iron poker was disclosed.

"Here's where he got his iron filings. I noticed the

corrugations on the tip. He had made it nice and black again, but pokers don't wear away in minute ridges. Elsie agreed with me. It wasn't like what it was before she went away, that it wasn't."

"And what, may I ask, was the meaning of the cable to Australia?"

"Do you remember another very intelligent remark you made on Sunday evening?"

"I made any number of intelligent remarks."

"Possibly. This was to the effect that Ogden's Americanese was too good to be true. It seemed to me no more exaggerated than the sounds that fill the English air in August, but after a bit I began to think you were right. I was sure of it when, under stress, he came out with a solecism. He said 'Good-oh.' Now 'Good-oh' is purest dyed-in-the-wool Australian. It is the Australian comment on every conceivable remark. If you say to an Australian: 'I'm afraid your trousers are on fire,' he replies 'Good-oh.' Mr. Ogden, on a different occasion, ejaculated 'Too right!' Another bit of undiluted Sydney. And yet when I asked him if he had been to Australia he denied the soft impeachment. So we've asked headquarters, Sydney, if it knows anything about a tall man with an American accent and skewbald eyes. It may be productive. One never knows. But the longest and sharpest tack is Madame la Comtesse de Barsac.

"From the fastness of her nursing home she has come out strong with a telegram that must have cost her a pretty sum. It is this sort of thing. 'Madame la Comtesse de Barsac has just learned of the death of Mademoiselle Cara Quayne. She believes that she has evidence of the utmost importance and urges that the officials in charge of the case apprehend one Samuel Ogden. Mademoiselle Quayne's letter of December tenth follows and will explain more fully the reasons that commend this action.'"

"'Struth!" said Nigel, "that puts the *diamanté* clasp on it."

"I rather fancy it does."

"I suppose it's the letter Cara Quayne wrote after she got back to the flat on Sunday afternoon."

"That's it. With the help of the bits we got from the blotting-paper I think we can make a pretty shrewd guess at what's in it. Cara may describe her visit to the temple, her encounter with Ogden and her fears for the consequences. She has gone so far with the heroin habit that she cannot face the prospect of being done out of it. She implores her old friend to help her, perhaps asks if Madame de Barsac could put her on to an agent for the stinking stuff. I hope she'll say he threatened her, specifically. If she does——"

"Yes," said Nigel, "if she says that it'll look murky for Mr. Ogden."

"There's another useful bit of information. Old Nanny Hebborn, as I think you heard her tell me, lurked in Mr. Garnette's parlour on Sunday night and saw the beginnings of the cup ceremony. She described the movements of the Initiates when they formed their circle. She said Ogden went up first. When Miss Wade and the Candour skirmished to get one on each side of Garnette, Ogden out-manœuvred them and himself got in on Garnette's right hand. Nanny said he deliberately stopped Miss Wade and took her place. Of course he did. It was the only safe place for him."

"I suppose Ogden's counsel will go for Garnette?"

"Oh yes. I've no doubt Mr. Garnette's trans-Atlantic origin and activities will all be brought out into the fierce light that beats upon the witness-box. I hope it will be the dock. Him and his heroin! Devil take me, but I swear he's the nastier sample of the two."

"Will he get the money?"

"Not if Mr. Rattisbon can help it."

The telephone rang. Nigel answered it.

"It's for you," he said. "Fox, I think."

Alleyn took the telephone from him. Nigel walked over to the window and stared out into the street.

"Hullo, Fox," said Alleyn, "you've run me to earth. What is it?"

The telephone quacked industriously.

"I see," said Alleyn. "That's all very neat and handy. Thank you, Foxkin. Are you at the Yard? Well, go home to bed. It's late. Good night."

He hung up the receiver and swung round in his chair.

"Cable from Australia. 'Sounds like S. J. Samuels, American sharp, convicted sale prohibited drugs. Two years. Involved Walla-Walla homicide case!'"

He paused. Nigel did not answer.

"And Mr. Garnette has decided to make a statement. He says he has had some interesting confidences from Ogden. Little charmer! What are you looking at?"

"I'm looking down into Knocklatchers Row. It's very odd, but someone seems to be taking away the Sign of the Sacred Flame. Only it's raining so hard I can hardly see."

"You're quite right. It's a man from the Yard. Crowds collect and gape at the thing. I told them to take it away."

THE END

Ngaio Marsh

'The finest writer in the English language of the pure, classical, puzzle whodunit. Among the Crime Queens, Ngaio Marsh stands out as an Empress.' *Sun*. 'Her work is as near flawless as makes no odds: character, plot, wit, good writing and sound technique.' *Sunday Times*. 'The brilliant Ngaio Marsh ranks with Agatha Christie and Dorothy Sayers.' *Times Literary Supplement*.

Last Ditch

Vintage Murder

Death and the Dancing Footman

Death at the Dolphin

Hand in Glove

Colour Scheme

Scales of Justice

Singing in the Shrouds

Spinsters in Jeopardy

A Clutch of Constables

Death in a White Tie

Dead Water

Fontana Books